KV-638-508

Stone cold dead

There should have been nothing but pleasure involved in an eighteenth birthday party combined with a formal engagement to be married. But Richard Patton and his wife, Amelia, find themselves in an unusual environment, in which the word 'flight' takes on a fresh meaning, and a 'pound' has nothing to do with money or weight.

Yet it is weight that defeats Richard when it comes to attempting to rescue what turns out to be a distinct embarrassment. Weight and cold. The water is taking on a surface layer of ice, and it is difficult to accept that people might live in this environment on their houseboats. Or even die on them.

The young woman whom Richard discovers is not dead, though very close to being so, and the discovery leads him on to ventures that threaten the basic moral values of their new friends at Flight House, and even restructure their lives.

When the truth is finally revealed, it still leaves two explanations to be made, and the only question remaining is who shall make which.

Also by Roger Ormerod

Newport Libraries

THIS ITEM SHOULD BE RETURNED OR
RENEWED BY THE LAST DATE
STAMPED BELOW.

STACK

1 4 JUL 2007

1 5 DEC 2007

1 6 JUL 2008

Please return this item to the library from which it
was borrowed

3/2a

NEWPORT BOROUGH LIBRARIES

0143062

Newport
BOROUGH
SIROL

STONE COLD DEAD

Roger Ormerod

Constable · London

First published in Great Britain 1995
by Constable & Co Ltd
3 The Lanchesters, 162 Fulham Palace Road
London W6 9ER
Copyright © by Roger Ormerod 1995
The right of Roger Ormerod to be identified
as the author of this work has been
asserted by him in accordance with
the Copyright, Designs and Patents Act 1988
ISBN 0 09 474010 0
Set in Linotron Palatino 10pt by
CentraCet Ltd, Cambridge
Printed in Great Britain by
Hartnolls Ltd, Bodmin

A CIP catalogue record for this book
is available from the British Library

1

What had been sleet, driving directly at the windscreen, became an agitated lace curtain of ice particles as we motored, more and more slowly, along the valley. The wind howled and buffeted around the car, and visibility was rapidly becoming impossible. The particles were hissing against the screen, trickling down the glass without aid from the wipers, and I reckoned we were lost.

'Nonsense, Richard,' claimed Amelia. 'We can't be more than a mile away.'

'We could drive right past the place, and not see it. What're we looking for, anyway?'

'It's called Flight House.'

'What I meant was: is it built right on the roadway, set back, or at the end of a long drive? The visibility's down to about ten yards. We could drive right past it, and not know.'

Amelia had been navigating for us, the map on her knees and a torch in her hand. She seemed quite confident that we were on the correct stretch of tarmac, and heading directly to our objective.

'Ruby said we can't miss it,' she assured me.

'Didn't you ever visit her, when you were at school together?'

'Not here. Richard, do use your imagination. She didn't live here at that time. But I'm sure we're about there now, so don't worry.'

Allowing the car to drift to a halt, I pulled over, feeling the nearside tyres run on to roadside grass. Clearly, we were in a country lane, and my impression was that nothing but fields and forested hills flanked us on both sides. With the car halted I sat and thought about it. Main beams on full did little more than throw the storm back at us as a white blanket. I could see nothing. I tried the foglights. The penetration was better, but too low to help.

'I think that's a signpost ahead,' I told her. 'I'll just walk along and check.'

Reaching back over the seat for my anorak and hat, I felt Amelia stir uneasily.

'Don't for heaven's sake get lost,' she said. My wife sometimes sees problems that don't exist.

'How could I? Leave the foglights on, and I can't miss it. And don't turn the engine off. I shan't be a minute. Oh – and I'd better take your torch.'

She put it into my hand. It was impossible to climb into my anorak in the car, so I had to get out to do it. The hat, yes. I managed to put it on, and a lot of good that did me! I stood out on the tarmac, and my hat was whipped away in a second. Turning quickly, I caught a glimpse of it in the torchlight in the fraction of a second before it was kited over the nearside hedge.

'Hell!' I said, struggling into the anorak. The ice particles threatened to peel the skin from my face, a thousand needles prodding me. The torchlight did little but dazzle. Cautiously, I trod forward, left foot on grass, right on tarmac. In that way only could I navigate towards what I had thought to be a signpost.

Thus, head down and with my scalp already aching in the penetrating cold, I moved forward, and almost walked into the back of what I took to be a car. A quick upward flick of the torch from the immediate front of my feet confirmed this. It was red. It could have been a Ford Fiesta, or a similar small hatchback. And yet . . . here?

Was it, I thought, someone else who was lost and marooned? Yet the engine wasn't running – an essential if the heating was to be maintained. Or . . . a courting couple? Surely not. It was far too bleak and unencouraging to provoke a stop for a bit of canoodling. Or was I getting old? In any event, the flick of the torch seemed to have indicated an emptiness.

Now, standing beside the driver's door, I could see, quite clearly with the torch, that the car had been abandoned. A breakdown? How appalling that would be on a night such as this and out in the wilds! And my sweep of the torch indicated that the keys were hanging from the ignition lock. That was strange. One did not, except in very unusual circumstances, leave a car abandoned and with the keys available. And, of course, the keys being inside, with the door unlocked. I tried the driver's door, and yes, it opened.

One of my weaknesses (and my wife can quote a considerable list) is that I can't, as she puts it, keep my nose out of other people's affairs. I feel uneasy in situations that, on face value, do not have a valid explanation. This didn't. I reached in and turned the key. The dash lights came on. The fuel gauge indicated half a tankful. I turned it another notch and the engine fired at once. The temperature gauge showed at least half its marked norm. I looked round. Somebody caught short, and nipped behind the high hedge just the other side of the car? Surely not. On such a night, it would be needless to nip behind anywhere.

Faintly, I heard my name called, the sound whipped away into the night.

'It's all right,' I shouted, and emphasized it with a swing of the torch. Then I switched off the car's engine, slammed the door, and left everything as I had found it. Head down, with my right arm round it for protection from the wind, now blowing from my right, I moved onwards as I had been doing before, one foot on grass and one on tarmac. And there it was, just as I had thought from no more than a vague impression: a signpost.

Here, there was a crossing of two lanes. The ancient, painted indications were barely decipherable, partly obscured by a layer of ice particles. But I caught sight of the word: FLIGHT. The word following that seemed to be: HOUSE. That cheered me up considerably. A quarter of a mile, it informed me.

I turned to trudge back. This necessitated re-crossing the lane that led to left and right. In those few yards I lost my sense of direction, this partly caused by a sudden and energetic gust of wind, which sent me staggering forward until brought up abruptly by a hard stone surface that thumped into my thighs. The torch indicated the curved top of a low wall, which led away to my right. As I knew I hadn't seen it on the way there, I left it behind me and plunged hopefully forward, blessing the abandoned car as it floated redly into the beam of the torch.

Now I was leaning sideways against the bitter wind, or it would have had me on my face. I skirted the car, and had Amelia's Granada in view as two low foglights stabbing at my ankles. I whipped open the door, fell inside, and slammed the door with relief. My anorak could stay on now. A quarter of a mile. We ought to be able to do that in no time at all.

'You were right,' I said. 'We're not lost. It's straight ahead. A quarter of a mile. Flight House, it's sign-posted. It must have the lane all to itself.'

'What was that you stopped for?' Amelia asked. 'It looked like another car to me.'

'That's right. It was.'

'So why did you waste time peering into it? Richard . . . it could have been a young couple, and how embarrassing that would have been. For you, too.'

'Nobody in it. Nothing wrong with the car, unless it's mechanical.'

'How very strange, Richard. Now watch yourself along here.'

'I'm looking for lighted windows. We don't want to drive right past it.'

'From what Ruby said on the phone, you can't do that. Not – she told me – without getting wet. I wonder what she meant, Richard.'

'A river, perhaps?'

'Oh no. There's no river shown on the map.'

'Well,' I said, 'we'll know in a minute. I can see lights ahead.'

I realized that this indicated an ease in the storm. The wipers were leaving a clear windscreen, and nothing in the way of ice particles or snow was now obscuring it.

'Yes. It's a floodlight or something like that.'

The first thing that emerged from the darkness, and facing us, was a blank and windowless end of a large house, mounted high on it a floodlight, throwing an orange glow on to a flat patch of hard earth and gravel. This was clearly used as a car park, because two vehicles were already parked there, nose-in to the blank wall. Or rather, I now saw beyond one of the vehicles, a blank end wall but with its surface broken by a single, narrow doorway. There was plenty of room for the Granada.

The dashboard clock indicated 5.30. Not bad, really, though the whole trip had been in the dark and in appallingly deteriorating weather. I hadn't wanted to stay over for the night, although Amelia's friend, Ruby Fulton, had well-nigh insisted on it. Now I was glad of it, certainly not wishing to drive the forty miles home in the sort of weather we had encountered on the way here. But here we were. Flight House. And frankly I would be glad of a hot drink, preferably laced with a shot of whisky.

We had gone there for a party. Not my line at all, parties, but Amelia would have driven here alone if I had resisted, and I couldn't have had that. But ... a party! That very day was the eighteenth birthday of Amelia's god-child, more correctly, I suppose, her god-daughter, name: Amelia Ruby Fulton. I had been informed that, in order to avoid confusion, she was called Mellie. And this day, too, was the day on which she was going to become formally engaged to be married. So it was to be a combined birthday and engagement party.

It did appear to me that formal engagement parties were rather old-fashioned. These days people seem to say, 'Let's get married, shall we?' And, 'Suits me.' And that's that. But no – not at Flight House, apparently. For here, I was soon to learn, they were all firmly and delightfully living in the past. The very situation of the house – at the end of its own lane rather than its own drive – seemed to have cut them off from life as it is lived today, and the party itself would no doubt be sedate and very proper. Dignity and probity would reign supreme, and ears would not be blasted inside-out by continuous outpourings of rock and pop. Ah well – that would suit me fine.

Amelia had found a bell button, which must have been working because the door was flung open and the two women were in each other's arms. I stood and waited until they had attention to spare for me.

'And this, Ruby, is my husband, Richard.' I always loved this phrase of Amelia's, because she usually managed to insert a modicum of pride. You need that little boost, from time to time.

'Richard! I've heard so much about you.'

This phrase is rather disconcerting, as it leaves you wondering just what was said. I smiled. 'And I of you,' I countered. I found my face wasn't as stiff as it felt, because I managed some sort of a grin. She pouted, then raised herself on her toes and lifted her cheek to be kissed. She was a neat little package with a slim, tidy figure, and barely a sign on her pert and roguish face of the passage of time since her own eighteenth birthday. Blue-grey eyes twinkled at me. I could have sworn she winked. So I reached my hands forward and beneath her armpits and picked her from the floor to my own level, then kissed her on the lips.

'Richard! You're like ice,' she cried.

And Amelia added, 'Seems rather too warm to me.'

I put down our hostess and she pouted. 'Just pleased to see you,' I apologized. 'I was beginning to wonder whether we'd ever get here.'

9

'Oh . . . has it been so terrible?' Ruby asked. 'We're very exposed here. Now – I'll show you to your room later, and you can get nice and warm in a hot bath. Let me take your anorak, Richard. No hat?'

'It blew away.'

'Oh dear. Never mind.'

'I'll nip out and get our things,' I said, 'while I've got the anorak on.'

'Oh yes. You do that. You'll find us in the lounge. Second on the left, along this hallway, Richard.'

We were, I realized, in their main hall, although it seemed so narrow. The floor was tiled, and a staircase clung to the right-hand wall, mounting into the shadows. So what I had taken to be a side door was probably their front and main door. It was a strange house. At this time I was somewhat disorientated, and all I could do was retrieve our two suitcases, lock up the car, and return inside. Then, I would do as I'd been told and find them in what she had called their lounge.

This I did satisfactorily. The storm had quite blown itself out, but had left a deadly cold behind it. Where puddles had lain on the gravelled surface I felt thin ice crackle beneath my feet. But the orange light was very helpful, and I was able to carry both suitcases in without any trouble. These I left at the foot of the staircase, and tossed my anorak on top of them.

Second on the left, Ruby Fulton had said. It was dim along that narrow hallway, but I found the door, opened it, and walked into a public house bar. I stopped. The blasted house was confusing me. Yet, there they were, waiting for me, waiting to enjoy my surprise. And laughing.

There was a long, slightly curved mahogany counter all along the right-hand wall, and behind it, wearing an apron now, was Ruby. Behind her was the original bank of mirrors and shelves, and on the shelves a display of bottles, these empty and obviously for display only.

Round tables with intricate cast-iron frames were scattered here and there, each with four chairs, and a long bench seat ran around three of the walls. Facing the counter, on the opposite wall, there was a row of half-frosted windows. Double swing doors, also with frosted glass windows, faced the centre of the counter. I looked about me in confusion.

Amelia was standing at the counter, a glass in her hand. I knew its contents would be her favourite long drink – Dubonnet and lemonade.

'What'll you have?' asked a man's voice from behind my shoulder. I turned. He was tall, slim, his general demeanour one of confidence, his expression grave, as though too many concerns rested on his shoulders. I stood aside for him to pass, and thus be in a position to welcome me. He offered his hand. This, I realised, had to be Ruby's husband. He withdrew his hand and used it in an embracing gesture, taking in the whole room.

'Whatever you like,' he said. 'It's on the house.' Which was a strange thing for a host to say. And he laughed. 'It's always on the house.' This was still more strange. 'You'll be Richard, yes? I'm Gerald Fulton, Mellie's long-suffering father.'

I had the impression that his joviality was slightly forced, and that his normal self would be somewhat dour. It was there in his deep-set eyes, and in the stubborn set of his jaw.

'Now that's not fair, dad,' called out a young woman I hadn't noticed. I was having to assimilate too much, too quickly.

'Then come and tell us why, lass,' he suggested. No, I realized abruptly, it had been an order. In this house, I felt, Gerald Fulton was in charge, and though his request to his daughter had been pleasant enough, it had nevertheless been an instruction.

This was a man, I decided, with a Position to maintain, and mentally he would spell it with a capital P. He was almost complacent in his dignity, and had offered his hand as though bestowing an honour. Head back now, eyes glowing, he smiled at his daughter. With obvious pride. She was *his* daughter, and the pride was self-congratulatory.

She approached. Clearly, she was a reincarnation of her mother, though Mellie was a little taller, her figure more generous and full. But the eyes were the same, and they glimmered at me with the same mischief as I'd recognized in Ruby's. Yet the line of her lips hinted at a frustration, something she resented. Perhaps she hadn't noticed the fondness with which her father regarded her, and had seen as too authoritative his doubtless anxious concern for her welfare and happiness. And there was just a hint in Gerald Fulton's expression, as he watched her approach, of a possessiveness that demanded only the very best for her in life, and a sure knowledge that only he could judge what was and what was not in her best interest.

With a sudden chill of understanding I realized that this

forthcoming event – the actual engagement, as signalized by the slipping of a ring on her finger – was not at all what he had wished for her. No doubt nothing could be good enough for her in his eyes, and he completely failed to realize that he could be alienating her to such an extent that she might run from his overpowering influence, and thereby plunge herself into a much worse situation than her father could have visualized. And from midnight onwards she would be legally free to do as she wished.

But my mind was running beyond control, building too much on too little. These thoughts had taken only seconds, as she was still approaching, and then she was holding out her hand, her left hand, palm downwards, so that I took it in my right, and found this to be remarkably more personal than the more normal greeting.

'I've so much wanted to meet you,' she said, a little breathlessly, though I couldn't see why. 'Aunt Amelia tells me you were a policeman.'

I smiled at her, still holding her hand. There was something, now, rather beseeching in this contact, something strange, as though she feared to release me, as though I mattered in her life. I found this to be embarrassing – and rather pleasurable.

'A detective inspector,' I told her. 'But retired now, a long while ago.'

'I have no great affection for the police,' said her father. He nodded, almost as though underlining it.

'Now . . . dad . . .'

'Young Ray Torrance is a policeman,' he observed, as though airing a grievance. 'The man to whom she's to become engaged,' he explained to me.

She tugged at his sleeve. 'Dad!' she appealed. 'You know you like him.'

'Oh yes. Yes, yes. I like *him*, certainly. A grand chap. But I could wish he was anything other than a policeman.'

It was time, I realized, that we dismissed this theme as irrelevant, otherwise it could cast a blight on the evening's festivities. I tried to laugh it away. 'May I guess,' I asked him, 'that you've been recently breathalized?'

'Tcha!' He abruptly dismissed what had been intended more as a pleasantry than a serious proposition. 'I am a solicitor. That ought to explain everything to you.'

And indeed, it *did* cast some light on it. He was probably a

12

country lawyer who specialized in criminal cases, thus bringing himself into opposition to the police. There would be plenty of crime in the district, placid countryside or not, you could reckon on that, and he would be the solicitor representing the accused. What might he have had to face? The theft of a van-load of sheep in the night, a boundary dispute that had erupted into violence? Always, Gerald Fulton would appear for the defence. Then he would exercise the exaggerated pose of self-confidence that I'd already recognized, in an attempt to disrupt the police case on technicalities he didn't really understand. How proud would he be to be able to press the local bobby into minor admissions of faulty procedures! How soon after the event had the officer entered the details in his notebook? That sort of thing.

I had, in my time, encountered all these problems, had stood in the witness box and attempted to retain my equanimity when alleged irregularities had been hurled at me. And I was supposed not to bandy words with the defence lawyer.

But recently, I understood, the police were becoming more adequately aware of the possible legal traps that they might have to encounter, could combat them with more expertise, and therefore arrive at the court with more confidence.

This might explain Gerald Fulton's attitude. He was not a man to accept defeat graciously. He must always prevail, but the odds were that he wasn't being too successful of late.

'But you like *him*,' I suggested blandly. 'It ought to be easy enough to forget that he usually wears a uniform, and just relax in the thought of Mellie's happiness.'

He pursed his lips. 'Words of wisdom from a policeman? How very novel! But believe me, the young fool won't let me forget. He seems to think it's amusing to dig at me with his really very immature authority. "I see your car tax is running out, sir," he'll say. Damn him – when I've already sent off for the renewal. Thinks it's amusing. And, "The tread on your off-side front tyre's almost illegal, sir." Blast him! Always "sir" – as though he's about to arrest me. Not with any sign of respect, you understand. And he grins at me. In a sort of challenging manner, I always think. But you haven't got a glass in your hand, my dear fellow.'

'It's all right. Plenty of time. But . . . is this the party?'

'Oh no. In an hour or so we shall sit down to dinner. Then afterwards we come in here for the party. And . . . ah, here he is now. Trust him! Just his measure.'

He had been looking past my shoulder. I turned. There was no need to tell me who was meant, as the young fool had turned up in his uniform. He was flapping his chequered cap against his thigh.

'Evenin' all,' he said. 'Is this bar licensed, may I ask?'

'See what I mean?' asked Gerald gruffly. 'Come along, I'll introduce you.'

The young man had entered by way of the frosted-glass swing doors, so he must have walked round the house from the parking space. Now he stood and waited as we approached. He was very nearly as tall as Fulton, a little shorter than me. And in his eyes there was something that I could not put a name to, possibly embarrassment at the lack of response to his pleasantry, or perhaps something deeper than that. His eyes would not meet mine; he seemed flustered. And the lines down from the corners of his mouth I recognized, from past experience, as being due to a repressed tension.

'I'd like you to meet a fellow police officer, Raymond,' said Gerald. 'Former Detective Inspector Patton.'

'Richard,' I said quickly, disliking the formality. It had been deliberate, of course. 'And here is my wife, Amelia.' She was now at my elbow, and held in her hand a whisky and soda, which I knew was for me. 'This is Mellie's fiancé, my love,' I told her. 'Ray Torrance, I understand.'

Gravely, young Ray took her hand. 'Pleased to meet you,' he said. 'You'll be the godmother Mellie's mentioned – yes? I reckon she might be glad of your support. And you, sir, how do you do?' Very grave, now, he was, and he almost clicked his heels as he reached forward with his right hand. And why, I wondered, was there that haunted expression he seemed not to be able to shake off? Why was his hand shaking as he offered it?

Gerald Fulton, I realized, had quietly left us, his action being very close to downright insulting to young Ray Torrance.

'Not "sir" please,' I said. 'And why the devil the uniform?'

'Just come off duty. And anyway – '

Then Mellie swept down on him and clutched his uniformed arm to her side with an almost predatory possessiveness. She shook his arm. 'You did it on purpose, Ray, didn't you? I know you. Just to irritate father. Now admit it.'

He grimaced at her. 'I wanted him to be quite sure you're going to marry a policeman,' he admitted. 'And I hope . . .' He glanced sideways at me. 'Hope I might be able to get some support. I'll feel better now, sir, with you here.'

'Richard,' I corrected patiently. 'And I've already had a few words with him on the subject.'

But Mellie wasn't going to allow Ray any distraction from the central objective of his presence there. 'You've brought the ring, Ray?'

'Of course.' He plunged a hand into his pocket and produced a small black cubical box, in which it presumably nestled.

'Let me see . . .'

He tossed her a teasing glance. 'You've seen it a dozen times.'

'No. Let me see it . . .'

'Not now,' he said, flicking a wink at me. But his words had been more abrupt than seemed necessary. 'It's supposed to be unlucky.' He managed a distorted grin.

'Oh – you!' She allowed him a brief frown, then pouted.

I had never heard of such a superstition, and when I glanced at Amelia she shook her head.

'Got to get it right,' he said, almost apologetically, 'if only for your dear poppa. All formal it's got to be. The ring on your finger and a toast to the happy couple. Later, my lovely. Later.' Then he thrust the box back into his pocket – and failed to meet her eyes. A nerve was flicking in his forehead.

'Oh . . . you . . .' she said, slapping the back of his hand playfully, but there was pain in her eyes, and a hint of distress in the line of her mouth. He had refused a request.

Fortunately, at that moment the scene was shattered by the abrupt, bouncing arrival of a stocky young man with a shock of untidy hair and a beard that seemed to be hanging desperately to his chin and drawing down his lower lip. Perhaps not young, though. The beard misled me; he would have been in his mid-thirties. He had Mellie's eyes – and there the similarity ended. There was no humour in the lines of his face, but a serious understanding, an almost heavy awareness of an authority that was not immediately apparent.

'Mother says I'm to show you the house and your room and what-not,' he told us, his gaze switching from Amelia's face to mine. 'You haven't even been allowed the chance to freshen up. No organization at all. Mother's hopeless, and father expects to be carried about. Come on. I'm Colin. Mellie's brother. And what the hell're you doing in uniform, Ray, you clown?' He turned back to me. 'You've got luggage?'

'It's in the hall.'

'Ah yes. Come on, then. Dinner's at around seven – in the dining room, of course – and the party's to be in here afterwards.' He glanced at his future brother-in-law. 'In uniform! That sense of humour's going to be the death of you, Ray.'

Amelia and I glanced at each other, and grimaced. We were in the safe hands of a man in control. I wasn't quite certain of what, at that point.

At the door into the hall, he paused to turn on a switch. It seemed to do nothing, certainly it didn't stir the shadows in the hall. He then operated more switches, and hall and stairs sprang into view. They were not the stairs I had previously seen, but wider, and directly opposite to their bar-cum-lounge.

'We've put you in what we call the front,' he told us over his shoulder, marching ahead of us with our cases, which he had retrieved from the side door, in each hand. I carried my anorak. 'Watch this step here, it's deceptive. Second door on the right,' he called out. 'I haven't got a spare hand.'

I reached past him and opened the door. It seemed remarkably bright in there, though the room lights were not turned on. As I reached for the switch beside the door, he said, 'Leave the lights off for a minute. There's something I want to show you.'

It was a special treat he had kept for us. There was a bright expectation in his voice as he led the way to the window. The curtains were drawn back.

'This is why it's called Flight House,' he said with hushed pride. 'That's the flight, down there.'

We were looking down – in a harsh white pool of light that must have required a whole bank of floods above us – on a canal basin, at what he had called the front of the house. There were three locks, rising from our left. This side of the water, and at the head of the lowest lock, there was a strange octagonal building, standing to one side of what looked like a footbridge, which ran over to the bank the other side of the locks. The two higher locks were directly opposite to us, and away to the right, just visible in the overthrow of strong white lighting, the upper canal ran away in a shallow curve to the left.

16

It was breathtaking, a study in black and white uncompromising practicality, which at the same time presented a special beauty in its balance and proportions. Amelia touched my hand, caught it, and squeezed it.

'It's well over 200 years old,' Colin said, his voice now hushed. 'James Brindley built this, the canal and its locks, and the toll booth. That's the octagonal building over there on your left – and this house here. It used to be a lock-keeper's lodge, combined with a bargee's pub, as you'll probably have guessed. The old stables for the horses are still standing, but they're at the far end of the house – to your right. You can't see them from here. We'd have converted 'em into lock-up garages, but it would've been a bit hairy, getting cars in and out. Width enough to drive along beneath these windows – oh yes. Eight or so yards. But backing out or backing in . . . that'd be a bit tricky. Inches to spare – and one wrong move and you'd be in the wet. We could really do with lock-up garages.'

He was silent. Clearly, he was devoted to the place. He loved it with a deep and reverent passion.

Just to break the silence, I said, 'It's what they call a staircase, isn't it? A staircase of three locks. Or a ladder – I can't remember which.'

'Oh no! Indeed it is not. It's called a flight. That's because of the two reservoirs between the locks. We call them pounds. It's all terribly complicated, but it's to save draining all the locks when a boat's moving up. It takes a bit of working out, I can tell you. That's why this is one of the few locks in the country that still has a lock-keeper. Most of the traffic's holiday boats, these days, which is summer stuff. March to October. But boats do come through in the winter. People live all the year round in their houseboats. So there has to be a lock-keeper. Permanent. This whole building is the lodge. They did their lock-keepers well in the old days. Paid 'em well. Now it's rent free to the present lock-keeper. And that's me.' He produced this with solemn pride.

'No salary?' I asked, and Amelia nudged me for asking personal questions.

'Oh no. Just the lodge. Mind you – there's a tradition. The lock-keeper gets tipped for helping the boats through.'

'Ah,' I said. I was beginning to understand the unusual set-up. 'And your father?'

17

He turned to me. His face was heavily side-lit, cutting his features into harsh angles. He twitched his beard with what could have been a grin.

'I'm the legal tenant. I let him live here, rent nominal, that's to make him a legal sub-tenant. I took over this job from my uncle, and he from my grandfather. It's been in the family since Brindley built the place. We don't operate the pub now, of course. I offered my father the job of bar-tender, but he wouldn't take it.' He threw back his head and laughed. 'He's now trying to buy the freehold from the present owners, but they turned him down. Now he's digging into obscure law to try to force them into selling. Not a chance! Don't you think it's a laugh? Don't you?'

'It is, indeed, a humorous situation,' I agreed, and Amelia appreciated the tricky problem with her own little tinkle of a laugh.

Yet it had its serious aspects, as Colin proceeded to explain.

'I've told him,' he said, 'that if he does any more to break-up the arrangement between Mellie and Ray, I'll ask him to leave. I'll *tell* him to leave. And he wouldn't like that. Not one little bit, he wouldn't. That's because *he* knows, being a solicitor, that I can have him out of here. I rather like my sister, and Ray's not a bad chap. They'll be happy. But dad's done all he can to break it up. Stupid man. Stupid self-opinionated nincompoop.'

I hadn't heard that word, nincompoop, for years. No doubt Brindley himself had used it in his time. Once again, I had to acknowledge that these people lived in the past. And perhaps that wasn't a bad thing.

2

After he'd left us alone, Amelia said, 'We've got our own bath-room. Isn't that splendid?'

'I suppose it is. You try it then, love. Me later.'

'I'll unpack first. What're you going to do?' she asked.

I tried her with a question. 'Haven't you noticed something that's missing? Or rather, several somethings.'

She shook her head. 'Now don't be so mysterious, Richard, please. Out with it. What's missing?'

'Ashtrays.'

'Ah!' she said, understanding.

I am a pipe smoker. My pipe has now become part of me, an integrated element of my persona. But I do not smoke my pipe in other people's homes unless they themselves are smokers. The evidence of this is in the presence of ashtrays. I hadn't noticed any here.

'So while you're having your bath, love, I'll just pop outside for a smoke,' I told her.

'Now ... that's ridiculous, Richard. You'll be absolutely per- ished. Your lips'll freeze to your pipe-stem.' She laughed lightly, and patted me on the cheek.

'What else, then? Do I open the window and put my head outside? In any event, I want to take a look at the locks. I'm interested in how they work – and I can't understand this business about pounds that Colin mentioned. How do they help? I don't get it.'

'Then at least put something over your head.'

'I've got a scarf.'

'Now *that* I would like to see. You'll look like a senile washerwoman.'

'Nobody will notice me. If they do, they'll think I'm the ghost of a bargee's wife.'

She pursed her lips at me, and stepped out of her slacks. 'Then give me a quarter of an hour.'

I nodded, slipped my anorak back on, and put the scarf, for now, around my neck. Then I hurried down the stairs, intending to go out by way of their bar. Or I would get lost.

This I expected to be empty, but it was not. Ray Torrance was still there. Where else would he be, I thought, as he was, it seemed, already clothed in what he intended to wear for dinner and for the party. I would have bet that Gerald was already dressing for dinner, indeed always did dress formally for dinner, and Ray would seem even more out of place in his uniform.

And he had been drinking. He had a spirit glass in his hand at that time, when I walked in on him, and had the grace to look guilty. He even blushed.

'Go easy on the spirits, lad,' I said. 'There's a long evening ahead.'

'I'll be all right.'

19

It is a recognized fact that such a claim is usually made by somebody who is far from right already.

'You'll be a fool if you give your future father-in-law the chance to criticize you,' I told him, nodding in emphasis. 'There's supposed to be a party coming up, and what a pity it'd be if one of the two most concerned can't even stand.'

He raised his eyebrows at me. 'Why don't you mind your own soddin' business?' he asked, but without heat.

'Because I like the lass. I'd hate to see her unhappy.'

He stared at me blankly, downed his drink in one swallow, and banged the glass back on the counter. 'Can't you find something to do?'

I noticed that there were ashtrays, after all, and here in the bar, not simply to complement the atmosphere of a genuine pub, but in use. This meant that I didn't need to go outside. In fact, I was wondering whether it might be best to stay and keep an eye on Ray. There was something about this young man that gave me cause for concern. He did not handle his glass with the casual ease of a person who was used to spirits, and he was drinking as one who sought oblivion. But that could surely not be so, when this evening was intended as a joyful episode in his life. And I could not dismiss the thought that he was a worried young man, who might be tremulously in the process of changing his mind and backing out. His nerves were certainly stretched tautly.

'Much more of that,' I said, 'and you'll not be able to drive home.'

He shrugged. 'I'm staying the night,' he told me, thickly, defiantly. 'They've got a room ready for me.'

'You won't be staying if you ruin the party,' I assured him. 'Don't kid yourself, laddie. Poppa Fulton wouldn't be pleased if you pass out, stoned to the eyeballs, before you slip the ring on her finger.'

I realized I'd gone a little too far. He stood there, tense, face white with a flare of red on his cheeks. For a moment he stared at his hands, noticed that they were shaking, and clenched them into fists. I gave him time to do something, anything, by pausing to fill my pipe, but he turned away abruptly and leaned against the counter, presenting his back.

I shrugged, and left him to it.

Outside, I stood in the cold white glare of the floodlights, which were way up beneath the eaves, and flicked agitatedly at my lighter. I had handled him badly, should have sympathized, and tried to discover what exactly was haunting him. After all, it was Mellie's happiness that was at stake, and I would have hated to admit that Gerald Fulton had been correct, after all, and that Ray Torrance, policeman or not, was not a fit person to marry his daughter. So far, he hadn't impressed me favourably.

I tried to thrust the incident to the back of my mind, and put the scarf over my head, tying it beneath my chin and tucking the ends inside my anorak. Then, hoping that nobody would see me like that, I got the pipe going well and set out on my peaceful stroll in the night.

It was now piercingly cold. The storm had blown itself out and the air was still, allowing the chill to press down on me, and on the locks. The floodlights were essential now, I realized, as I walked the twenty feet to the lock closest to me, the top one. The upper rim of it was constructed from blue coping bricks with rounded edges, which didn't encourage too close an approach, especially as the surface beneath my feet felt slippy. One peep over the edge was sufficient for me. The light didn't even reach the water at the bottom, as the level was low. The feeling was claustrophobic, if only by suggestion. I would have hated to be down there, even safely in a canal boat, though it would be logical that some sort of ladder would be provided, in case of accidents. I couldn't see one, but the shadows were heavy.

A spark fell from my pipe and spun down, down into blackness, my own tiny satellite disappearing into eternity – finally to be extinguished.

I moved along to my left, to the central lock, where the water seemed to be even more distant. It was separated from its upper mate by a smaller chamber, which must have been one of the pounds that Colin had mentioned. I nearly stumbled over an awkward and ugly erection of ironwork, almost waist high and in the form of an ungainly rack thrusting upwards, held by a ratchet, but with a toothed pinion to lift it or to lower it. I couldn't understand its use. But the huge, true gates, as I knew them, were familiar to me, their long arms reaching out, black and white. There was always this total lack of colour. White on black. It was probably the reason why canal boats are traditionally brightly painted – a reaction, a rejection.

Here, between these two locks and spanning the pound, there was a six-foot wide footbridge. There seemed no reason for me to cross, to what seemed to be nothing but a stretch of grass, so I continued onwards, keeping to the safer side where I could watch where my feet stepped.

I was now opposite the end of the house, so that the orange light above the parking space shaded into the white. Shadows became heavier, taking on a shade of blue. Here was the octagonal toll booth. From this, Colin would be able to scan the full extent of his domain. The white light slanted from behind me, my own shadow purple.

Ahead of me there seemed to be nothing but darkness. No hint of light now softened the solid blanket of the sky, and all impression of colour was bleached from the angular shapes around me. Water rustled, but I could locate no source of the sound. I stood, held my breath, but nothing save a bitter, chilling sigh of leaking water broke the silence.

More from a sense of proximity than from sight, I came to realize that there was no further access beyond the toll booth, certainly not on that side of the locks, but a squat, humped shape led away into darkness on my right. It seemed to be another bridge, but narrower. Hadn't I seen this from our bedroom window? I felt for a parapet, and it was there. Gently, I eased along, until the surface below my feet was level. Its peak. I leaned forward and peeped over.

Here, I seemed to be poised over a depth I could not estimate, and from which rose the water trickle, a hollow sound now, caught and trapped. Not removing my hand from the parapet, I moved along until the surface ran down to what had to be the far side of the locks. At this time I dared not move without my hand touching something for reassurance, something solid, the slimy surface of bricks, which, for some reason linked with memory, felt blue – or the rough and crumbly surface of eroding stonework, then the colder but more reassuring curve of metal, a handrail beneath my left hand, leading downwards.

I paused and looked back, just to orientate myself, and was surprised that the house was closer than I'd expected. Venturing out into unknown shapes and shadows, I had felt as though lost there, poised over a fathomless pit, from which the rustle and tinkle of water came as a whisper. There is more, it hissed to me, more. Not to see, though, as the light snagged and trapped itself amongst the man-made angles and projections of stone and metal.

Yes, metal this was beneath my hand, clammy and slippy, with a feel of all-pervading damp, or perhaps ice, and now not so reassuring as it had been at first touch. Angling down and away. A way. A prepared way, waiting, just imploring to be explored by a tentative foot. There were steps. They were barely detectable as steps, except that one level felt lower than the previous level, but the impression was blurred by the fact that there were no edges. Two hundred years of fumbling clogs to blundering hob-nails had rounded the treads. Each almost ran into the next, until it seemed like a slope, only barely impressed into a mockery of a run of steps.

It lured me onwards. It was only on and down, it seemed, that I would be able to progress at all. The water echoed as in a hollow chamber, a minor leak that took on the guise of a torrent pouring free, and now, down and to my left, I caught a glimpse of it as it captured a ray of amber light and converted it to liquid, flowing gold. But . . . so small, this flow, a spurt, a trickle, but beating in my mind louder and louder.

I paused, recognizing this feeling of intensification. It arose from an awareness, possibly an intuition sharpened and honed by my late profession. Now, although only a bare suggestion of light slanted and reached inside what seemed to be a cave, I could detect that this was in fact a squared and angular man-made recess, this the second of Colin's pounds.

I stood very still, afraid to move, because my impression was of confinement. Water seemed to surround me. There was a whispering, creaking sound, hiding behind the brittle water trickle. When I turned my head, I realized it was the hiss of static water in the bottom lock, as it eased its surface into an ice layer.

There was now a level footing. This I felt through the soles of my shoes. The angular shape which was almost touching my knees I now realised was one of the rack and pinions. But – why here? Why low-down, almost beneath the footbridge that I'd walked across? It seemed to have no purpose, to be lost and abandoned. In this pit, the trickle of water seeming to be a constant echo completely surrounding me, I stood. The cold reached out to me; the rustle of water took on its own voice, and shapes were beginning to correlate. I felt that if I remained there it might engulf me. Yet I could not move.

23

If I stood very still, would the slanting orange glow venture closer? If I concentrated, would I locate the source of the water's trickle, and would I be able to reconcile a feeling of uneasiness?

And indeed I did detect movement, way down, down in the whispering blackness, as an oily disturbance of the black surface. A crisp packet, discarded six months before, a mile up the canal? A beer can? No. No, not so symmetrical. And there it was again, lifted free of the water, turning restlessly, disturbed by my presence. Something white.

I bent closer, as it had seemed to beckon. Fanciful, Richard, fanciful.

It was at this thought – the choice of beckoning as a simile – that I recognized the fact that what I could be seeing, though my logical mind rejected it, was a human hand.

I crouched, then knelt, on the hard stone surround to the pound, peering and staring. Then again the water surface, two feet below me, stirred lazily and heavily, and a smoother shaped blackness seemed to bulge for a second on the oily flat surface. It moved, rolled, disappeared. And the whiter shape again flicked at me, beckoning, reaching. It was definitely a hand.

Scrambling in the confined space, I managed to stretch out on to my chest. To my left was the rising face of the footbridge, and to my right, most awkwardly, was the strange shape that I now knew to be a rack and pinion. There was barely enough space for my shoulders to edge past it. All I could do was to lean forwards and stare at the blackness, and wait, wait for the surface to break again, so that I could reach down . . . and as I thought that, it did. Definitely, now, I recognized it as a human hand. It could be nothing else.

I raised my head. Never before had I had to shout for help, but now I did. 'Help! Help me!' The sound I managed to produce seemed pitifully weak, lost in the chambers of the locks. Then somebody, no doubt Colin, switched off the white floods, as though my voice had signalled it. 'Oh God!' I groaned, and, 'Help!' I bellowed. It was a useless, baffled appeal.

I was clearly not sufficiently low even to touch the water surface. All I could do was stretch out, rolling on my left hip, my left hand poised to plunge at the very first sign . . . but still the water was too far below me. Further over, now, I twisted on my stomach, legs spread behind me, my right arm hooked round the solid metal of the rack and pinion. I was poised, aching, my eyes straining for any movement, and I dared not raise my head.

Then again the hand appeared. I plunged for it, but managed to do no more than touch the fingers. Then they twisted away. The water surface was too distant, down in the blackness, and I had to slide forward, the edge of stone almost down to my waist now, with the solid edge digging in beneath my ribs. My right arm slowly slipped from the rack. I had to allow it to do so. It was the only remaining chance of reaching far enough, and I tried to control the slip until my fingers, groping, locked themselves into the teeth of the rack. Slippy, slimy teeth. I hung on desperately, poised above the black water, the dead black water that now released stagnant fumes, foul and gassy.

The hand! I plunged as it turned to sink, up to my elbow in iced water now, and felt the arm. My useless, frozen fingers failed to grip, and the arm, the hand, the fingers slid away from me. There was no longer any sense of touch in my left hand. I was soaked to well above my elbow and the cold was its own agony, gnawing away at my reserves of strength.

It turned up again, raised high to the wrist from the surface of the water – a corpse's last desperate attempt to be withdrawn to safety. I thought I detected a spark of light, and I slapped my left hand against it. In only that way could I detect that I had touched it. My mind instructed my fingers to close, and they seemed to obey, but achingly slowly.

I thought then that I had the hand. Long, slim fingers were locked in my left palm, and I concentrated all my efforts on lifting, pulling, fighting against the weight of a body with its saturated clothing, and fighting the cold that was robbing me of strength. I heaved, groaning, and the hand barely lifted clear of the surface. My right hand, I was aware, was slipping away from the rack.

Then, with no sensation of anything but agony from my fingertips to my shoulder, I knew that the hand was sliding finally away. I tried to grip more firmly, but my hand was useless, and the fingers slid from my palm. I drew back. Pain shot through my spine, and my right hand seemed frozen into the teeth of the rack. I lifted my head.

'Help!' I whispered hoarsely. 'Help me!'

No more than a feeble bleating sound emerged, drowned by my own mental curses of frustration. There was an awareness of a great loss.

Time elapsed as I attempted to extricate myself from the restricted space. My left arm was useless, and I had to rely on my right. The fumbled grip on the rack proved to be impossible in taking my weight. My fingers slipped from it. I had to force my mind from the necessity of its being greased, and I cursed it for that necessity. The difficulty was in backing out. Slowly, I edged away until I could turn, still clumsily, and heard, as a distant and plaintive cry, Amelia calling out, 'Richard, Richard! Where are you?'

But my throat was constricted; I could do no more than whisper. Back, back, a few inches at a time. Then, my reaching left fist, which I seemed not to be able to open, touched something. I recognized it. The handrail.

But the hand, which had clung to the wrist and slid from the fingers, still stubbornly refused to abandon that task. Right hand, then. Right hand crossed over my chest to the rail, I told myself, as my aching legs straightened. Greasy fingers to the rail. I could feel no security. Crawl up the steps. Yes. That would be best. Head down, I crawled. One step, two steps ... My left hand still would not open. I had to allow knuckles to take the weight.

'Richard! Oh ... Richard!'

Now her voice was closer, panic in it.

'Here!' I shouted. It emerged as a whisper, drowned by the rustle of running water. Crawled up another step. 'Here!' I croaked.

'Richard ...' She was now directly above me, horror in her voice.

'Fetch help,' I whispered. 'Don't come ... closer. Get help. Colin. Get Colin.'

Amelia is very sensible. No arguing. She could see she could not help me physically. 'I'll be back,' she said. 'Rest. Wait. A minute. Just hold on, Richard.' But her voice was unsteady.

There was an age in that minute, a doddering old minute that took an eternity to absorb all sixty seconds. Then the white lights snapped on again, voices were raised. Shouting. Torches threw their weight around, and Colin was looking down at me from the footbridge.

'What the hell ... Ray, you come down with me. We can get behind him. Lights down here. Let's see what we're doing. Lights!'

They came round behind me, two strong young men, one of whom knew every indentation of the worn steps, where to put a foot, in which direction to lift me, turn me, roll me, until others could find footroom to take my weight.

Colin's head was close to mine. He was whispering encouragement, and my legs were beginning to operate, weakly, but it was a relief to have confirmation that they were still attached.

I managed to croak a few words. 'Somebody in the pound,' I whispered. 'Couldn't have left him. Or her. Her, I think. Slim hands, couldn't hold on. Phone the police.'

'All right,' he said. 'In a sec'. You first. That's it. Can you take your own weight? You're doing fine. But you've got to keep moving.'

Then Amelia was at my side. 'Oh Richard, just look at you! What've you been *doing*?'

I think I smiled, but if so it had to squeeze past the agony of my left arm. They got me into the bar. Oh, blessed warmth! Everybody was there, staring at me as though I was a demon raised from the depths. They sat me down. I could hear Colin on the phone, and I wondered how they would manage to retrieve the body. There was a pain in my left thigh.

'You're *sure* it was a person – somebody?' asked Amelia anxiously.

'Yes!' I had spoken it with bitterness, and went on more gently. 'Yes, love. Certain.'

Ray Torrance held out a glass of whisky, offering it to my left hand. I shook my head, and put out my right. Now, with the circulation returning, my left arm was a rage of agony. I could barely restrain a cry of pain. But the spirit hit me, and the warmth flowed – inside, anyway. It would take a while to reach my fingertips, or relieve a strange, hard pain in my left palm. My hand was still a frozen fist.

They removed my anorak carefully. It was completely ruined, black grease all over the right side and the right arm, soaked and dirty all down the front. It wasn't until Amelia gently removed the scarf from my head that I realized I was still wearing it.

'My pipe,' I said cautiously, my voice still unsteady.

'In your anorak pocket,' said Amelia. She drew it out in two halves. 'I'm afraid it's broken.'

That accounted for the pain in my left thigh, I realized. I'd been lying on my pipe. It was my meerschaum, too.

But now I was too busy trying not to cry out as my whole left arm went into a riot of pain. Still, my left hand wouldn't open.

27

'How on earth did you come to be down there?' asked Gerald. He was clearly not pleased with the turn of events. It would disrupt the party, and cast a shadow on his daughter's formal engagement.

So I told him my story in between sips of whisky, how I'd seen a white shape, why I had been so certain it was a hand – because I'd grasped it in mine – why I thought it had to be a woman's, from the long, slim fingers.

'She couldn't possibly have been alive,' I said. 'Even when I first saw the hand, she couldn't. I was just plain stupid. I could have done nothing for her – but I felt I had to try.'

If I hadn't, I would have found it difficult to live with myself.

'Try a cigar,' Gerald offered.

'Thank you . . . but no,' I said. I can't smoke cigars. 'There's a spare pipe in the car.'

'I'll get it,' Amelia offered.

'No,' I said, sharply, quickly. 'It'll wait.' I tried to smile at her.

I didn't want her to leave my side. There was something I had to say, for her ears alone, and as soon as the opportunity presented itself.

'I think I can walk now,' I said optimistically. 'The feeling's come back into my legs.'

Somebody helped me to my feet. I saw that it was Colin. We tried it together round the bar floor, his hand to my elbow, with everybody watching us anxiously, me limping.

'Yes,' he said. 'You seem fine. Come along – the stairs could be tricky.'

On that point he was correct. My thighs and knees had been in contact with bare stonework. I ached. Head to toe, I ached. But we made it up the stairs and to our room, where I sat with a thump on the edge of the bed.

'Thanks,' I said. 'I'll be all right now. Don't let it interfere with your dinner.'

'We'll wait. There's no hurry.'

'No . . . really.'

'I doubt anybody will feel like eating,' he said, 'knowing that there's somebody in that pound. I'll leave you now – and look in later. They're coming.' He cocked his head.

I could hear the sirens too, and see the reflected blue flashes of their warning lights.

'Did you tell them what they've got to contend with?' I asked, and he nodded. Then he left us.

I waited until the door closed behind him, and stared at my left fist. The pain was receding, and the fingers were capable of movement. Enough feeling had returned for me to detect clearly what I'd felt before, but at that time only vaguely. There was a hard object digging into my palm.

'I'll run you a bath,' Amelia said. 'You'd better get those clothes off.'

I saw then that she must have had her own bath, as she was wearing the dress she'd brought for the evening. Over it, she had thrown her anorak. Hers had a hood. She must have failed to see me walking around outside, and had come to search me out. Luckily for me.

'In a second,' I said. 'There's something else.'

I reached over with my right hand and slowly, painfully, began to lift one finger at a time from the clasped left hand. Then paused. Footsteps raced up the stairs, and there was a tap at the door.

'Come in,' I called.

It was Colin again. 'Ashtray,' he said, waving a large glass one. He put it down on the bedside table. 'Now all you need is the spare pipe.' He grinned. 'See you later.' Then he was gone.

It had been his hint that I need not venture into danger again, simply for a peaceful smoke. Smoking can be dangerous.

'The car keys?' asked Amelia.

'Anorak pocket,' I told her. 'But leave it for now. The anorak's in the bar. There's something I want to say.'

'Oh . . . mysterious.' She was humouring me. 'Say on.'

'You'll have talked with Mellie,' I said, and waited for her nod. 'Of course you would. And – two women together – I expect the engagement ring was mentioned.'

'Of course.'

'Described? Did she describe it?'

'What *is* this, Richard? What're you getting at?'

'So?' I insisted. 'The ring.'

'So – exactly what?' she demanded. 'She told me how generous Ray had been. £800 for a ring! That's a bit much for a policeman – a constable. But apparently he insisted, because she liked it. I mean . . . oh, you know how it is.'

I grinned at her. 'It amounts to emotional blackmail, but all the same it's a fair sum to carry around on a finger.'

29

'What're you getting at, Richard?' she demanded. 'Please don't criticize her. I'm told he's picked up a nice little inheritance recently.'

I nodded. 'I see. And . . . correct me if I'm wrong – you have to be measured for a ring. It'd never do if it was too loose. It could slip off.'

'Oh, Richard! You know all this. Yes, she had to be measured. They slip different sized rings over your finger to get it right.'

'And . . . then he pockets the ring? The man does.'

'Well – I don't know how it is these days with young women. I reckon most couples don't bother with engagement rings – and if they do they probably slip them on in the shop, and that's it. But these people here . . . well, you've met them, Richard. It all has to be traditional. She gets the ring on her finger this evening.'

I nodded. 'All being well.'

'And what does *that* mean?' She was clearly losing patience with me.

'Did she describe it?' I asked. 'Oh . . . she's sure to have done.'

'Yes. If you *must* know. It's naturally got a ruby. Her second name. It's a ruby with a circlet of diamonds.'

She waited impatiently for my response. I had to decide exactly how to put it. So I approached it from a different direction.

'Have you noticed – young Ray Torrance has been acting rather strange all evening, from the moment we first met him. He refused to open his little black box and show Mellie the ring. He's been looking harassed and worried, and he's drinking too much. I did wonder why. But I think I know now. Call it a guess.'

It was a guess inspired by multiple suggestions. A ring that Ray refused to produce, and his weak explanation that it was unlucky – the fact that rings are bought as a proper fit – the fact that the hard shape now in my palm had slipped away from the dead hand so easily – and the fact of a tangible atmosphere of something untoward.

'*Do* tell me, and then get to your bath.' Amelia was impatient.

But I wasn't ready. 'That hand in the pound . . . I thought it was a woman's. Long and slim fingers. I also thought that I caught a spark of light down there. Then I couldn't keep hold of the hand any longer. It just slipped away, being all wet and my fingers numb. But as I lost the hand I felt something hard in my palm. It's still there. And I couldn't open my hand when I managed to get out of there. But . . . . I think I can now. Shall I try it?'

She stared at me, her face rigid, eyes huge. Down below, beneath our windows, I could hear the police vehicles arriving, their sirens yawning down to a growl.

'Try it,' she suggested softly.

I did. My fist opened, and in the palm lay a ring. It was a ruby with a circlet of diamonds.

'Oh Lord!' she whispered.

'You think this could be the one?' I asked.

'Oh yes. Yes.' But her voice wasn't steady. 'It must be, otherwise the coincidence is too great.'

'And also, of course,' I pointed out, 'the ring was not a perfect fit for the finger it was on. So – what do I do about it? That's where I want your advice, my love. A woman's view of the problem. If it's *the* ring, then how did this other woman – assuming it is a woman – come to be wearing it? But if it *is* the ring, that would explain Ray's attitude, if he came here this evening with an empty box in his pocket. He would *have* to come, ring or no ring. How he thought he was going to wriggle out of the situation I can't guess. I reckon he couldn't, either. The last I saw of him, he seemed to be drinking himself into a stupor. Better *that* scandal, I suppose, than having to admit he had no ring to place on Mellie's finger.'

'So now you'll be able to ease his mind,' she said lightly. 'That should please you, Richard.'

But she had not allowed her mind to probe the background implications, and perhaps was not taking me seriously. So I decided not to pursue it at that time.

'Hmm!' I said. 'I think I'm ready for my bath now.'

'You're putting it off!' she cried. 'The ring, Richard!'

Did she intend me to rush out of the room and hunt for Ray? I shrugged. 'I need time to think, my love. I'll do some thinking in the bath.'

'*Is* there anything to be decided?' she demanded. 'If that's the ring Ray bought for Mellie (and how it could be I can't imagine) then you must take it to him. Shall I do it? Give it to me and . . .'

I shook my head, smiling to reassure her. 'But you see – ' I found I could get to my feet quite easily and stand without too many pains. 'I'm in an awkward spot, my love. I'm an ex-policeman, and I've removed evidence from what seems very likely to be the body of a woman. I've removed a ring. And we don't know what she was doing here, or how the ring got on her finger, or how she got into the pound. An accident? Or was she pushed? The parapet on that footbridge over the pound is only about thigh height, so it could have been an accident. The ring is evidence of ... well, something. So my obvious duty is to hand it over to whoever turns out to be the officer in charge of ... whatever it turns out to be, and in the circumstances, with the background evidence, the implication is murder. So – am I to be responsible for withholding evidence in a horrible crime, just to help out a young man I didn't meet until an hour ago? Ask yourself, my love.'

'But ... Mellie!'

'I know, I know. But think about it, while I have my bath. And bear in mind what a terrible death that must have been, if she wasn't dead when she went in.'

'I'll go down and try to find your other pipe,' she said, somewhat distantly, clearly not wishing to allow her mind to dwell on the nature of the death. Then she left the room abruptly, obviously annoyed with my attitude.

3

I did not run my bath immediately, but went to stand at the window, watching what was going on below. Whoever was in charge seemed to know how to go about it. Or perhaps he wasn't in charge, because Colin was down there. They were his locks, and he would know best what to do.

For a few minutes I couldn't detect what they were doing, but then I realized that there was an obvious approach to it. They had the gate at the head of the bottom lock open, Colin in charge at that time, and were flooding the pound in order to float the body out to a more exposed position in the bottom lock, from where they could approach it more effectively.

The white floodlights were now switched on again, and supplemented by lights from two of their vehicles. It was like working in full daylight. Almost beneath my window, they were rigging a square of canvas, with ropes. Once they had a sight of the body, if no more than a gentle roll to the surface, they would be able to work the canvas to a position beneath it, and lift it out. It ... it ...

I couldn't prevent myself from thinking in this way. There had been only the shape of a hand and fingers on which I had based my decision, and it was perhaps too little on which to form a firm basis as to sex.

Yet ... there was the ring. Would a man wear such a ring? These days, perhaps. Ah yes.

I turned away. The ache in my fingers had become no more than a stiffness. I decided on the bath.

This was the biggest bath I had ever seen. I wallowed in it gloriously. The residual aches disappeared, and I could exercise all my faculties. It seemed to me that I was being manoeuvred into a position that all my instincts told me was wrong. If it turned out that the death had not been accidental, I would be compounding a crime. Or did I wait until somebody in authority made the decision? And then decide. That was a very weak way round it, and would be recognized as such. Procrastination, it's called, but in this instance it could be the thief of my self-respect rather than my time.

Amelia had been a long while. I was towelling myself when she called from the bedroom.

'I've brought your pipe, Richard.'

'Did you have any difficulty finding it? You've been gone quite a while.'

She didn't answer directly. Or rather, she answered in an evasive manner.

'The dinner's going to go ahead, as planned,' she called out. 'They've actually got a gong. Gerald's acting as though everything's normal, and what's going on outside is of no interest to anybody inside. It's just as well we packed your charcoal grey suit, I must say. It all sounds as though it's going to be very formal.'

I wandered into the bedroom. 'Think I'd better have another shave?' I asked, rasping my hand around my chin.

'Oh no. You'll do.' She hadn't even cast me a glance. 'But I've been talking to somebody who says he knows you.'

'Have you, indeed?'

I might have guessed that she would have moved around, trying to get together as much information as she could. No doubt she would have had a few words with everybody who would listen, if only to gather evidence that there would be no harm whatsoever in my returning the ring to Ray Torrance.

'His name's Slater,' she told me. 'Inspector Ted Slater, he told me. He wasn't wearing a uniform, so I suppose he's a detective inspector. Do you think?'

'Yes,' I said. 'I knew Ted. I'd better get out there and have a word . . .'

'Richard! It's still cold out there, and you haven't got a coat to put on. You don't want to get a chill, and after what you've already been through – '

'Yes, yes. Maybe I can borrow an overcoat. It can wait, anyway.'

'And I looked into the bar,' she told me. 'They call it a lounge. Anyway . . . I looked in. Mellie was in there, talking to Ray.'

'And?' I had to prompt, because she didn't go on.

'She was close to tears, Richard. I could tell that. And you were quite correct. There *is* something strange about Ray. That *must* be her ring.'

She pointed at it, where I had left it on the bedside table.

'And I'm sure Mellie's feeling that there's something wrong,' she added.

The way she had spoken, the way she pointed, indicated that I was in severe dereliction of my obvious duty, which was to put an end to the distress.

'I will not have her upset, Richard. I will *not*.'

She does not usually flare up at me like that. Any other time, she would have respected my reason for hesitation. But this was brushing too close. I turned away, not wishing to look her directly in the eyes. Instead, I went to the window and looked out.

In the time I'd taken with my bath, they had succeeded in the task for which they'd been preparing. They had captured the body in their canvas sling, and had brought it, dripping, over the footbridge, to where there was more space to spread it out, and more light. It was indeed a woman, as a skirt was twisted clammily around her legs. So I had been correct in my guess. Both skirt and jacket were dark. Now black with water, they were nevertheless recognizable as the uniform of a woman police constable.

Two men were crouched over her, one clearly a doctor, with his bag beside him. He was not the medical examiner I'd known in my time.

'I'll be a minute,' I said.

'But Richard . . .'

'Only a minute.' And I rushed out, down the stairs and through the bar, out into the cold night. The men were packing their equipment away; an ambulance was waiting to receive the body. I walked up to the two men. As my feet came within the orbit of Slater's vision, he looked up.

'Who're you?' he demanded.

'I'm the one who spotted her, and tried to get her out. I've got a personal interest – '

'Then take it somewhere else,' he told me flatly. 'You're Patton, aren't you? This isn't for you.' His tone wasn't encouraging.

'Proprietory interest,' I suggested. 'And why the CID?'

'I told you. It's none of your affair.'

'She fell in. Easy enough – '

'Somebody phoned in,' he interrupted. 'Said she'd been killed. So the CID it had to be. And it turns out it's in the family. This is Woman Police Constable Clare Martin. One of ours, Patton, one of ours.'

'An accident . . .'

'There is what looks like a depressed fracture of the skull,' the doctor observed, his head down, as though telling WPC Martin how she'd died. 'And there are thumb marks on her neck. Looks like thumb marks. For now . . . I'd say she was strangled before she entered the water, and got a blow on the back of her head going in.'

Slater cocked his head at me. 'Satisfied, Patton? Satisfied?'

'I would be, if you'd found her cap.'

'What?'

'Her peaked cap with the checkered band,' I explained. 'If she'd been wearing it, perhaps you wouldn't be looking at a depressed fracture. No sign of it?' I asked innocently.

'No sign,' said Slater shortly.

'That's strange,' I remarked, and turned away back to the house.

When I walked into the bar, Amelia was tucked away at a corner table and talking quietly to Ray. I had to hope she wasn't telling him I had the ring, as I was planning to use it as a form of blackmail. Then, perhaps, I would be able to force out the truth and make up my mind as to my future actions.

Colin was standing with one foot on the genuine, old and worn, brass rail around the base of the counter. Morosely, he was drinking something that appeared to be beer. When I asked, he said it was shandy, but it smelt stronger than that. Brandy in it, perhaps.

'Got to keep a clear head,' he told me, but his pronunciation wandered.

He stared past me at Ray, frowning. Then he put his huge hands over his face and rubbed his features vigorously, as though trying to enliven them towards something. Or away. Away, perhaps, from the distress of a sudden death, one within his own domain.

There was anger in the set of his jaw. 'Look at him,' he mumbled. 'Nothin' matters to dear old Ray. Somebody dies, and right outside there ... but does he care? No. Not him. He chats away as though it's nothing. Nothing!' He swept his arm violently, sending his glass flying, to crash to splinters behind the counter. I pretended to ignore it, though Amelia's head had lifted, startled.

'How long have we got?' I asked, changing the subject. Then, at his blank expression, I amplified, 'Until the dinner gong.'

'Oh ...' He shrugged. 'Say ... a quarter of an hour. Twenty minutes. Or more. When last sighted, father was dressing. Mother said he was tying his bow tie. Never a made-up tie for him, you understand. He despises them, he says, though how you can despise an inanimate object I don't know. Don't worry. I've known it to take half an hour.'

'A perfectionist,' I murmured.

He made a sound of disgust. 'It's typical. Nothing has to interfere with his plans. There's going to be a dinner and then an engagement party. The fact that somebody's met with a horrible death out there – oh, he's already forgotten that. You can bet.'

Not, I thought, a perfectionist, after all. More closely I'd call him self-opinionated. Everything revolved around Gerald Fulton. And it revolved at the pace suitable to him.

'Is your mother having to do all the cooking?' I asked, just to change the subject. 'On her own.'

'Oh no. She's got help. She fixed it up. It'd never occur to my dear father. Mrs Phipps from the village. Marvellous, she is. And her daughter, Betty – she's going to do the serving. It'll all be absolutely correct, you'll see. Dinner *and* party. Has to be, if father's got anything to do with it. It's not every day, he said, that you have a daughter getting engaged.'

The thought crossed my mind that this evening he might be disappointed, as what was possibly the ring was still in my pocket.

'And is the young lady prepared for the ordeal?'

'Ordeal? Funny way of putting it.' But he looked away from

36

me, he too aware that there was something off-key with such an arrangement. In fact, he made an attempt to rationalize the situation.

'Of course,' he said, 'something just *had* to crop up and spoil everything.'

He was attempting to be annoyed about this, possibly adopting his father's attitude. But it was false. Distress was in his set expression.

I tried this out, saying casually, 'You're thinking about the death?'

'Yes,' he snapped. 'That. Of course.'

I leaned back against the counter, casually eyeing Ray across the room. I raised my voice a little.

'They've identified the poor woman, you know. They've managed to get her out, and she's known. One of Ray's fellow-workers. One of your friends, Ray,' I called out.

'What?'

'The dead woman.' I tried to ignore the fact that Amelia was staring at me in amazement. 'She's a policewoman, Ray.'

It was Colin who reacted most forcefully, taking my arm and turning me to face him. 'Who?' he demanded. 'Do they know her name?'

'It doesn't really concern us,' I told him, glancing down at his hand. 'Ray, perhaps. If he knows her.'

Colin reached for a clean glass. 'I'll have to get out there. Ask 'em . . .' He'd already forgotten the glass.

'They're busy. I wouldn't interrupt, if I were you.' I tried to change the direction of the conversation. 'It was you who phoned them, wasn't it?' I asked.

'Yes, yes. Why the questions? I'll have to get out there.'

'No. I wouldn't do that.' I clamped a hand on his wrist.

He jerked it free. 'Take your hand off me.' Now his voice was dull, almost toneless. 'I've got to know.'

'Why?' I demanded.

'A policewoman . . .'

'Her name was Martin,' I told him. 'Clare Martin.'

Then Colin was off and away towards the door, and I caught him by the arm just as he reached it. He turned, his eyes wild. 'Take your hand off me.'

I shrugged, and released him. 'You knew her?' I asked quietly.

'Yes.'

37

'Then my advice is to wait until somebody comes along and asks.'

Relaxing now, he allowed himself to be moved back towards the counter. 'Advice?' he asked. 'From an ex-copper? I don't like the sound of that. You're making it sound all . . . well, all kind of serious. Sort of.' He managed to pour more beer into his fresh glass. 'She fell in, didn't she? An accident.'

I shrugged. 'Who can say? So far, I know next to nothing. We'll soon hear all about it, more than we want to. But relax, Colin. It's a special evening.'

'Special . . .' He groaned.

I made an attempt to divert his mind in a slightly different direction, and repeated what I'd asked before. 'Was it you who phoned the police?'

'Of course it was. It's *my* flight. My responsibility.'

'But why did you use the word killed? I mean, most people would have said drowned. You said killed.'

'She was killed by falling in, wasn't she? Does it matter?'

'Only that you gave the impression that there was violence involved, so instead of the regular force, you've got the CID, and they have to justify their existence by asking questions.'

'Oh . . . come *on*,' he cut in. 'The poor woman fell in – didn't she? What she'd be doing here I can't imagine, but here she was. And she fell in. I can't see why anybody . . . I mean, it's dreadful, but it's got to be an accident – hasn't it? The bridge parapet's low. It'd be easy enough. An accident. Too much fuss – that's all. Too much . . .'

He stopped, shaking his head violently as though trying to dismiss it.

'Well, for one thing,' I said, 'she was a police officer. For another, there was a heavy contusion on her head, and for – '

'Heh, heh!' he complained. 'Take it easy. You're making a bloody mountain – '

'Out of nothing?' I cut in. 'Oh no, Colin. There's trouble on the way, and I'm simply giving you the tip-off. That's all. For now, from just a quick check, the doctor's suggesting she could have been strangled. The blow to her head could well have been inflicted when she fell in. Or,' I amplified, because his blank expression suggested he was rejecting everything I said, 'when she was thrown in.'

'You're ex-police, sure enough,' Colin stated tersely. 'It must get into your blood. Obsessed. You lot see nothing else but trouble, everywhere.'

'Just warning you,' I told him casually.

'*Warning* me! Are you saying I could be responsible?'

'Don't be an idiot. I'm only asking you to be prepared. There could be upset and unpleasantness. You might pass the word along to the rest of your family, and prepare them for it. I don't know what you'll do about your father, though. But let him know how things stand. He mustn't get the idea that if he ignores it, it'll all go away.'

He downed the rest of his drink, twisted his head so that he was eyeing me quizzically, and asked, 'You'll be around, Mr Patton?' Red showed in the lower lids of his eyes.

'Yes. As long as is necessary.'

'Then we'll have somebody to turn to.'

He went away, leaving me feeling empty. Why should he assume he could rely on me? I could do nothing to help him and his strange family, which seemed so defenceless all of a sudden. Then I realized why I had thought of them in this way. The ambience of their lives; the fact that Colin was employed in an environment established over 200 years before; the fact that the father's direction of thought was as ancient as the laws he lived by; the fact that the physical isolation cut them off from the present pace of life: all these rendered them helpless when tossed into the brisk and impersonal routine of a full-scale modern murder investigation. They would be lost. I could not desert them now.

Particularly at this time, I could not desert them, because I had in my possession a definite and positive item of evidence relating to what could have been the murder of Clare Martin. If I handed this over to Detective Inspector Ted Slater, my involvement, and my personal illegal action in retaining it, would be rationalized. Wiped clean. And the dissolution of the family could well begin, I felt.

More than that – if I failed to hand over the ring, it would toss the responsibility directly on to my shoulders to discover the murderer, and I would have to pray that it didn't turn out to be one of the family, as this, too, would destroy them.

Amelia, although apparently absorbed with Ray, noticed that I was now standing alone at the bar, and lifted her head. 'Have you seen Mellie, Richard?'

'Well . . . no. Not recently.'

'I'd better go and see if she's all right. I mean, help her if she's in trouble. I mean, help her if she's needing advice with her dress . . . or anything.'

She hadn't done that well. It was too obviously an excuse for leaving me alone with Ray. I had something to give to Ray, and I'd better get on and do it. That was what she was telling me.

'See you later then,' I said, and I strolled over to where Ray was sitting. He stared morosely at the table surface. His fingers were pushing around an empty glass. I could see he was aching for another drink.

I sat opposite to him. I could have done with a drink myself, but at least I had my pipe, and could fill it and light it; anything to occupy my hands.

'Have you been outside?' I asked.

'No.'

'I thought you'd be interested,' I told him casually. 'Lots of your mates are out there. Detective Inspector Slater's in charge.'

His eyes darted up beneath lowered eyebrows. 'The CID? What're they in it for?'

'I assumed you'd know. You'll never make a good copper unless you're inquisitive. Perhaps you'd rather not know – is that it?'

'Can't say I do.'

'Oh?' I had to take into account that he was so far down in the morass of his miseries that nothing outside touched him. 'They think it's murder, you know.'

'Gerraway!'

'It's true. And she's somebody in the force, too, so they're going to tear the place apart for clues.'

'In the force?' His voice was dead and toneless.

'Yes. You probably know her. Clare. Her name's Clare Martin.'

Now his head was raised, his eyes wide and startled. He licked his lips. 'Clare?' As though he hadn't heard me when I'd told Colin. Perhaps he hadn't been listening.

'You know her?'

'Of course I do. I worked with her.' His eyes wouldn't meet mine. 'We're both on traffic patrol.'

'Were,' I corrected. 'She's dead. And I believe they're treating it as a wilful killing. Murder. For now, anyway.'

'Murder?' It was a whisper.

'And there's a possibility she was strangled. The doctor saw signs.'

He attempted to clear his throat, possibly a psychological reaction to the thought of choking. 'That can't be true,' he managed to say.

'It's the situation, as at this moment. When they get down to the post mortem examination, then they'll be certain. Whether or not she was dead before she went into the water, I mean. If so – the strangling – it would've been a very silly thing to do. A good push, and she'd have been in that pound, and she wouldn't have been able to get out.'

He was shaking his head emphatically, and slapped the table surface to put a stop to me. 'What the hell're you on about?' His voice was slightly more firm now, more assertive.

'I'm just saying that in any circumstance requiring that she should be killed, it would've been simplicity itself to push her into any of the locks. The temperature of the water would have finished her off before she actually drowned, I would guess. And so simple. So . . . I wonder why she was strangled. That's all.'

'How would I know?' he demanded plaintively. 'And why're you going on about it like this?'

'I thought you'd be interested. I mean – if she *was* strangled, she could have been brought here – already dead.'

'Could she? You getting to something, are you?' Now there was a hint of impatience in his voice. 'If so – why not say it?'

I smiled at him. 'Yes I am. Has she got a car?'

'Yes. I mean . . . I'd think so.'

'You mean yes. And is it a small red hatchback?'

Now he glared at me. 'How the hell could you know that?'

'Because we passed it, coming here. Abandoned – or rather, left. At the top of the lane leading down to here. By the crossroads. Now . . . from the run of the canal, and how it relates to this house, it seems to me that it would run right past that crossroads, so there'd probably be access on that corner to the tow-path. Yes?'

He simply stared.

'And perhaps that was how she got here. Not brought as an already strangled woman – it's probably a bit too far for that – but on her own two feet along the tow-path. Tricky at night, I'd have thought. But it's a fair guess. Wouldn't you say it's a fair guess?'

'If you like. I suppose this means something? Getting some-where, are you? If so, you'd better get on with it, because that bloody dinner gong'll be going any time now, and nobody – just nobody – ever dares to ignore Poppa Fulton's instructions. Believe you me.'

Anger had now distracted him from his mood of despair. I didn't know whether or not I wanted him angry, though people at such a time are apt to be indiscreet.

'There's time enough for what I want,' I said. 'It'll take no more than a few seconds to show me the ring.'

'Ring? You mean the engagement ring?' He stared at me as though bemused. 'Why would you want to see that?'

'I just do.'

'Then you can manage without. And why'd *you* want to see it? It's females who go all sloppy over jewellery. I suppose you aren't . . .' His eyebrows shot up.

'No. Not at all like that. Describe the ring, then, if I'm not to see it.'

'Heaven help us! What's the matter with you, all this – '

'Describe it,' I snapped, getting annoyed by his evasive tactics.

On this he now seized. Perhaps it would keep me quiet. 'It's a gold ring like any other ring, with a ruby in the middle, 'cause her second name's Ruby, and some little diamonds all round it. And you'd never guess how much it cost! The bloody robbers!'

'It sounds as though it'd be worth about £800,' I said.

He stared at me. 'Who told you that?'

'My wife, and she had the information from Mellie herself. I do hope you haven't lost it.'

'I . . . no . . . what the hell're you talking about?'

I put my right fist on the table, knuckles down, then opened out my fingers, the ring in my palm. 'Is it like this one?' I asked gently.

'What . . . what . . .' he gabbled. Then he shot out his hand, and I closed the fist. Having closed it, I thought I might as well use it, so I waved the fist under his nose. 'Is this your ring?' I asked gently. 'It slid off into my hand when I was trying to pull her out. WPC Martin, that is.'

He stared at me blankly, and strangely I caught a light in his eye that was very different from the despair I'd expected. His lips twitched, then he said, 'No.'

'No? You mean this isn't your ring?'

'Of course not.' Now he was positively grinning, and I was beginning to get the impression that he'd led me into a trap.

'Then what . . .'

'You've been jumping to conclusions, Mr Patton, haven't you! This is the ring.' He reached into his uniform pocket and produced his little black box, flicked the lid open with a finger, and slid it on to the table beneath my nose.

The ring was magnificent, catching the lighting and winking it back at me.

'Go on,' he said, enjoying himself. 'Take it out of the box. It's not going to crumble into dust. That's right. Now put your cheap masterpiece beside it. That's right. Here . . .'

He reached over and put his right hand in a cage over both of the rings, and shuffled it around, then removed the hand. 'There. Any doubt about which is which?'

There was no possible doubt. One was alive, the other dead. I picked up the genuine one and carefully fitted it back into its box.

'Put it away,' I said. He did. I went on, 'Now tell me what the hell's been nagging at you all evening, and why you've been hanging around like wet drawers on a clothes-line. I can't see any reason . . .'

'*That's* your reason,' he told me, prodding a contemptuous finger at the fake.

Now that I'd acquired a little basic experience, I was wondering how Amelia could have mistaken an obviously cheap ring for a genuine diamond and ruby one. But of course, the implication had been there, that the ring was deeply involved with what had been going on. We had linked suggestion with truth, and deceived ourselves.

'You expected something like this ring to crop up – a fake – to disrupt the smooth course of the party?' I suggested.

'Not . . .' he said, peering at me from beneath lowered eyebrows. 'Not exactly a ring. Something. Just something. I'll have to tell you – '

'You most certainly will, and be damned quick about it, before that dinner gong cuts it short. Think what Gerald would say if we're late.'

'As quick as I can. There's not much. It's just that I knew the bitch would try to do something to spoil it for me.'

'The bitch in question being Clare Martin?'

'Yes. We worked together, you know. A team – traffic patrol. It's . . . well, you share experiences, and grow rather close. You could say this for her, though, she was a damned fine partner. I'd

43

rather have had her at my elbow than a man, if there was trouble, I can tell you that. Oh yes, we were a grand team, but it got so that she wanted to make it a permanent team. And that I certainly didn't want.'

'Because of Mellie?'

'Yes. Mellie.'

'So Clare knew about her?'

'Oh yes. Of course. A lot gets said during a full shift in the car. Clare knew . . . and she bloody-well hated it. Hated.'

'Hmm! Yes.' And I could've bet he'd been too naïve, and told her too much.

'But she was still trying,' he said. 'Tried everything, she did. But . . . frankly, she was a bit overpowering – always had to know best – bossy, you know. Imagine six hours together with that sort of thing – and yesterday was as much as I could take. On about the engagement, she was, every minute. I was right fed up with it. And then she said she'd see me later that evening, at my place. Last night, that was. For what she called a farewell performance.'

I cut in quickly before he could go into details. 'Are you telling me that you had her in your bed on the night before you got engaged to another woman?'

His eyes were wide, his mouth loose, perhaps in surprise at my anger. 'It's not as though I was getting married today. Just an engagement. I thought – '

'Never mind what you bloody-well thought. You ought to be ashamed – '

'I've got this little flat – '

'Never mind explaining your life-style, either. What I can see is that you've got a barefaced cheek – '

'It's all right for you to talk! I tried to chuck her out, and she was a right handful, I can tell you, and it got to be all-in wrestling, and it's not far from that to – '

'Let's not have a round-by-round commentary. I think I'm wasting my time here. D'you know . . . and shut your mouth and listen, you young tyke. I've taken evidence from the body of a young woman, and I haven't handed it over. This ring. It might not matter, but then again it might be the most important clue there is. I did that for *you*. No! No, I didn't. I did it for Mellie. But now I'm beginning to think you're not worth it. She deserves better. Much better.'

'Now you just hold on!' he cried. 'For God's sake . . .'

44

'I've a good mind to take this ring to Inspector Slater, and tell him the truth – that it slipped off her finger and into my hand, and let *him* enquire about it. And d'you think he'd worry about Mellie finding out how and why it got ... How *did* it get on to Clare Martin's finger? Did you buy it for her as a consolation prize?'

He made a sound of disgust. 'You trying to be funny?'

'How did it get on her finger?'

'There's the gong,' he said, half raising himself from his chair.

'To hell with the gong!' I snapped, leaning forward and clamping a hand on his shoulder. 'Sit down, damn you. The ring – the ring. Explain.'

He shrugged, looked disgruntled, grimaced, and said, 'I told you. Clare almost forced her way in, and I'd got the box open, on my dressing table, and she saw it. She would. Women's eyes go straight to that sort of thing. And she did her stupid squeak and said, all sloppy, "Oh, is that for me?" Knowing damn well that it wasn't. And she tried to make off with it . . .'

'Steal it?'

'Had it on her finger, she did. That was how the barney started . . . and it finished – well – on the bed.'

'And this, I suppose, took place with the ring still on her finger? She smiling at it past your shoulder – '

'You crazy or something? The bloody gong's gone.'

'Out with it, or I'll tell the lot to Mellie.'

'Oh Christ! I got it back. In the end. Got it off her finger, and managed to chuck her out of the door. Had to near as dammit throttle her unconscious . . .'

'What?' I whispered.

'Got my hands on her throat.'

I groaned. 'But you got the ring back, and she left? And . . .'

A door was opened. I detected the movement on the edge of my vision. 'The gong's gone, Richard.' It was Amelia.

Not for one moment did I take my eyes from Ray's. 'And the other ring?' I made a gesture towards Amelia, one she would understand.

Ray sighed. 'Ain't it obvious? She must've bought a cheap copy. Paste, they call it. Bought it from memory. That'd be easy enough. Women remember that sort of thing. Yeah – that'd be it. Then, I suppose, she intended to come and flaunt it here – and make a farce of our engagement.'

'But you managed to stall her off, by throwing her in the – '

45

'No! You must be crazy. Why the hell would I have had to go that far? I'd have got that ring off her, somehow. If I had to knock her down and take it by force.'

'Richard . . . the gong!'

'I'm coming.' I got to my feet. 'We're coming. Come along, Ray. On your feet. And smile, damn you. Smile at your host and hostess. Apologize for keeping them waiting. And kiss your fiancée . . . if you've got that much bare-faced cheek.'

I didn't glance sideways to check whether he was smiling. Amelia led the way. I had no idea where their dining room was situated.

It was a big room, almost square, its walls surprisingly undecorated with pictures. Large, blank expanses of Regency stripes cried out for something to dislocate the symmetry. Faces turned to us as we entered. Ruby seemed tense, and Mellie was decidedly drooping. Amelia took the seat she had obviously been occupying before having been sent to locate the miscreant husband and almost-fiancé.

There were seven of us, three women and four men, so that it was inevitable that two men should sit together. I was one of them, and sat between Amelia and Ray. But before taking my seat I bowed formally to Ruby and Gerald, two bows, and said, 'I apologize most sincerely for keeping you waiting, but I was engaged in a most serious conversation with your future son-in-law, and there were matters that had to be settled.'

Gerald grunted, then nodded. Ruby smiled weakly. We sat, Ray and I. A glance sideways confirmed that he was blushing. For some reason I didn't understand, it seemed that the delay had now been universally accepted as due to my advice to Ray on the facts of life. If anybody didn't need advice on the practical aspects, it was Ray. On the application and timing of his expertise, he still had a lot to learn.

'You may serve the consommé, Betty,' said Gerald.

I was teased by a terrible urge to point out to Gerald that his black bow tie was inaccurately tied, one wing being larger than the other. But such urges have to be restrained, and I contented myself with concentrating on my spoon and its journey to my lips. It was not until this moment that I realized how very hungry I was.

Conversation bubbled around the table. Not one word was spoken about the death of a young woman, virtually on their

46

doorstep. There seemed to be a bland assumption that the incident would not in any way disrupt the smooth tenor of their lives. A woman had died. Her silly fault, it had been, and nothing at all to do with the occupants of this house.

The meal was superb, the wines that accompanied it were of the finest vintage. I drank sparingly. The evening threatened to present many empty hours that required filling, and I had a good idea that only a small part of them would be occupied by the engagement ceremony. Somewhere in the near vicinity would be Detective Inspector Ted Slater. Waiting to pounce. By now (not a thought to be entertained in the middle of a meal) they would have the body of Clare Martin laid on a slab. Though a full autopsy could not be expected until the following day, the ME would by then be able to express himself with more confidence as to whether thumbs had or had not been applied to Clare's neck with violence, and the forensic team might by then have searched out a wooden or stone edge that could match the blow to her head. Tomorrow would reveal more positive evidence as to whether the blow to the head or the thumbs to the throat had brought about the death.

My guess was neither. The water had killed her. But it was no more than a guess, and the only certainty was that Ray (sitting at my right and now chattering away as though there was nothing at all that need concern him deeply) had certainly had his hands to her neck.

Fingerprinting is becoming very sophisticated these days. Maybe they could now lift prints from flesh. In any event, they would have a definite shape of both thumbs to go on. Life could well become very tricky for Ray ... and decidedly tragic for Mellie.

Throughout these troublesome thoughts, I managed to smile here and there and add a comment when required. I still hadn't decided whether or not to hand the ring over to DI Slater.

Across the table, Colin, looking very drawn indeed, said not a word. And there was still Ray's involvement to worry about.

The ladies eventually retired to another room for coffee, leaving the gentlemen to their port. We really were doing it in a grandly dated manner. The port was sufficiently aged in oak casks to fit into the era of the proceedings, and it rotated in the correct manner.

And still, I thought, no mention had been made of the death in

47

the locks. It was not to be allowed to disturb us. But in this I was wrong. The four of us left the dining table for more comfortable chairs, a small table at each elbow now, and warmed by the flames of a large wood fire. There would be no clean-air restrictions in this isolated country setting. Gerald lit a cigar. I lit my pipe. Then the formality flowed from him, and he allowed his concern to raise its head.

'I hope we're not going to be disturbed by this tragedy outside,' he observed.

'I'm afraid there'll be questions asked,' I told him, surprised that Ted Slater wasn't asking them already.

'And why should that be?' he asked, very smoothly indeed.

'The woman died on this property. She didn't come all the way here to commit suicide in the locks, with all those miles of canal to use. I think we can assume that. She must have come for some other reason, for some more sensible and specific reason.' Which I thought I knew, but had no intention of bringing out into the open. For a second, Ray leaned forward in his chair, protest all over his face. Then he relaxed. Colin was eyeing him with a certain amount of suspicious interest.

'Reason?' Gerald demanded. 'What reason could there have been?' His eyes were firmly on me.

I didn't answer directly. 'There's been a suggestion already that foul play was involved. Indications are that she was strangled. But of course, she could have been killed elsewhere, and her body brought here. That would have been difficult. It would require a car, and any vehicle arriving here, at the house, couldn't have hidden the fact.'

'That sounds very logical to me,' Gerald observed, smiling thinly at my specious attempt to steer the murder well away from his immediate environment. 'And of course,' he went on complacently, 'we get quite a number of strangers around here.'

'But not at this time of the year, dad,' said Colin. 'In any event, she's been identified.'

'Has she?' Gerald drew on his cigar. 'Quick work, then.'

'Not really. The police knew her. She was one of them, a policewoman. Her name's Martin.'

Colin took a quick drink. His voice had been unsteady.

'Clare Martin,' put in Ray flatly, realizing that he couldn't make a secret of their partnership.

'You *know* her?' Gerald was suddenly struggling for his self-control. His voice was slurred. It was not good form to know a murdered person.

'Oh yes, sir,' said Ray blandly. 'I've worked with her, as partners, on traffic patrol. Two of us . . . always. She's been my partner for . . . oh, over a year now.'

'Indeed?' There was almost a sneer in that single word.

And Ray, recognizing this sour approach, Gerald's attitude having turned Ray's remark into an admission, struck back. To Ray, this man, who was to become his father-in-law, was a pompous idiot. It could be a convenient time to make his attitude clear. Yet his approach was soft, gentle, and unaggressive. His restraint surprised me.

'You know her too, sir,' he said, his angelically innocent expression no doubt boosted by his alcohol intake.

'What?' Gerald leaned forward. 'Of course I do not. I would deny that.'

It was strange that he should suggest he might need to.

It was the confidence in this statement that, I thought, pushed Ray over the edge, the brisk rejection, the condescension. I sat and watched it happen, the opportunity presented and the wicked smile as Ray seized it. And what an angelic smile Ray could produce when he tried! He had been worried all evening, in a very specific way that possibly involved the ring, and now, with that problem behind him, he had swung like a pendulum in the opposite direction. Confidence, blended with aggression, was in his smile. An attacking angel. Mockingly, he raised his glass to salute Gerald.

'I didn't mean that you'd met her socially,' he went on, smiling. 'Of course not. But there have been a great number of times you've faced her in court, she as the charging officer. Minor offences, of course. Traffic offences.' He flicked a dismissive hand. 'Nothing that would've needed a defence barrister. Routine stuff. Anybody could handle it.'

He paused to draw on his cigarette, and watched the smoke all the way up to the carved ceiling. It had been a neat little dig at Gerald, on whose cheeks had bloomed two bright patches of colour.

But there had been a sad undertone to Ray's voice, a hint of his admiration for his late partner, Clare Martin. This he was not doing for himself, was the suggestion, but on behalf of a dead woman, who would have been quite capable of handling her own attack resolutely – but now could not.

Ray stared at the ceiling, deliberately prolonging it. Gerald's lips formed a tight, straight line.

'Go on,' he murmured, danger in his voice.

Ray managed a sloppy grin. 'Traffic offences . . . as I said. That day, she was the charging officer – the witness for the police. Oh . . . you must remember the case. Can't have forgotten. That smile of hers, and her confidence in the witness box. WPC Clare Martin. No?'

'How can you expect me to remember all the police witnesses I've led into admissions – '

'Oh, but not with Clare,' Ray cut in rudely. 'You couldn't lead Clare by the nose. You *ought* to remember. That whole column it got you in the local paper. Her name was quoted. And yours, sir. And yours.'

'I think we've gone far enough with this.' Gerald clearly remembered, and very painfully, too. 'Shall we join – '

'But it was the high-spot in your career,' Ray cut in again. 'And if it hadn't been for Clare you wouldn't have got a quarter of a column. The way you tried to get her to admit your client wasn't driving dangerously until we began the chase! And she could quote the exact speed when we set out after him, and the exact speed when we caught him. Very good at that, Clare was. I was driving. She could concentrate on speeds and distances. But . . . the best bit of the whole hearing was when you waved the statement your client had signed, and pointed out all the changes in it. And she . . . oh, this was the big laugh . . . she pointed out that he'd initialled every alteration.'

'Young man – I think we must join the ladies.' Gerald's smile was a grimace.

'You really think the ladies would like to hear this? No? But you would, Mr Patton, wouldn't you? And you too, Colin.' He waited for my nod. He had no need of it, as he was in full flow now. Ray was clearly upset by Clare's death, which would seem to mean that he had not brought it about – or he wanted to spread that idea around.

'And have you ever seen a magistrate laugh, Mr Patton? Really laugh. But Clare . . . oh, nobody could bully Clare. You should really have eased off before you tried to imply she was lying, sir.

And that was simply because she wasn't reading from her notebook. Don't you remember? It was you who pointed that out. But she told you that her notebook was *hers*, to use if she needed it to refresh her memory – and she didn't need to. A wonderful memory, Clare had. And when she said perhaps *you* would like to have her notebook, and you'd then be able to get your facts right! That was when the magistrate really laughed. And your client lost his driving licence for a year. Solicitor Fights A Losing Battle. That was the headline. Surely, sir, you must remember Clare Martin.'

Gerald had to say something to silence Ray. He didn't give his words enough consideration. 'It is not considered good manners,' he said flatly, 'to criticize the dead.'

It was a comment on the stress he was feeling that he chose the wrong objective.

'Oh, but it's not the dead I'm criticizing, sir,' Ray told him with sweet gentleness. 'And you know it.'

There was a silence. Gerald had slid down into his chair, his eyes burning and his cheeks sunken and white. 'I remember,' he said softly. 'I wrote to your Chief Constable, who appeared to be just as intractable as your Clare Martin. You say she was your partner? It's perhaps as well that you'll soon be having a more compliant and pleasant partner, if not in your police car, at least for the rest of your life in your home.'

And, considering that such a man must have been hurt to his very core, he had done well to come out of it reasonably well. I wondered whether he realized that Ray had just given him a reason for having killed Clare Martin, because Gerald clearly remembered that episode very comprehensively. He would no doubt have remembered her face, too, had he been confronted by it. But could it be considered as a valid motive? I thought not.

Ray had not exactly made a good start to his relationship with his future father-in-law.

'We must join the ladies,' said Gerald. 'The party, and the engagement . . . Something else we must not forget.'

His voice held all the sweetness of a green lemon.

51

4

Led by Gerald, we joined the ladies. We walked in on them, and they were on their feet in a moment. Mellie ran to Ray, and they clung together as though each feared that something might try to tear them apart. We all went through into the bar.

As this was also a birthday, there were presents to be opened. Packages and parcels were arrayed on the mahogany surface of the counter, Ruby clearly having arranged for this to be done while we were eating. Mellie, herself somewhat mellowed by the wine she'd drunk, swooped on them with an eek of delight, and all we had to do was stand and watch, as wrapping paper flew in all directions. It was clear she had a passion for personal adornment, and that this was widely known, as most of the presents, even those sent from afar by distant relatives, were in the form of costume jewellery of one sort or another. And once again I had to admit that Amelia was so well equipped with imagination when it came to her choice. We had bought Mellie a wristwatch, but not one that required a battery to keep it going, but one that contained tiny gears and a thing that went tick-tick, and which wound itself. I didn't know how Amelia had divined, or discovered, that this would accord so splendidly with the obsession for the past and for tradition that pervaded the family, but in the event Mellie was enchanted with it, and even Gerald, to whom she handed it for his approval, was delighted. To my surprise, he not merely smiled fulsomely in our direction, but so far unwound as to offer a wink. At least, we had him in a good mood now.

Then, with glasses of various intoxicants in our hands, we chanted: Happy birthday to you ... She blushed. She was very close to tears. And Gerald went round to make sure that all of us still held plenty of liquid in our glasses, a brandy decanter in his hand.

It was at this moment that the swing doors opened quietly, and DI Slater eased his way inside. I had to admire Gerald, then. He took it in his stride, fetched an empty glass from the bar, thrust it into Slater's hand, and murmured, 'Say when.' Nothing, he implied, was going to distract from the happiness of his darling Mellie.

Slater grinned. 'I'm on duty, sir, but . . .' One eighth of an inch from its rim, he added, 'Thank you, that'll do fine.'

'Now . . . friends, folks, ladies and gentlemen,' Gerald chanted, himself intoxicated by the ceremony, 'I would like you all to drink a toast to my daughter, Mellie, and to Raymond Torrance, on their engagement. I give you: the happy couple.'

'The happy couple,' we all chanted, then we sipped at our glasses. Mellie, flushed and confused, also drank a sip, toasting herself and Ray.

And Ray went along with it splendidly by placing his glass on the bar and producing the little black box like a conjuror, and the ring from the box with a splendid gesture, took her extended hand in his left palm, and slid the ring – on to the wrong finger.

'You . . . idiot!' she screamed, caught in a magic delight, and Ray managed comic grimaces of apology as he finally got it neatly settled where it belonged. Then they kissed. As a tribute to the family's love of the past, she bent up her left leg while the kissing was going on, and we all cheered. By this time, everybody was clearly intoxicated by the occasion. I noted that the term 'everybody' now included two women, one busty and elderly, the other Betty, who had served us at dinner. Mellie spotted them, and went over to kiss each of them on the cheek.

Then there came the inevitable hiatus, when the excitement had fled into the past, and general conversation was on the agenda, but hadn't yet flourished. Into this, Inspector Slater slid a confident yet soothing voice.

I had met Slater at one time, as an officer ranked rather lower than myself. It had not been necessary to know him then, as our paths had rarely crossed, but there was one thing I could remember about him, and his present attitude brought it all back. This was his quiet and almost diffident self-confidence. He always ventured to express an opinion, but had no reason to raise his voice in order to support it, as he was so clearly understood to be correct.

'I don't want to put the mockers on your celebration,' he said, 'but there're certain things to be said, and while you're all here together it might be a good idea to say them now. Then I'll only have to say them once. After that, you'll see the back of me, for now, anyway.'

'I really must protest,' put in Gerald, half-way between right-eous anger and trepidation. 'This is a private party.'

'I'm aware of that, sir. Mr Fulton, you would be? Colin Fulton?'

'That's me,' put in Colin. 'No need to trouble my father . . .'

'Ah – thank you. I had the name of the lock-keeper, the resident of this property, and I rather assumed . . . Very well, Mr Fulton,' he went on, now addressing Colin and leaving Gerald somewhat confused, if his high colour was any guide, not certain whether to protest, and angry that anyone in authority should not be certain about his own status.

'Very well, Mr Fulton,' went on Slater to Colin, dismissing Gerald as being unimportant. 'I'm afraid I have to inform you, formally, that a young woman, a policewoman, has been found dead in one of your locks, as you no doubt already know.'

'It's called a pound,' said Colin flatly. He was stiff and formal, but his voice was not steady. 'And we already know about it. Even her name, Clare Martin, who worked with Ray, here, on traffic patrol. There's really not much the rest of us know about her. As a person. Mr Patton . . .' He nodded towards me, and I flipped a hand at Slater, to confirm. 'He tried to get her out. It's all very depressing, but I don't see how we can help you. In any way. Unless there's something you've got in mind.'

Colin looked round at us, nodding. We all murmured some-thing suggesting agreement, and Slater smiled.

'I didn't ask for help,' he said. 'Maybe later . . . maybe. But there are things you need to know. As matters stand, there's a distinct possibility that she was strangled.' He paused. Mellie gave a cry of distress, then bit her lip. 'But there's no certainty. Tomorrow, perhaps, we shall know more. But I've found it necessary to bring in a scene-of-crime team, who'll be working out there for some time. They will not interfere with you in any way. It will, however, be necessary for me to take names and addresses, but you, sir, and you, ma'am, are clearly Mr and Mrs Fulton, and living here, and I gather . . .' He lifted his glass and smiled. 'That I've just drunk a toast to Mellie and Ray. Ray I know as PC Raymond Torrance, and Mellie . . .'

'My name,' put in Mellie with dignity, 'is Amelia Ruby Fulton. We must get things right, mustn't we!' There was disgust in her voice, a little hysteria, and an upsurge of choked anger that her party had been ruined.

'We must indeed.' It had slid right past him. 'And Colin Fulton I already know as the lock-keeper. That leaves you and your wife, Mr Patton.'

'I am Richard, as you very well know, Ted, and this is Amelia, my wife. We're visiting.'

'Two Amelias?'

'Yes.' I left it at that, but gave him our address.

'Is it possible you'll be available here, tomorrow?' he asked.

'I don't know.' I glanced at Amelia. We had intended to leave directly after breakfast.

Gerald put in, 'I would like you to stay, Richard. A little while, if it's at all convenient.' It was the tone he would have used when asking a magistrate for an adjournment.

I glanced at my wife. She inclined her head. 'It can be arranged,' I said to Slater. 'For now, this is our address.'

'Then . . .' Slater looked round at our very silent group. 'Until tomorrow . . . I'll wish you all good-night.'

As quietly as he had entered, he slipped out again into the darkness.

'Well . . .' said Gerald, having given Slater time to get clear. 'It seems our little party has been spoiled by that clearly unnecessary intrusion. I'm sorry, Mellie.'

'It's all right, dad,' she said. 'Don't worry. It'll all blow over, and at least he waited until we'd really and properly got engaged.' She lifted her hand and jiggled her finger, so that the ring sparkled. 'Thank you, darling,' she said to Ray.

He grinned, though his heart wasn't in it. 'D'you think I ought to leave, precious?'

Bewildered, she looked across at me. I had rather gathered that the party had been expected to be prolonged, and that Ray had his own room available at Flight House. That would explain Gerald's reaction when Ray had appeared that evening in his uniform, the basic idea being that Ray had facilities for changing into a normal suit.

'You're not due to go on duty, Ray, are you?' I asked him.

'Oh no. I've got a couple of days' leave.'

'Well then . . .'

He looked at Mellie and grinned. 'Just checking,' he assured her. But the implication was that he wasn't certain where his position stood, on the family's side, or that of the police. This was not a situation I cared to encourage.

'It's where you feel your duty lies,' I told him, at which he smiled broadly, and winked at Mellie.

'I'll stay, then,' he said, seeming to relax.

Gerald had clearly not been paying attention, his own situation being paramount. 'Perhaps Richard could advise us. I've never been personally involved in anything like this, and we don't know what to expect.'

I tried to laugh lightly, but even to me it didn't sound good. There was an aura of anxious trepidation in the room.

'Well,' I said, 'there's nothing really to advise. It will all, no doubt, be unpleasant, but that's for tomorrow, not this evening. And I expect in the morning that you'll all be asked a lot of questions. What each of us – yes, they'll question my wife and myself, too – what we saw and heard and noticed. That'll be up to Inspector Slater. Nothing in that. You simply answer the questions. It'll be a nuisance, but there's nothing more easy to say than the truth. It happened out there at the locks, and although Colin has control of them it's really not much different from a public highway, like a street. Nobody here needs to feel responsible for what goes on out there. Not even Colin can be involved, because his responsibility is for the locks, not the people. And that's about all I can say. Oh – one more thing. What happened to my anorak?'

'It was completely ruined, Richard,' Amelia told me. 'I threw it away.'

'Ah!' I said. 'Hmm!' I added.

'Now what?' she asked.

'I rather wanted to go for a stroll outside.'

'And find another body!' Amelia protested.

'Oh . . . I trust not.'

Colin said, 'I've got a duffle coat you can have. One toggle missing. Will that do?'

'Excellently,' I told him. 'If it's big enough.'

He hurried away in order to search for it, and when I looked round I saw that Amelia and I were now alone. The party was dead. The leading cast, Mellie and Ray, had retired to some convenient and quiet retreat, where they might congratulate each other on their engagement in the approved manner, and Ruby and Gerald Fulton had disappeared.

'We'd better phone Mary,' I said.

'I'll do that.'

'Tell her . . .'

'I know what to tell her, Richard. She's so used to you getting mixed up in crimes that she'll be expecting it.'

'It's not my fault,' I protested.

Mary Pinson owns part of the house we live in and is our friend, and she was at that time looking after our two dogs. She has always worried over our welfare ridiculously, so that it was necessary to put her in the picture.

There was a phone on one end of the counter. I nodded towards it.

'Oh . . . but I'd better ask permission first,' Amelia said. 'And I don't know our area code, anyway.'

'Do you really think they would object?' And I told her the code.

'All the same . . .'

Fortunately, Colin came rushing in at that moment, carrying a duffle coat. I therefore asked permission for Amelia to use the phone.

'Of course. Help yourself. This is a bit scruffy, I'm afraid. It's what I wear when I have to go outside in rotten weather. For the boats.' He eyed my bulk with uncertainty. 'Try it on, anyway.'

I tried it. There was, as he'd said, a toggle missing, but it was a central one, which allowed for the fact that I'd been putting on a little weight recently, and was developing a minor pot.

'Mary understands,' said Amelia, replacing the phone. 'She says she expected it. And she's a little worried that we might not have brought enough of what she calls our bits and pieces. Oh . . . that suits you, Richard. A bit tight, perhaps. You're putting on weight, darling.'

'And I found you this,' said Colin, with an air of triumph. 'See if it'll do.'

What he was offering was a green corduroy peaked cap. It had a plastic top.

'Waterproof,' he told me. 'Useful when I have to go out in the rain.'

It smelt musty. Maybe that had to be expected of something whose whole working life had been spent in the rain. One had to be sorry for it, and I adopted it in an instant. 'Just what I wanted.'

'Do you *have* to go out?' Amelia asked. 'You can smoke in here.'

I shrugged. 'I only want to see what's going on out there.'

'Just like old times.' She pouted at me.

'It's not raining or snowing now, anyway, and we didn't have scene-of-crime teams in my day. Why don't you put on a coat and come with me?'

'Thank you, no.' She was quite definite about that. A certain amount of mental and emotional effort had gone into being involved with the engagement, and she was suffering from after-effects, in sympathy. 'I'll wait in here.' She waved a hand grandly. 'Look at the drink I've got, and all to myself.'

I grinned at her, kissed her on the forehead, and went out by way of the bar doors, pulling on the cap. It was a little tight, but, even though it wasn't raining, essential. There is a vast amount of body heat dispersed by the head, and it helps if you conserve it with a covering.

The area of the pound was bathed with light. A motorized generator was putt-putting away, providing the power for half a dozen floodlights. I approached.

They were down at the lower level, down where I had been, but in no danger of falling into the water as they had it roped off. Six men – no, I realized, five men and a woman, each uniformly garbed in black jackets and slacks, and covered by yellow slickers and yellow floppy hats. Internally, they would not be cold. One can work up quite a sweat in that kit. I stood on the narrow footbridge, smoking placidly and looking down at them. A flash-gun probed the deepest corners, every smallest detail to be captured on film.

I realized, then, that the tow-path, at this point, changed sides. From the lodge behind me and up along the canal, the tow-path was on the house side. From this bridge it was on the other side.

This seemed to have been necessitated by the positioning of the toll-booth. And now, too, I understood the necessity for the wider bridge between the top and middle locks. It had been to enable the horses to cross to the house side, the stable side if they were lucky, and it happened to be bedtime.

The thought crossed my mind that, if Gerald Fulton wished to cling so desperately to the past, he ought to restore a couple of the stables and install two shire horses, if only for show, though Colin might discover some novel way in which they might assist the boats through the locks.

I was still developing this theme as I watched the work below me. In the summer, with holiday boats coming through, happy families loaded on them, there might be many who would dearly love to be towed a little way, say to the next lock along, just for the joy of being propelled by a genuine old-fashioned horse. Charge, say, £1.00 for the tow, and pick up a return trip to make it viable. A job for Gerald? I grinned to myself.

'Heh!' A shout interrupted these lofty thoughts. 'What the hell d'you want?'

I realized this was meant for me. I peered down at the team. 'Just watching. Learning. No scene-of-crime teams in my day, you know.'

He'd got the hint that I was ex-police, and his attitude softened a little. 'Watch if you like, but don't move from there.'

'I didn't intend to. A bit tricky, isn't it?'

I knew that they were searching for any tiniest piece of evidence, possibly as insignificant as a single half-inch of hair or a chipped fragment of wood, anything that linked the contusion on Clare's head with the fall.

'Nowhere to put our bloody feet,' he said with feeling. 'And there's no damned room to get at it.'

'That was what I found out,' I told him.

At once his attitude changed to interest. 'It was you tried to fish her out?'

'That's so. I'm Patton. Richard Patton.'

'Sergeant Berry,' he said. 'Charlie. Hold on a sec', I want to ask you something.'

'Sure. Come on up here.'

Carefully, he manoeuvred himself past the others, and came up at the far side of the bridge. 'I'd shake hands, but I'm losing the feeling in my fingers. Can't work in gloves. Too clumsy. What I want ... I was told you were down there, trying to reach her. Exactly where were you? It's all right, you can put your hands on the parapet. We've done that.'

We leaned over together, but cautiously. With the pound bathed in bright light, and with barely a shadow, I was at last able to see why it had been so difficult for me. The bottom lock itself had gates, separating it from the pound. This meant that one of the large arms had been the first of my obstacles, once I'd got down there. In the dark, it had been something I'd scrambled over.

'There were white floods on from the house,' I told him. 'High up under the eaves. And the amber one from the side. You can see that from here. But you can imagine, not much light got through to this place.' I pointed to it. 'I didn't even know what I was climbing past. Feeling my way around, sort of. Then I thought

I saw movement, then something lighter, and I had the idea it looked like a hand, then I was sure of it, so I had a go at getting further down there and checking it.'

He glanced at me. 'How'd you get there?'

'Down those narrow steps, with the handrail.'

'Hmm! There's an easier way. A bit further along, down to the level of the coping stones, and back this way.'

'I didn't know that. Just worked my way down.'

'Then what? The arm of the big gate would be in the way.'

I tried to remember. 'I think I edged past it, or clambered over it.'

'Lifting off the chain?'

'Chain?' I turned to stare at him. 'What chain?'

He pointed. I could see it now, hanging limply from a staple in the bridge wall. About two feet of chain, and very rusty.

'I didn't notice it. I wouldn't, would I! I was concentrating, trying to edge past that iron rack and pinion.'

He stood back and eyed my bulk. 'A bit tight, wasn't it?'

'It was. Had to edge forward on my side, sort of. I didn't even know what I was edging past.'

'And the chain wasn't fastened? Jennie lass, we'll want some of that grease from the rack.'

Taut, pinched features were raised to us, half hidden by a yellow hat. 'Already got it, Sarge.'

'Good. And rust from the chain.'

'Just going to get it, Sarge.' There was a sharp tang of annoyance in her voice. The sergeant noticed. 'We're just about finished here, and not before time. There's a limit, in these circumstances.'

Then I ventured into realms over which I had no authority. 'If you'll come over to the house, I think we might fix you all up with hot coffee and a drink or two. Okay?'

'Lor-love-us – that'd be a rare treat. But we hadn't finished. You and me. The chain wasn't fastened, you say?'

'Couldn't have been, or I'd have noticed. Couldn't have got past it. Where does it fasten to?'

'A hook on that arm to the main lock gate. And there's a bit of a notice that says: "Please re-fasten chain." I've worked it out. It's to hold the gate when the lock's full and the . . . pound, is it? Yes, when the pound's empty.' He said this with a certain amount of pride. 'But if it was unhooked when you did your rescuing bit . . . well . . . why?'

60

'It's a point.'

'You're sure it wasn't hooked on?'

'How would I have got past it?' I asked.

'Depends how far you got.'

'All the way, Sergeant. All the way, till I was reaching over with my right hand hooked in the rack, that's how far.' I held out my right hand. 'Haven't got all the grease out of my nails yet.'

'You went that far?'

'I had hold of her hand, but it was all too heavy for me. The saturated body. Too heavy.'

'With one hand, yes. And what were you wearing at that time? What you've got on now? No ... couldn't be. It'd be a bit of a mess.'

He was the leader of the team. That meant he was CID, and his detective instincts were strong. He knew there would be some garment or other carrying traces ... of something or other ... which might link with something else, somewhere along the line in the investigation. He didn't miss a point.

'I was wearing my anorak, and it was in such a mess that my wife's thrown it away. We'll have to rescue it for you, Sergeant. If you want it.'

'I most certainly do. But you did get my point? If the chain was unfastened, then the suggestion is that it was done to give a bit more room ... I'm trying to say, it suggests she was shoved in this way, not toppled from the bridge parapet. From here.'

'Good point,' I said. 'Listen. How long before you're through, here?'

'Oh ... a few minutes.'

'Right. Now – you see those lighted windows, over there?' I pointed. 'Get closer and you'll see the words Public Bar on them. It used to be a bargee's pub, but now it's private, but looks like a pub bar inside. I'll go along and see if I can rustle up some hot coffee or the like, and these people living here are a good lot, so I wouldn't be surprised if a drop of brandy or the like doesn't get spilled into your glasses – if you all happen to have one in your hands at the time. Get my point? And I'll locate the anorak for you.'

'Give us ten minutes – and by heaven I'll personally tear up your next ten parking tickets.'

I slapped him on the shoulder and marched away, almost as though it was my house, my kitchen, and my brandy.

'Now what, Richard? You look as pleased as a dog with two tails.'

I told Amelia about it. 'Six of them, absolutely frozen and miserable. D'you think your good friend Ruby could fix something up? I realize it's a bit of a cheek, but I happen to know only too well what it's like to be absolutely chilled to the bone.'

'She won't mind. Ruby'll love it.' She turned away.

'Oh ... and sweetheart,' I called after her, 'what did you do with the anorak?'

'It's in a black plastic bag, just outside the door where we came in,' she called back.

'Right. I'll get it.'

The access to this door, which I remembered how to locate, led me, I discovered, right past the kitchen. In there, Amelia and Ruby were already chattering away, arguing as to whether or not to use the percolator, as there were ... They saw me passing.

'How many did you say, Richard?'

'Six.'

Ruby looked round and smiled at me. 'It'd better be mugs, I'd say, so we'll make it artificial coffee, as dear Gerald calls it, though they do say on the jar that it's made from real ground coffee, but for the life of me I can't see how they do it. Do *you* know, Richard?'

'Know what?'

'How they make this quick coffee stuff from real coffee.'

'I'm not sure. They probably percolate it first, and do some magic trick of drying it. The mysteries of modern technology are way beyond me. But as long as it's hot, I doubt you'll get any complaints.'

'And hot milk,' said Amelia.

I left them to it, and recovered the bag from outside the door. It seemed that my absence had not been noticed, because, as I passed the kitchen door again, Ruby was saying, apparently to me, 'And if you'll look behind the counter – or is it bar? I never know. Anyway, you know where I mean. You'll find plenty of spirits. Brandy and whisky and the like. I'm a duffer at names, because I don't drink spirits. It's not really ladylike, I feel, though I do believe that gin and lemon doesn't taste too bad. I hope nobody wants gin and lemon, because we've got no lemons.'

'I'll tell anyone who fancies gin that they'll have to take it as it comes,' I assured her. 'I don't imagine there'll be any complaints.'

Then I took the bag back into the bar, half lifting the anorak out. It was, indeed, beyond all possibility of reclamation. I saw then by the change in the light beyond the windows, that the team was packing it in, then, after the minute or two it took them to stack away their specimen wallets (clear plastic with a sealing edge) and their lights, they stumped in, preceded by Sergeant Berry's head. There was much flapping of arms.

'This where you meant?'

'It is,' I told him. 'Come along in. Coffee in a minute, and I'm looking to see what we've got in the way of spirits. I ought to explain to the rest of you that this is a private residence, and the reason for all the booze is an engagement party we've been having. Plenty left ... ah, here's your hostess. Mrs Fulton. Ruby. And my wife, Amelia.'

They swept in, each with a tray, one bearing mugs, cream and sugar, and a huge jug of steaming hot coffee, and one bearing sandwiches, which they'd whipped up somehow in the short time available.

Ruby said, 'Now, you're not on duty any more. Do take those yellow things off, they must be most uncomfortable, and I'm sure you can all find seats.' She stood, smiling as they slipped out of over-trousers and slickers, and Ruby cried out, 'Why, one of you's a woman!'

The girl laughed. She couldn't have been more than in her mid-twenties, a well-built young woman with sharp features and dark eyes, and, I saw when she whipped off the hat – very much like a fisherman's – dark hair that cascaded down to her shoulders. She shook her head, and it swirled out the full width of her shoulders.

'There are women in the force now, you know,' she said. 'And I rather like this job. It's like scientific detection, and I got my degree in science.'

'Well ... things are different from my days,' I told her. 'Now ... coffee for all of you, and you'll have to help yourselves to cream and sugar, and sandwiches. And brandy – is there brandy, Ruby?'

She nodded, smiling. I would plead ignorance when Gerald blamed me for wasting his oldest and most revered brandy on a gang of those pestilent police, as he no doubt considered them. To Ruby, they were half a dozen people who needed warmth and kindness. She was enjoying herself immensely.

It was when Sergeant Berry was duly satisfied, two mugs of hot coffee inside him and a brandy in his hand, that he decided he had to offer collective thanks to Ruby. He got to his feet.

'I'd like to say, ma'am, that we would all wish to thank you most sincerely for the sandwiches and the rest, and if my super finds out I'll probably be back in the ranks tomorrow, but that's tomorrow, and for tonight – thank you most sincerely, ma'am.'

The rest of the team joined in. Inspector Slater would have had a fit. As far as he was concerned, this was a house absolutely full of suspects, not to be approached for any reason whatsoever.

Then it was that Mellie walked in, closely followed by Ray. They stopped abruptly, faced by a small pack of strangers. Strangers, rather, to Mellie, though Ray would probably know most of them.

'You here, Ray?' said the sergeant, surprised.

I put him in the picture. 'The drinks are lying around because this evening we've had a party. I think I told you, Sergeant. A party to celebrate the engagement of Mellie, here, and Ray Torrance.'

Berry was still on his feet. 'But I thought you were getting engaged to . . .' He stopped, and took a sip from his glass. Perhaps at my expression, or catching the flip of my hand.

'Tomorrow,' Berry finished it. Then, confused, unwilling to look Mellie in the eyes, he raised his glass to his lips again, to put a full-stop to his sentence, then raised it higher to eyelevel, and said, 'Our best wishes to both of you. And now, we must get off. Ready chaps? You, Jennie? Good. Oh . . . this the anorak, Mr Patton?' He nodded round in all directions. 'Good-night, all.' And he ushered out his team ahead of himself. I heard him call out, 'Who's fit to drive?'

I realized I was still wearing the duffle coat and the strange cap, which was beginning to give me a headache. Something was, anyway.

5

Breakfast, the following morning, was a rather disorganized meal. We had not been told when or where. So, while Amelia was completing her preparations for facing the world, I nipped down and scouted out the situation.

It was to be in their capacious kitchen, and was being prepared by Ruby and Mellie. Ruby was busy, chattering away to her daughter and receiving no responses. Mellie had her head down, and was occupying herself with cutlery, moving it here and there, and back again without any obvious gain or loss. She darted me a quick glance. It might have been make-up, but her eyes seemed bruised and too bright. But not evening make-up so early in the morning, surely.

Eventually noticing my presence, Ruby said, 'A quarter of an hour, Richard.'

'Thank you. I'll tell Amelia.'

Again Mellie's eyes were raised to mine, questioningly, even imploringly. But without a direct question I couldn't do much about answering, so I nodded. No response. Tried a wink. She looked away abruptly.

I didn't know whether Ray had stayed here the previous night. It did seem, though, that he was on duty this morning, though he'd mentioned two days' leave. He had left behind him a number of unanswered questions, because Mellie had not been able to put them into words, more than likely, and had sought for explanations of what she could only feel, and not express.

But I was fantasising again, and on very little evidence. It was a habit I seemed to have acquired lately, and really, I would have to control my imagination and stick to logic and facts.

With my mind, therefore, firmly clamped on realities, I returned to Amelia and told her how things stood.

'Really, Richard, I ought to be down there, helping. Oh . . . why didn't you tell me?'

She rushed out of the room before I could exercise any of my logic on her.

It was a bright and sunny morning, the hills the other side of the valley apparently swaying as mist patches lifted, drifted away, disappeared. Two tiny dots moved on the bracken-strewn slopes. A man ... a dog. I saw no sign of sheep, so that was exactly what it was, a man and his dog – though it could have been a woman – taking their early morning walk. As I would be doing at home at around this time, with our two boxers, Sheba and Jake. Except that we had the river Severn on which to look down, and here there was only the canal. Brindley would be turning in his grave at my use of the word: only.

And down below, I saw, at the locks, was Colin. Was it part of his duties as lock-keeper, I wondered, to take a morning patrol around his empire, checking that everything was as it should be? He would no doubt consider it so, in any event. His responsibility, it was, and everything had to be correct. This morning, too, he would have to make a special check, that the intrusion of a woman's body, and the subsequent invasion by the police squad, had left nothing out of its proper place or disturbed the precise levels in all three locks and the two pounds.

Nodding to himself gloomily, he tramped round and round, earning his right to occupy this house on this site. He would resent the interference. Something decidedly distressing and unpleasant had cast a shadow over his placid life.

I went back downstairs, put my head inside the kitchen door, and was greeted by Amelia asking, 'Where have you *been*, Richard? You'll have it all go cold.'

And Colin followed me in, looked round, smiled bleakly, and said, 'Early breakfast, isn't it, ma?'

'Your father wanted to get away to his office.'

'It's Saturday. He doesn't go in on Saturdays.'

'He said he wanted to.'

'Then why isn't he here, fussing and grumbling – '

'He's here now,' said Gerald from the door, gently closing it behind him. 'And I'd like a little more respect from you, my lad, if you don't mind.'

Colin grinned at me, and winked. I shook my head. Gerald was clearly not in any mood to accept a ribbing this morning. He'd had enough of that from Ray, over the port the previous evening.

Ruby at last could sit to her own breakfast. 'Must you really go, Gerald?' she asked.

'Yes.'

'You know ... surely you must realize ... those policemen are sure to be here this morning again.' She was quietly pleading with him, but shrank from intruding anything unpleasant into the atmosphere, which was taut with overtones already.

'I'm sure Richard can handle things, better than I could, anyway.'

Gerald looked across the table at me. There were hard vertical lines between his eyes, and a muscle twitched in his left cheek. 'But I'd like a word with you, Richard, before I leave. If I may?'

It was only as an afterthought that he managed to convert it from an instruction into a request. And it had been an effort to make it.

'Of course,' I said.

'Before I leave.'

'I'm available any time.'

So it was reduced to the simplicity of my sitting there, imbibing tea until he was ready, asked to be excused, got to his feet, and nodded to me. I slipped a wink to Amelia and she looked down quickly, then I followed him out.

He had a study. I had to accept that he was the kind of man who would, though probably no work was ever done in that room. No studying. Certainly, there was no evidence of a rewarding occupation, no filing cabinet, a desk that was a table pretending to be a desk, a blotting pad with leather corners, and nothing in the way of mirror-image words visible on its surface. A wickerwork wastebasket was empty beside the swivel chair, in which he might sit and do no more than swivel. I could see no sign of legal tomes. This, no doubt, was why he wanted to retire to his office in town. He wanted to read up the law of evidence, and the right to silence, perhaps. There had been recent talk of abolishing this right, but he might find he had to resort to it in the near future. Oh yes, I could understand what he had in mind. Trepidation.

He did, however, have facilities for two people to sit comfortably in his study – two leather, studded, easy chairs. He gestured now towards one of them, politely waited until I'd slumped into it before he took the other, then he said, 'I rather wanted a private word with you, Richard.'

'I did realize that.'

'Then perhaps you can understand why?' He looked mournful, pitiful. It was costing him a great deal to defer to a policeman, even though only an ex-one.

'It did occur to me', I admitted, 'that you'd like to know how you're going to handle an interview with Inspector Slater.'

'Yes.' He looked surprised at this inspired guess.

'And you realize you're in a rather difficult situation . . .'

'It's not that,' he cut in. 'I really do have to call in at the office.'

I took him up on that briskly. 'How often do you need to go to your office on a Saturday?' I asked.

'Well . . .' He waved a hand vaguely.

'Never?' I didn't wait for an answer. His eyes told me all I wanted to know. 'But today? Well now, let me make a guess. You find you've got to get away, by yourself as I said, in order to work out how you're going to behave when Inspector Slater turns up and starts to ask questions.'

'I've already said – '

I still wouldn't allow him to go on. 'And perhaps you're wondering whether your future son-in-law would think it his duty to remind Inspector Slater of that little upset you had in court with the dead woman – Clare Martin?'

I paused there to allow him to put in a word or two, but he was silent. His cheeks were grey. I could see his jaw moving as he chewed away at nothing, unless it was anger.

'I wouldn't be surprised,' I told him, trying to be kind, 'if you still have that cutting from the newspaper, locked away in your office drawer.' I saw that this was so. His eyes wouldn't meet mine and he licked his dry lips. Once. 'And you want to go through it again, just to check whether it reads the same. Whether, in fact, the incident could constitute a valid motive for something as serious as murder. Isn't that what you've thought?'

'It was wicked of him,' he whispered.

'Who?'

'Ray, of course. Wicked to toss that at me. I was never keen on him as a suitable husband for my daughter, I'll tell you that for a fact. But I've kept silent about it. And then . . . for him to throw it in my face as he did!'

I had my own opinion of Ray Torrance, but I didn't think it wise to express it, just at that time. In practice, I found myself excusing him, or at least justifying his outburst. 'He'd drunk too much, in the bar and during the dinner, and he knows you don't like him. He resents it, and it's been bubbling away inside him – then suddenly he saw his chance to get back at you . . . to denigrate you. And after all, it was to no one else but your son, Colin, and myself. It was still a tight little secret, if that's how you'd like it to be. At the worst, it was a tiny incident from the past.'

'But . . .' He shook his head, unable to take it on.

'But the young woman is dead,' I said for him, 'and here, on your doorstep.'

'What would she have come here for?' he asked.

'I don't know,' I lied. 'She *was* here, and you can't get round that. But it's a weak sort of motive you're thinking you've got.'

He held up his hand, almost as though in protest. 'But it's *there*. A reason . . . a motive, and you know very well, Richard, that a motive isn't a fixed thing. Good or weak . . . to a person who kills, *their* motive is what matters. And I haven't been able to get that woman out of my mind . . . to this very day.'

He shook his head, shook himself to silence, and wouldn't look me squarely in the face.

There is such a thing as too much righteousness. A man who prides himself on his probity, who builds his very life on an exacting code of correctitude, has to stand very firmly on his self-erected pillar of dignity, because the higher he builds it the more easily it will topple, and it takes very little to shake the confidence that maintains the balance. Clare Martin had reached out, that day in court, and the pillar had shuddered. To him, it would seem to be a terrible attack on his very existence, and he would not realize that it could constitute only a little amusement in his social circle, and then be forgotten.

Yet still the degradation would gnaw at him. To Gerald Fulton, he had a true and strong motive for having killed Clare Martin.

I smiled in an attempt to encourage him. 'It's not really acceptable as a valid motive,' I assured him. 'How long ago was this court incident?'

'Oh . . . eight months or so. Perhaps a little more.'

'Well then. Even if you'd now been presented with the opportunity – '

He raised a hand, halting me. 'But I was. I saw her. From the bedroom window, I saw her. She was near one of the footbridges. Standing there . . .'

'You saw her? Recognized her?'

'She was in the light from my amber parking lamp. I knew it was Clare Martin.'

'All right. So the opportunity was presented.'

He stared at me.

'You didn't ask yourself why she was there?' I asked.

'Well . . . no. If anything, I sort of linked her with Ray. It did cross my mind that she'd come to tell him he was wanted . . . his job . . . you know.'

'It doesn't work like that.'

'No. Stupid of me. But that's what I thought. In any event, she was his friend, his partner, so she might well have come along to congratulate him. On his engagement. Something like that's occurred to me.'

'Yes. Something like that,' I agreed, taking my pipe from my pocket, putting it back. 'But all the same, you knew she was there . . . here. And you feel you ought to tell this to Inspector Slater?'

'If he asks. Of course. I am, after all, an officer of the court. I would have to tell the truth, Richard. You must see that.'

I laughed. He stared at me blankly. I explained.

'If you felt you had to tell the truth, why are you speaking to me now? Wasn't it your intention to discover from me how far you dared to wander away from the truth?'

'It was not.'

'Then what?' I demanded.

'I wondered if I'd have to tell him about my motive. If he doesn't already know all about it, of course. They probably laughed their heads off at the police station when that case was reported.'

'I think he'll know,' I told him quietly.

I was quite certain that Ray would find an opportunity to bring it to the attention of Inspector Slater, but I didn't think I ought to say that.

'And if he knows?' He shook his head. 'Mr Patton . . . Richard . . . I have a reputation in this district, one I wish to retain. I wouldn't want it spread around that – '

'That what?' I was rapidly losing my sympathy for him. 'That you have a motive? Nonsense. People don't think in that way. They don't whisper to each other: "Oh, but he had a good motive, that Mr Fulton. That court case, you know." Rubbish. The public wouldn't get interested unless you were arrested. Or . . . at least . . . taken in for questioning.'

'Arrest?' His fist thumped down on the arm of his chair. 'They can't . . .'

'Oh, for heaven's sake! I said: *unless*. Unless that happens. And people don't get taken in for questioning unless there's a damn good case to answer.'

He shook his head. 'There is,' he said miserably.

'There's a paltry motive.' I had difficulty in not shouting at him. 'You might well have disliked her, but you had no reason to see her as a threat, at this specific time. Naturally, you'll be asked questions. But here. Possibly in this very room.'

'Questions?' He looked startled.

I almost laughed out loud. 'Damn it, man, you're a solicitor. You've asked your own questions in your time. You simply answer them, and that's that.'

'What questions? What?'

'Are you asking me to put to you the questions that I'd do if I happened to be in charge of the case?'

He looked offended, then was abruptly eager to try it. 'Yes. You do that.'

'So that you'll have your answers ready?' A little sarcasm had crept in there.

'If you don't want to – '

'For pity's sake, Gerald, this isn't a quiz game! It's real. It's serious.'

'I am quite aware', he said severely, 'that it's serious. I'm in a difficult situation. I was here – on the spot – and I had a motive for killing that young woman. Please do what I'm asking, Richard.'

I could tell him that Ray had a motive a damned sight better than his silly court episode, if Ray had really thought she intended to disrupt the engagement party in some way, and that his thumb marks would be on her neck. But murderers don't think: my motive isn't as good as so-and-so's, so I'll leave it to him. Their own motive is overpowering. I sighed. How to start?

'We don't know exactly what time she went into that pound,' I reminded him. 'The police might get a more exact time of death. But . . . for now . . . we'll assume sometime in the last hour before dinner. Right?'

He nodded.

But it was *not* right. I had been thinking sloppily, not concentrating on facts. If that was Clare's car, the one I'd found abandoned with the engine warm, then it had been left there at 5.00 to 5.15 pm. If she'd walked down to the house – lodge, as Colin called it – she could have been at the locks at around 5.10 to

71

5.30. Gerald had been in the bar, shaking hands with me, at around 5.40.

'No,' I said, 'we can be more exact than the last hour before dinner. Let's concentrate on the time between 5.10 and 5.30. I've reasons for believing that. So – you saw her. When?'

'I was in my bedroom. Getting ready. I told you that.'

'*Your* bedroom? Not "ours"?'

'I do not share a bedroom with my wife, Richard. Please leave it at that.'

I was only too pleased to do so. I doubted that Slater would be.

'All right. Your bedroom. Getting dressed?'

'Yes. For that hour or so you mentioned.'

'An hour to get dressed?'

'Yes. Well . . . laying out my evening suit.'

'That took a whole hour?'

'One way or another, yes. Getting dressed in my suit for when you arrived. Laying out the evening suit, as I said.'

'And your window . . .'

'Overlooks the locks. As does yours, Richard. I thought you'd ask that.'

'So that you *could* have seen her down there, irrespective of the fact that only your orange light was on at the time?'

'If I'd looked.'

'But you didn't look?'

'No.'

'Because you didn't need to, having arranged a meeting . . .'

'No! That's not true.'

I held up my hand, halting him. 'There you are, you see. You've just had a practical demonstration of what happens when you tell lies.'

'I haven't – '

'A little while ago you told me that you'd noticed her. Now – because you lied about it, you've got yourself all tied up in excuses and denials. We'll go back a bit. You've said your window overlooks the locks. So you could have seen her down there. *Did* you see her, Gerald? Remember, I'm pretending to be Inspector Slater. So . . . did you see her?'

'Yes, yes. Let's get on with it.'

'Now you're allowing yourself to become agitated. Take it steadily. Just the truth. It's quite simple. Get angry, and you start making mistakes. Tell lies, and that's the worst mistake you can

72

make. Or does a solicitor, working mainly as a defence lawyer in criminal cases, get to the stage where truth is only what your client dares to admit? It's not like that in a murder case, I can assure you. Shall we go on? You're now talking to Inspector Slater. All right?'

He nodded reluctantly.

'So ... I'm Slater now ... so you saw her standing below, near the locks?'

'Yes.'

'And you could recognize her?'

'Oh yes.'

'In dark clothes in orange light – looking down at an angle?'

'Yes.'

'As a woman?'

'Of course as a woman.'

'They wear slacks these days.'

'She wore a skirt. The woman I saw ... she had on a skirt.'

'All the same, it could've been any woman, in dark clothes.'

'She was wearing one of those caps with a checkered band round it.'

'So ... having recognized her ... you had time to go down there and confront her – '

'I didn't.'

'Didn't what? Go down, or have time?'

'Both, damn it. I didn't go down. If I'd wanted to, I didn't have the time.'

'How is that?'

'I just didn't have the time,' he repeated.

'You said you were in your room, for a whole hour. More, perhaps. And what took all that time? You were laying out a suit, and the rest, and your dinner jacket, fancy shirt ... and whatnot. An hour! And you would need no more than two minutes – all right, five at the most – to get down there and push her in – '

'I didn't *do* that!' He seemed frantic, holding up his hand to stop me.

'But you did have enough time,' I pressed him.

'No!'

'You could have run down. The side stairs, out at the side of the house. One push – '

'That is not so.'

'Where are the shoes you were wearing?'

'What? Shoes?'

'What *were* you wearing?' I was deliberately impatient, in my persona as Slater.

'I was dressing . . . dressing . . .'

'Dress shoes, then. Soft? Black?'

'Yes.'

'Which have been cleaned?'

'Yes.'

'Why clean them, if you didn't go outside?' I challenged.

'I'd clean them anyway, if I'd worn them just to meet you, and to the dinner.'

'An excuse. You ought to do better than that, sir.'

'Sir?' His eyebrows shot up.

'I'd call you that, if this was a true interrogation. You had the time to do it. Admit it.'

'I was dressing,' he said wearily.

'An hour? Nonsense.'

'I had difficulty with my bow-tie.'

'That was later, and you rushed it, anyway. It wasn't tied correctly. One wing was larger than the other.'

'No!'

'Oh yes. I noticed.'

'Oh my God!'

'And I'd say that in *my* statement, when I'*m* interrogated.'

I sat back, allowing him to gobble, in what could have been anger or indignation.

'Why are you saying all this?' he whispered at last.

'Because you wanted to know what you were going to say to Inspector Slater. Now you know.'

'But I can't . . . it's not true . . . I didn't.'

I laughed. 'You asked. You were worried about this paltry motive you've got. So I thought I'd show you. Means, opportunity, motive. That's the formula. And I've shown you. You had the means – a push, and she'd be beyond recall. You had the opportunity . . . in all that time you used to titify yourself.'

'Titify?'

'It's a version of tittivate. Let me say this. You had the means and you had the opportunity. But my dear friend, you haven't got a motive worth considering. You and your silly motive! Rubbish.'

'But when I'm asked?'

'You answer questions, as you've been doing, Gerald. Every-

74

body – and don't forget that that includes people not resident here – had the means for the killing, and no doubt the opportunity. And I'll bet, when Slater gets going, he'll dig out no end of motives. So you're way down on the list. Relax. Just tell the truth.'

I levered myself to my feet. Why did I feel so stiff? 'Now you can get along to your office.'

He gave me a thin smile. 'I don't think I need to go now. Thank you, Richard.'

But it wasn't thanks I saw in his eyes, it was resentment. I had not told him what he'd wanted to hear, that he was clearly a person of respect and authority in his own sphere, and no one could seriously consider him as a suspect in a murder case.

I had not said it, because it wasn't true.

I paused at the door, and turned. 'And Gerald, you still haven't told me all the truth.'

'I have.'

'You said you saw her. Noticed, was the word you used. But I have reason to believe she must have been here, at the earliest, at about ten minutes past five. At the latest, five-twenty. The storm blew itself out at about five-twenty. So . . . how could you have seen her, let alone recognized her, when the storm was still blowing?'

'I saw', he said painfully, 'a woman. Distinctly a woman. Who else could it have been?'

I shrugged. Who else? A great number of possible people. Yet . . . she had been Clare Martin to Gerald.

6

When I returned to the kitchen, I asked Amelia, 'Feel like a walk, love?'

She seemed surprised at the suggestion. 'It's too cold, Richard.'

'Haven't you looked outside? It's a grand morning for walking.'

There was that doubtful look in her eyes. 'It *seems* fine, but outside the door I'll bet it's perishing cold. And anyway, where is there to walk?'

'The tow-path. It's sure to lead somewhere.'

'Such as?' She was considering me with her head tilted, a tiny smile on her lips. This expression was used whenever I suggested anything in which she saw no point.

'Well,' I said, 'I was thinking of trying to get a new hat. The one Colin lent me makes my head ache.'

'Oh . . . surely you can manage until we get home. And where, around here, do you expect to buy *anything*? It's nothing but hills and trees and grass.'

'I can ask Colin.'

'You do that, my pet.' I half expected her to pat me on the head.

'And if there *is* somewhere?'

She gave that a certain amount of thought, then shook her head. 'No. I think I'd better stay here. It's all right for you, with all your experience. Dead people, you take in your stride. Murdered ones you seem to take for granted. But it's upset poor Ruby no end. And Mellie's going around like somebody in a trance. No. I'll stay here, if you don't mind. But by all means go on your own, if you really feel you must.'

I gave her my best grin. 'Oh . . . I do.'

What I really wanted was a valid excuse to take another look at that abandoned car. If it *had* been abandoned, that was. It quite naturally fitted a scenario in which Clare Martin had wished to reach Flight House without drawing attention to herself. If that happened to be her car, then she would probably have had direct and discreet access along the tow-path from the car to her place of death.

But, in that event, why had she not locked the car and pocketed the keys? It would have been a natural, even instinctive action. That was what was troubling me.

And behind all my reasonably logical intentions was the thought that I would like to avoid Ted Slater just at that time. I was painfully aware of that ring in my jacket pocket, and the fact that I was withholding evidence. The longer I kept it, the greater my culpability. So . . . a discreet walk was indicated.

I searched out Colin, as a first move, and found him, as I'd expected, prowling around his locks. He was standing now beside the stark rack and pinion opposite the lock gates between the top and middle locks. He looked at me hopefully, as though I might be of use to him.

'What d'you make of this?' he asked, pointing to the rack and pinion. 'Somebody's pinched the handle.'

'What handle?'

He sighed at my ignorance. 'Look – there's a squared shaft on the pinion, and a ratchet. There's a handle that keys on that square, a winding handle. It raises the smaller gate, way down below, to ease the water pressure against the main gates. Now it's gone.'

'What does it look like?'

'Oh . . . a steel shaft about eighteen inches long with the square hole in one end and at the other a two-fist sized handle sticking out.'

'Heavy?'

'Weighty. It's got to be strong, you see.'

'But Colin, there're several of these rack and pinion things. I've noticed 'em myself. Perhaps it's on one of the others.'

'No it isn't. D'you think I haven't looked? Searched. It's gone missing, and that's that.'

'But you must have a spare.'

He sighed at my ignorance. 'You don't need a spare. One to do the lot. I've been using that one for years. And who'd want to pinch it, anyway? Any boats coming through – and there hasn't been one for nearly a month, now – they've all got their own winding handles. I just don't understand it.'

I glanced sideways at him. He seemed genuinely concerned, but there was more than that revealed on his face. In one night it had become haggard. When he spoke, he emphasized every word with nervous gestures of his hands.

'Colin,' I said. 'You're forgetting. There's been a fatal accident . . .'

'Forgetting!' He made a wild toss of his head. 'I'm trying not to think about it . . .' He allowed that to tail away.

'We don't know yet how she died,' I told him easily, softly, to give the impression that this could not deeply concern us. 'But there's been mention of a blow to her head.'

'Who's said that?' He was suspicious.

'The police. They fished her out. All we know yet is that much. There's a contusion. But just imagine that you wanted a weapon to use for that purpose . . . this handle you've been talking about – wouldn't it be just the thing?'

He choked. 'I . . . I suppose. They're weighty.'

'And how best to dispose of it afterwards than by tossing it into the nearest lock? There'll be a few feet of water down there . . .'

'Five or six feet. Always. You can't run 'em dry – you'd have to pump it out.'

'There you are, then.'

'Oh Lord! I'd better . . . better . . .' He didn't know what he had better do.

'Order another,' I suggested.

'Yeah. I suppose. But they won't like it.'

'Who won't like it?'

'The people who own the canal.'

'People? I thought these canals belonged to authorities. Shropshire and Union. That sort of thing.'

'Can't we go inside out of the cold?' he asked.

'Why not? It's your place.'

'It's theirs, theirs!'

I couldn't see why he should be upset about that fact, but he certainly was not his usual placid self.

'Anybody in the bar, d'you think?'

'Shouldn't be – at this time.'

'There, then. And you can tell me all about it,' I said comfortingly.

He looked at me doubtfully, but nevertheless led the way through the swing doors, which went wump behind us. There, I sat him down at one of the tables. He sagged loosely.

'A drink?' I asked, but he shook his head.

'No. It's too early.'

But it did seem to me that he needed one. Slowly, I filled my pipe. 'Why don't you tell me?' I suggested, while my eyes were concentrated on my hands.

'The canal – '

'No,' I said. 'Not that. Tell me why you're all of a fidget and upset, I meant. And don't tell me it's because of your blasted winding handle.'

He had his hands clenched together on the table surface, but he couldn't control his fingers. They locked, they unclenched, they writhed. He stared down at them, frowning as though he commanded them to be still, and they would not.

'You can't know about this canal,' he said stubbornly, refusing to face a different concern that I felt was haunting him. 'It's one of the few privately owned canals in the country. It could be the only one, now, for all I know. Thirty-three miles, that's all it is, from

78

end to end. In the old days, it used to link a colliery with a clay pit and pottery place, then later on with a power station, but now there's no colliery, and the power station runs on gas. But it's always belonged to that one family. They're the ones who financed Brindley to do his early experiments with canals and locks. There's a thirty-foot rise here, and that would normally need five locks – a staircase. So he thought up this arrangement with the pounds in between. It only uses three locks. Getting his eye in for the Bratch Flight, he was, on the Staffs and Worcestershire canal. But this one came first. And the canal's been owned by that same family who originally owned the colliery. In those days, it would've brought them in a good income.'

'Sounds as though it did.'

'Plenty of traffic, then, but at that time it was all commercial. Now it's entirely holiday boats. They pay a fee for the use of the canal and its locks. There're nineteen, as well as this flight. But it couldn't be very profitable, 'cause there's always mainten- ance of the waterway and locks to be done. That's why I don't get paid, except for the tenancy of the house. This house. The lodge.'

'So how do you make any money out of it? You'd need money. *Some* money. Even if your father pays you a nominal rent.'

He managed a distorted grin. 'It's a tradition, you see. That toll booth used to be just that. Each boat paid a toll, which went to the owners. Now ... well, it's the same tradition, but twisted around a bit. The boat-hire people tell them all – the people who hire their boats – what is expected of them. So it's generally known that the lock-keeper at Flight House should be tipped, for his help in getting them through. Because – and you can believe me – they'd get themselves in a hell of a mess if they tried to do it themselves. Probably flood the lot. So they tip me. Usually a quid. A quid out and a quid back. And that's my source of income. Though why I'm telling you all this I don't know.'

'Perhaps there's something you're getting round to.' I made this a bland suggestion.

He tried to smile, but it didn't work very well. 'It's the family that still owns it, the ones that're left. Two sisters and an elder brother. Add up their ages and they could easily match the age of the canal. And old-fashioned! You'd never believe it.'

'Oh ... I think I would.' I smiled at him encouragingly. There had been a warmth in his voice when he'd spoken of the present family.

'They visit us once a year,' he went on. 'Friends of *this* family, you see. They come to see how things are going along, even though I keep 'em in touch. They still use the Rolls they bought in the thirties, and driven by the old chap who drove it home for them from the suppliers. He's been with them for ever. And ... strict! Oh dear me! They belong to some obscure religious group – and I'm dreading it.'

'Dreading what? Are they due for another visit?'

'No, it's not that. But I have to send them reports on what's happening, if there's anything at all out of the ordinary. So ... I'll have to send a report on *this*. A fatal accident...'

'Not an accident,' I put in quietly.

'Whatever you like to call it, to them it'll be shocking. I suppose ... to anybody, really. But you know what I mean. And they'll be distressed. It'd be like defiling the place – an insult to dear James. That's James Brindley. Heavens, he died over 200 years ago, but they look on me now as the guardian of his blessed memory. Dear James would be upset, they'll say, wherever he is now, and I shouldn't have allowed it to happen. Oh ... they'll be along, you can bet. Probably erect a memorial stone to ... to ... Clare, right by the pound.'

His voice had fallen so low that I had to lean forward, closer to him.

'I like them, you know,' he said softly, after clearing his throat. 'And I think they like me. But everything *does* have to be right and correct. And murder isn't. If it *is* murder. They won't like the fact that I failed to prevent it. *Everything* that happens, there has to be a report. If I wanted ... wanted to get married, they would have to know. They'd be here, to meet the young lady. We'd have tea and toasted pikelets.'

'Pikelets?'

'Crumpets to you. And they would have to approve of my choice.'

I cocked my head at him, trying to suppress a smile. 'And d'you think they would?'

'What?' He looked up, directly into my face, the first time for some minutes.

'Approve of your choice – if you wanted to get married.' I tilted my head at him. 'And do you want to?'

'Well ... yes.' But he didn't smile as he said it, not offering me a share in the pleasure of it. His hands were kneading away at each other on the table surface.

'And have you consulted the ruling family about it?'

'Not yet.'

'And – why not, then?'

'There'll be trouble. I'm trying to think of a way round it.'

'Trouble ...' I was finding it difficult to get anything in the nature of personal information out of him. 'In what way – trouble?'

'She ...'

'This is the young woman you have in mind?'

'*Will* you let me say it!' he complained, as though I hadn't been struggling to tear it from him. I simply nodded.

'It's more than likely they would disapprove,' he told me miserably. 'I told you. They're old-fashioned.'

'I did get that point.'

He still seemed hesitant, and I had to prompt him yet again. 'Why might they disapprove?'

'Because she's already married.'

'Ah!' I said. 'Yes. That would certainly be a problem.'

'With a youngster,' he added.

'Ummh! A child complicates things, I can quite see that.'

'So you see – '

'I can understand now that you'll have to consult them. Oh yes. But Colin – didn't you say that you'd have to report on that fatality we've got here?'

'Yes. I'll have to do that.'

'And that will probably bring them sailing along?'

'Sure to.'

'There you are, then. Pick the right moment ... and your personal problem will prove to be very minor – '

'Minor!'

'In comparison with a dead woman in your precious flight.'

He thrust his locked hands on to his lap, beneath the table, as though restraining himself from assaulting me, then looked up with dark eyes beneath his bushy eyebrows and asked, 'Are you trying to be funny, Mr Patton?'

'Richard, please. And I'm on your side, Colin, I assure you. Put in your report to this ruling family of yours, and tackle them on the other subject when they turn up here. You're sure they will?'

Then he managed at last to smile. 'Oh yes. I'm certain they'll be along.'

'Then I'll wish you the best of luck,' I told him, and with complete sincerity. Colin, I had decided, was a solid rock on which his employers had come to realize they could rely. I could see no problem facing him.

It occurred to me that the younger members of the Fulton family did seem to be having trouble with their chosen mates. Mellie had her Ray – but did she even imagine that he had been indulging his sexual inclinations with Clare on the night before their engagement? To Mellie, with her quiet and placidly contented mother, and her father so rigidly strictured to the path of probity, such activities would be unthinkable, and completely unacceptable.

And Colin – well, his was not quite the same problem. Men did fall in love with other men's wives, and vice versa. You see it going on all the while. But, to the ruling family – as I was now thinking of them – such deviations from an accepted moral code would seem to be sinful. Thou shalt not covet thy neighbour's wife. Had dear James done it? Almost certainly not, they would chorus. In any event, he'd been too busy digging canals, and all he'd have seen about him would have been men. Irishmen. Tough Irishmen, digging miles of canals without the aid of any tool but a shovel. The Irish Navigationals – later to be called Navvies. Dear James's horizon would not have included an acceptable female.

Considering the background, I had to accept that Colin seemed to have a serious problem on his hands. When I looked up from these contemplations, he was eyeing me with concern.

'We're kind of engaged to be married,' he said softly, awed by this fact, as soon as he was certain he had my attention.

'Are you?' I tilted my head at him. 'Engaged to a married woman? That's novel.'

'I gave her a ring.'

'Kind of plighting your troth?'

'All right.' He was mildly irritated. 'Put it like that. It was – how can I explain it? – something she could have with her for reassurance. While we waited.'

'Waited?' I thought about that. 'Waited for what, for heaven's sake?'

'For the right time. I mean ... there's been Mellie's engagement. I couldn't do anything till that was out of the way. Now could I? And breaking the news to mother and father. That'll be tricky.

Dad would have to think around all the ways it might affect his . . . his . . .' He bit his lip, shaking his head.

'His standing in the community,' I suggested.

'Yes. That.'

'But he's in the position to put you in touch with a good solicitor, one who's an expert on matrimonial affairs. You'd need a good one. I mean, you and the young lady you have in mind, you and she would be the guilty parties, if she simply walked away from her husband, and though it's reasonably easy, these days, to get a divorce, there'll be the custody of the child. Boy or girl?'

'It's a boy. Dennis.'

'Right. Custody. It usually goes to the woman, though. Still . . . you must bear in mind . . .'

'Why the hell're you going on like this?' he demanded impatiently.

'I was simply giving you an idea of the problems you might have to think about.'

'Oh . . . thank you! Thank you very much. As though I don't bloody-well know!'

'And you've told nobody but me?'

'Not yet. I couldn't risk it. You're the first.'

'Risk what?'

'Bringing her here, to the house.'

'Couldn't you?' I was unable to get much life into my voice.

'No. I *wanted* her here. With me and the family.'

'But the other family, the three old dears who own the canal, wouldn't they have to be told? You did say that.'

A cloud brushed across his eyes. That jaw, square beneath the fuzz of beard, seemed to harden.

'They'd have to accept it.' There was defiance in his voice.

'To approve . . .'

'Yes. And they'd have to.'

'Or search for another lock-keeper?' I said this lightly, gently ribbing him, and was therefore jolted by his positive reaction.

'Let 'em search,' he claimed with a hint of pride, a challenge. 'They're thin on the ground, the ones who've worked a Brindley flight.'

'You mean – thin on the water.'

'Hah! Bloody amusing.'

'And if they failed to approve?' I asked, very gently indeed, stroking his ego, as he seemed very touchy this morning. 'They could surely ask you to leave? You've got no right of retention ... In fact, I suppose they could give you immediate notice to quit. What then?'

His beloved flight of locks, or his beloved whoever she was?

'I'd give ... I'd ... I'd. Oh, damn it, I don't know.'

'But so far it hasn't arisen, has it? The choice, I mean.'

'No. You know that damn well. What *is* this?'

I shook my head. 'Nothing. Just vague thoughts.'

'No. Not vague. Come on – out with it,' he demanded. I seemed to have got him in a fighting mood.

'I was just wondering whether your young lady knows all about the conditions attached to this arrangement with you.'

'Arrangement? Damn it, we're engaged. I told you that.'

'Engaged,' I said emptily.

'Properly. I gave her a ring.'

'Yes. You said that.'

'One like Mellie's. That was what she fancied.'

I didn't like the sound of this at all. 'How did she know, this young lady of yours ... what Mellie's ring was like?'

'Well ... Ray showed it to Clare, and Clare told Helen all about it. Described it. They're sisters, you know. Clare and Helen.'

'Ah!' I said. 'Yes. Helen being this married woman fiancée of yours?'

'That's the way it is. But of course, I couldn't afford anything so grand. A pretty poor thing, really. But it's not the value, is it? It's what it stands for.'

Naïve Colin! 'No, it's not the value,' I assured him stolidly. 'But it looked like it?'

'Sort of. Cheaper, of course. But they *did* say they were sapphires, in a circle outside. Not a real ruby in the middle, though. A garnet, I think they called it.'

'I see.'

'And she didn't wear it on her finger, of course. *He'd* have noticed.'

'Her husband?'

'Yes.'

'Quite frankly, I'm not sure a husband notices such things.' I said this in reassurance, and hoping that I would, should the circumstances arise. 'Where *did* she keep it, then?'

He smiled bleakly. His eyes were hunting the room, as though looking for some work he ought to be tackling. 'In her bra, or something – I think.'

'Hmm! Next to her heart,' I said brightly.

He gave me a sickly smile. 'Keeping it kind of a secret. Only Clare knew, apart from Helen and me, of course.'

I nodded. 'Yes. A secret.'

'Had to be. You can see that.'

I stared at him, confused and angry, not knowing what to say. Colin was completely honest and reliable, and he deserved better than all this deceit and emotional upset, into which he had plunged.

'A secret,' I said in disgust. 'Until you've cleared it with the three old dears, *and* their chauffeur, *and* the bloody Rolls Royce, I suppose?'

'What're you talking like that for?' He was frowning heavily, tilting his head and considering me as though he doubted my sanity.

Because I wanted to bounce to my feet and stalk around smashing things, and raving against the unfairness of life, that was why.

Sighing, I put my hand in my jacket pocket, then held out my palm. 'Is this your ring, by any chance?'

'Yes, yes,' he gabbled. 'But . . . but . . . how'd *you* get hold of it?'

'It slipped off Clare's finger into my hand, when I tried to pull her out,' I explained to his blank, bleak face. 'Because it wasn't a correct fit for her finger, which it wouldn't be if it hadn't been bought for her. Do you understand what I'm saying, Colin?'

'Well . . . yes.' He stared at me from beneath his eyebrows. 'Of course. Thank you.'

Yet he had not understood, not fully considered it, hadn't even asked me to explain how it'd come into Clare's possession. I didn't know that, unless Helen had asked her to keep it safe for her. They had been sisters, after all, and perhaps Helen had realized it was not safe to have it in her own possession, with a husband around.

I was pleased to get rid of it. No longer would it haunt me as possible evidence in a murder investigation. It was Colin's ring, and there was no necessity to tell him that the odds were that Clare had intended to flaunt it at the engagement party, and use it to claim her own engagement to Ray. If that was what her intention had been, though I couldn't imagine it would have done her any good. It would so clearly have been seen as a pitiful attempt at disruption.

But I was no longer certain about any aspect in the set-up.

Then, 'Ah . . .' said a voice behind me. 'Here you are.'

I twisted round in my seat. Ted Slater was standing behind me, smiling a very cool smile. He had the drawn and bloodshot look of a man who hadn't come in contact with his bed during the preceding night.

He stared past me at Colin, and made a dismissive gesture. 'Do you mind?'

'Yes, I do bloody mind,' said Colin, whose nerves were drawn tight, and who didn't intend to be ordered around. 'This is my property. I haven't even invited you past that door.'

'I just want a few words with Mr Patton.' Slater was heavily patient.

'Then do it elsewhere.'

'Now you just listen here . . .'

'No. You've got no legal right to walk in here and take over.' Clearly, Colin was in no mood to be pushed around. His temper was on a short rein.

'Unless you've got something in your pocket that gives you legal right of entry, Inspector,' I said. 'Which I'm sure you haven't.'

'Aw . . . for Chrissake!'

I laughed. 'We'll go outside, Ted, if you want to talk.'

But Colin gestured wearily. 'Oh . . . never mind. What does it matter? What does anything matter?' He turned to me. 'I want to make a phone call, Richard. I think that report had better be treated as urgent. Can't wait for the post . . . I'll phone the old dears, and . . .' He returned his attention to Slater. 'And if they decide to take a little trip here, you'd better watch your step, Inspector. Oh yes.'

Then he marched out into the hall, and I had visions of two old ladies waving umbrellas beneath Slater's nose, and an older gentleman making lethal threats of phoning the Lord Chancellor, or some such boyhood friend.

'Yuff!' said Slater, taking the vacated chair. 'Not much co-operation around here. It's a good job I've got you, Richard. I'm sure you'll know what it's all about. Oh . . . this is WDS Tomkinson. She's here to take notes.'

Woman Detective Sergeant Tomkinson was a large and imposing woman, at that moment seeming even more bulky because she was wearing a padded anorak with a hood, this thrown back from her head and revealing a tangle of auburn hair. Now *that's* what I need, I thought, an anorak with a hood. Two birds with one purchase. She might have observed my attention, because she frowned and turned to move a chair to a point just beyond my shoulder, so that I would always be aware of her presence, but would have no impression, from her reactions, as to whether or not what I said might be pleasing to her cherished inspector. And – oh yes she did cherish him. That much had been obvious from what I'd seen in her eyes, and noted from the discreet flexing of her lips. For me, her presence would have been distracting, because she was plainly a woman by whom one would not wish to be cherished. She would devour you, engulf you, and heaven help you if you resisted. Fourteen stone of solid woman, that was what Slater had with him, a block of a woman in a two-piece tweedy outfit with three large buttons on the jacket (revealed when she threw off the anorak) which had padded shoulders. Unless that was all muscle. I wouldn't have been surprised. And Slater was splendidly unaware of her dour devotion.

'I take it', said Slater, leaning forward, 'that you've been feeling out all the possibilities and discovering what's been going on.' He twisted his lips into a sour smile, then he nodded knowingly.

'We've naturally been discussing the tragedy,' I said. 'Of course, I've listened. And of course I've drawn a few conclusions and discovered a certain amount of background information.'

'So? Let's have it, Richard.'

'In confidence,' I said.

'You can't expect to talk to me in confidence, for God's sake. How can we talk in confidence with the WDS here?'

She spoke up. It was a remarkably soft voice, and musical. 'I could leave, Inspector.' And take her notebook with her? Slater would not be able to permit that.

'No need, no need,' I said, gesturing towards her. 'The inspector misunderstood. When I used the word "confidence", I was explaining that what I've been told was in confidence. As a friend of the family, Ted, that's how I've heard things. So of course, I can't repeat any of it to you.'

'Now you listen here . . .'

'Oh . . . and I can tell you that there's been a certain amount of rehearsal involved.'

'You've had the bloody nerve to brief them!' he shouted, staring at his sergeant, to make sure she had heard it. She pursed her lips in disapproval.

'I've had the nerve, as you put it, to listen to what they had to say, and to advise them that their best and proper course is to tell the truth. You ought to be thanking me, Ted. I've done a lot of groundwork for you, and nothing I've heard can be of any help to you.'

It's practice that does it. I could now tell lies with fluent and nonchalant ease. Perhaps I was assisted by the knowledge that if I told him all I knew he'd be overwhelmed by useless detail. I could, however, tell him various facts without violating any confidences. I would have done so, but he burst in, furious with me.

'You've got a duty!' he shouted. 'You're an ex-copper . . .'

'Ex. Ex. True. But now I make my own judgements.'

'Much more of this and I'll have you in for a bit of serious questioning, Patton.' He nodded in emphasis, and he looked as though he'd like to strike me down.

'Nonsense. You'd have to be prepared to charge me. And I've got a top-line solicitor, here on the premises, who'd tell you where you get off. Now cool down, Ted. I can tell you, for instance, that Clare Martin was seen – by that same solicitor – standing down by the locks at some time between five and five-twenty yesterday evening. At that time, the storm was still blowing, so it's unlikely he'd get a definite enough sighting, and there was only that orange floodlight at the end of the house to help him out. It's my opinion that he couldn't have identified anybody with any accuracy. And that's the only sighting of Clare Martin that I've discovered. Nobody's going to say they actually spoke to her. Now . . . are they? But, you go around and do your questioning act. They're all still here, except young Ray Torrance, but I expect he's on duty at this time. But he'll be available eventually. Are you getting all this, Sergeant?' I asked, turning to face her.

'Thank you, sir, yes.' Only her lips moved. No hint of expression dared to invade her craggy face.

'Now . . . tell me, Ted,' I went on, 'what you've done about the car. I *can* give you information there, because there's only me involved. And my wife, of course.'

'Car?'

'At the crossing, the other end of the lane from here. *Her* car, I'd have thought. Clare's. I came across it at about five-twenty, yesterday evening. I assume you've taken it in for examination? Is it hers?'

'I don't propose to discuss the investigation with you, Patton. Especially if you're not prepared to co-operate.'

'I *am* co-operating.' I grinned at him. 'What did you make of the fact that the door was unlocked and the keys left in the ignition lock?'

He licked his lips, glanced at his WDS, and said, 'I didn't make anything of it.'

'Nothing? Well, I ought to tell you that you'll find my prints on the ignition key, the door handle, and probably on the outside of the door. They're on file, of course.'

'What the hell's all this?' he demanded. Anger rumbled deep in his throat. He thought I was playing games with him.

'I'm telling you, if you'll just listen. I got out of our car, because I was looking for a direction pointer. This was on the way here, you understand. *That* car was there. I noticed it'd been left with the keys in the ignition. I tried the engine, but there was nothing wrong there. So I shut the door, and left it as it'd been. Now – can you think of any explanation for that strange fact? *Is* it hers? Or should that be: was it?'

'It was her private car,' he told me stiffly.

'And the set-up didn't strike you as strange?'

'No. No, damn it. And you're only trying to distract me.'

I shrugged and pouted at the WDS, but she didn't react. So I went on, 'I'm not trying to distract you, Ted. I believe this could matter. Just think about it. Any driver, leaving a car – especially out in the wilds – almost automatically takes the keys out of the ignition switch and locks the car door. Right? So why was it left like that? And I'm not even talking about the reason the car was left there.'

He tried a smile, but it didn't actually bloom. 'Now Patton . . . you're forgetting. How many reported stolen cars do we get, where the keys have been left in? Dozens, every week. Right?'

'But not – surely not – by a trained police driver.'

'So what the hell're you getting at?'

'Just that it's got no logical explanation, so that makes it interesting. Just imagine it. *How* would that have come about? I can think of only one way.'

He sighed. 'You're doing your best to distract me.'

'Trying to help, Ted, help. I was just thinking . . . if you were getting out of a car, a heavy weight in your arms ... Are you seeing this, Ted? Are you? The ignition key wouldn't be reachable if both hands were full, and perhaps with the weight being lifted out heavy and bulky, and the door would have to be shut by leaning on it, or nudging it with a hip, say.'

'It's if this, if that, all vague and fanciful, Patton. You're trying to distract me.'

I shook my head, and waited.

'Then what the hell're you getting at?' he demanded, angry now.

'I've been wondering whether she could've been dead at that time, that's what,' I told him. 'How big was she? How heavy?'

He shook his head.

WDS Tomkinson spoke distantly. 'She'd barely have made the regulations. Seven stone – a flipperty slip of a girl.' There was perhaps envy in her voice, annoyance anyway.

'Have you got that down?' I asked her. Her own words – would she have recorded them?

'I have, sir.'

'No difficulty with "flipperty"?'

'Thank you, Mr Patton, no.' And no hint of a smile either.

'So you see,' I said to Slater. 'A strong man, her corpse in his arms, and with access to the tow-path. He could've carried her as far as the lock.'

And at last Ted Slater was pleased. 'Not exactly logical, Patton, surely.'

He shook his head in mock sorrow. 'All the way – a quarter of a mile – to get rid of her, and the canal itself within a few yards! With a bridge over it, in fact. He could've just shoved her over the parapet. Have you got *that*, Sergeant?' he asked.

'Indeed, sir, yes.'

'Then underline it.'

He smirked at me. I refrained, therefore, from suggesting the alternative explanation, or pointing out the basic fallacy in what I'd described. It was simply that Clare had been seen alive at a time at least several minutes after I'd peered inside her empty car. Seen by Gerald Fulton.

But Inspector Slater hadn't been listening to me, anyway. Not seriously.

'Now ... if you'll excuse me,' I said, sliding back my chair and getting to my feet.

'We hadn't finished.'

'No. Of course not. I haven't asked you if you've got a more definite cause of death.'

'I'm telling you nothing.'

'I rather thought I'd send Colin in to see you, and he can arrange interviews with everybody – but if you're going to be stroppy . . .'

'All right! All right! She drowned. She was knocked unconscious first, then dumped in the water. That do you?'

I nodded. 'Right. Then I'll go and dig out Colin Fulton, and send him here, and perhaps he can arrange for you to interview everybody in the building, those who were here last night. One at a time . . . however you fancy. You don't need to go through the premises, I wouldn't think, though Gerald Fulton (that's the solicitor I mentioned) might agree to taking you up to his room and showing you where he was when he thought he saw Clare Martin. And where she was, at the time. But do it how you want to. Colin will fix it for you, I'm sure. Just try to get off the site before the owners arrive.'

'Owners?'

'Of this place. Of the whole canal and all its locks. Two elderly ladies and an old gentleman. From what I could gather, they wouldn't want to discover police personnel on the premises, and you wouldn't want to upset them, I'm sure.'

'What the – '

'I'll send Colin to you.' And I walked out into the hall.

'Oh . . . Patton.'

At the shout, I turned back. 'Yes?'

'I was forgetting. Something I intended to tell you, then you'll know the lot. Clare was two months pregnant.'

And how would this news be received by the two elderly ladies and their even older brother? And how by Mellie, if she had any inkling about Ray's activities with Clare?

7

'They're coming,' cried Colin, striding purposefully along the corridor, as though he must alert everybody for this momentous occasion. I was surprised he hadn't banged the gong to assemble us.

'How long?' I asked.

He paused, caught in mid-stride. 'A couple of hours. One to get as far as the Rolls and load all the luggage they'll think they might possibly need, and one to drive here at the regulation speed of forty miles an hour.'

Poor old Rolls, I thought, just dying to show what it could do, and restrained to forty.

I walked in on Amelia, who was standing at our window and frowning.

'I can't decide,' she told me, 'whether that's the most ugly view I've ever encountered, or the most splendid.'

'It rather depends on the viewer, I'd have thought.' I stared down at it. 'Whether you get the sense of sheer magic at the imagination and accomplishment involved, or see it as shapes and proportions and practicalities. Romantic or pragmatic.' I didn't tell her my choice as to which was which. 'I've just been told we've got two hours of grace. D'you still not fancy a walk?'

'Two hours? Of grace?'

'The owners of this little lot, plus about nineteen ordinary locks and thirty-odd miles of canal, are due to descend on us in order to find out what's going on. Two old ladies and an older gentleman. It's *all* theirs. Locks, canal, water . . . the lot. And now – a murder.'

She turned to face me. 'That's certain, is it? Murder, I mean.'

'In practice, she drowned. A blow to the head, which must have knocked her unconscious, and then she was dumped in the pound. Then she drowned. There's nothing positive, though. She could have simply fallen, hit her head on the way down, then drowned. Could have.'

'It's all most unpleasant.' She wrinkled her nose at me.

'So why not come out for a walk? Get away from it all, for a while. As I said before, it's a lovely morning.'

'No, Richard, I don't think so. Poor Ruby will need help. There'll be rooms to be prepared, and a lot of other things to be thought about. I'll stay, Richard, but that needn't stop you from going. If you want to.'

'I'm not keen on being seen in this duffle coat – and it's too tight. I would like to buy a new anorak, one with a hood. Then,' I said with triumph, 'I shan't need to bother with a new hat.'

'What a clever idea! It's obvious you've been a detective. No ordinary person would have thought that out.'

Amelia had been developing a pert little habit of tossing at me these random sarcasms. Her eyes twinkled, her lips trembled as though just about to produce another little gem. So I kissed her quickly on those lips, getting in first, and she said, 'But do try to be back for when the old people arrive, Richard.'

'Don't worry. I'll ask Colin where's the nearest likely source of one anorak, with hood. Detachable, in brackets. And if it's too far . . .' I shrugged.

'You could use the car.'

'But that wouldn't be the walk I've been promising myself.'

She laughed. 'Of course. Silly of me.'

I found Colin in the bar, chatting away amicably to Inspector Ted Slater, as though they might be discussing a local football match. From the expression on Slater's face, and the tense concentration on the face of WDS Tomkinson, it was clear that in any event Colin was not sticking to Slater's prescribed programme.

'D'you mind if I put a word in, Ted?' I asked.

He scowled at me. 'Go ahead.'

'It's Colin I want to speak to. I want to go and buy a new anorak, Colin,' I explained. 'Is there anywhere within walking distance?'

'There's Crayminster. But I hope you can get back . . . they'll be here in about two hours, Richard.' He was looking very hard pressed.

'How far?'

'A mile and a half, or so. Along the tow-path. You come out in the centre of the town. Walk up the ramp to the street, turn right, and you'll find Fenton's, on the second corner to your right. He sells everything. Everything. You're in a farming district, you know.'

'Ah!' I said. 'Fine.' A mile and a half. I'd do that in about half an hour, a brisk trek on to Fenton's, half an hour back. 'I'll do it easily.'

I left them to it. Colin was trying to get across to Slater the point that his winding handle was missing, and it could make a very good weapon of offence. I walked out into the thin, chill winter sunlight, then put my head back inside.

'Which way?' I asked.

'Right – from here.'

This was the opposite direction to the one by which we'd arrived. I stepped out jauntily. I was wearing the duffle coat, but without the scarf over my head, and proposed to work up enough body-heat to keep the tired old brain working.

This was, in accordance with Colin's set-up of the flight, 'up' the canal. The water lay, of course, absolutely level. Therefore, the tow-path also ran level. I stepped out ahead smartly, trying not to think about the death of Clare Martin. Usually, it's the other way round; I try to concentrate on a problem, and get no answers because my eyes are everywhere, seeing this, observing that. Now I couldn't relax, couldn't even arouse any great interest in the pair of ducks paddling away from me to the far bank. No, not swimming. They seemed to be walking on the water, but then I realized that there was a thin ice layer, out here in the open. Thin ice, ice that floated, with here and there the water lying on its surface. Black ice, it seemed – it was still transparent. What were they, that pair of ducks? Mallard? Or teal? I'm not very well up on my bird recognition.

They disappeared beneath the overhanging trees on the far bank. I paused for a moment and looked back. Already, Flight House had disappeared. I hadn't realized that the curve in the canal was quite so extensive. But there I was, out in the open and all by myself. No traffic whipping past, no bustling and thrusting shoppers. Just a pair of ducks, who had now disappeared, and whose feet must have been very cold. I walked onwards. Better not hang around, I thought, or I might not be there to welcome the people who owned this paradise.

You could live happily here, I realized, puttering along from lock to lock as the mood dictated. Peace. But . . . there would be drawbacks. The cold, for instance. Weren't the modern boats steel-hulled, and wouldn't they be terribly cold in the winter, Calor gas heaters or not? And it would be somewhat cramped. Yet (and hadn't Colin said this?) people did live the year round on canals. It would be a quiet hideaway for a criminal on the run. Who would think to search the canals? It would – if I developed the theme – be a novel way in which to transport drugs, say. Slowly, but gently and innocently. Would the police think of this? I wondered. Maybe I would encounter . . .

And as I thought this, the steady bend revealed just such a craft. It did, too, seem smart enough to be almost new, such as drug traffickers might well be able to afford.

Developing this theme in my mind, I strode towards it. It was not alone, I saw. Beyond it were three or four other craft, though

94

looking rather scruffy in comparison to the lead boat, which was clean, bright with its yellow/gold and black main hull, red and orange for its cabin. Smart, even with lace curtains to its windows and a pot of what had been flowering plants on the cabin roof, and indeed it was being lived-in, because one of the mahogany-framed glass doors, which opened from the cabin on to the prow, was a foot ajar. The vessel was firmly tied, fore and aft, to two iron bollards.

Just in case somebody had seen me, I made a friendly gesture in its general direction, but all that attracted was a young brown and white cocker spaniel, which darted out of the door, barked a couple of times, darted back, then burst out to add another couple of barks.

'It's all right,' I said to him. 'I'm not going to touch anything.'

He was still barking as I walked on.

The next four boats were very nearly wrecks, each tied to a bollard, but I couldn't imagine them going anywhere unless it was to the bottom. The last of the run was a very fast-looking motor cruiser, which wouldn't be allowed to use its speed on the canal. It was firmly cocooned in stretched canvas.

I marched onwards, paused to get my pipe going, and with shoulders back lost myself in the peace of it. And I completely forgot that I was bang in the middle of what looked like a murder. Murder. Violence. How alien that was to these surroundings!

On exactly the half hour, by my watch, I reached the concrete ramp, marched up it, and was abruptly thrust into the same old rush of traffic. I had encountered three more locks on the way, but simple, single-rise ones. Turn right, Colin had said. At least I wouldn't have to cross the road. Crayminster, it was called. It was half-way between being a village and upgrading to a town. Very soon I came to what might have been their market square. It was still cobbled, but no shoppers could stand there for a prolonged or even a brief natter, as the traffic used it as a slight widening of the roadway, where a quick and horrifying overtake might be accomplished. Second to the right, Colin had said. Here was the first. A quick look along it revealed a cobbled surface again, but this was strictly pedestrians only. Motorcycles might have got through. Prams might encounter difficulties. Anything much wider would get stuck.

I turned away, preparing to head straight to Fenton's, and a police patrol car drifted to a halt at my elbow, its horn giving a

95

short, warning pip. I paused, glancing at it. Ray was driving it, and he was alone. He grinned, unclipped his seatbelt and climbed out, walking round the car to confront me. He was in uniform.

'Mr Patton . . . You shopping or something?'

'Shopping, yes. And I'd prefer Richard. I'm just hoping to find something to replace my ruined anorak.'

'It's Fenton's you want for that. You're nearly there.'

'I know. I've had full instructions,' I assured him. 'And you . . . I thought you'd got time off.'

He shrugged, grimacing. 'Got caught, didn't I! I just dropped into the station to make out a report. You know . . . about Clare's death, and what I know. Keep it official, I thought, do it by the book.'

'That's always the best course,' I said. 'But there's not much you can say, is there? In this report of yours, I mean.'

He shrugged. 'Well no. What else would I be thinking about at that time but the engagement and what-not! Good Lord – did you see how Mellie's dad was rigged out? He doesn't live in this century.'

I smiled at him. He wasn't qualified to criticize, he turning up in his uniform. 'And now?' I asked. 'Where're you off to now?'

'Hell. You know how it is. Put your nose in, and suddenly you're back on duty. The super's car's broken down, way out in the wilds, Crofton Magna way, so I'm going to pick him up and bring him home to his office. I'll make it a fast run, and . . . well, tell Mellie, will you. I'll be along.'

'I'll do that.' I watched him get back in the car, and drive away, and there it was, Fenton's. Exactly where Colin had said.

Although it occupied window space in both streets, the narrow doorway in the corner was squeezed even more narrow by the displayed, hanging garments that almost filled the space. Trousers – corduroy and thick tweed.

Leather coats. Leggings. Sturdy, heavy boots. I edged through and pushed open the door. A bell tinkled above my head, as it had probably tinkled for over a century.

There was a smell of leather, of damp tweed and dry rot. The ceiling was festooned with hairy garments, hacking jackets, fawn waistcoats, waterproof trousers, rubber boots that would reach your waist. For fishermen, these.

'Can I help you, sir?'

The crumpled old man was leaning forward over what was

visible of his counter between a display of riding breeches and one of leather jackets. I ducked my head, and approached.

'I would like,' I said, 'an anorak, preferably with a detachable hood.'

By that time I didn't fancy my chances. Anything not to be worn for riding horses, or fetching in and milking the cows, or wandering the hills in pouring rain or a foot of snow, searching for sheep, was not likely to be there. He smiled. The rubicund face cracked open. 'Your size, sir ... um ... ah ... tricky.' Then, by some magic related to a stage illusion, he disappeared, and as abruptly appeared at my elbow.

'Something like this, sir?'

He was holding up a coat that I would not have called an anorak. But as that fellow said – what's in a name? It was in a fabric I had not previously encountered, looked a little like tarnished steel armour, and was indisputably, as he put it, 'Completely waterproof, sir.'

'It looks as though it would be,' I conceded.

'Shall we try it on, sir?'

We tried it on. By some miracle, or from his experience of heaven knows how many years, it did fit. It was a little longer than what I usually wore, even than my warmest overcoat. 'That's to stop the rain dripping into your gumboots, sir.'

'I don't usually wear gumboots.'

'I could find you a pair. Just your size, sir.'

'No, no. Has it got a hood?'

'Oh yes. Detachable. There.'

He swept it over my head. It was a little large, but ... 'It is usually worn over a woolly hat, sir.' This, not entirely to my surprise, he produced with the air of a magician, clamped it over my head, and ... surprise ... surprise. The hood now fitted perfectly. He then demonstrated the locations of the seven commodious pockets, and pointed out that the padded lining was detachable.

I was quite convinced by this time that it was completely waterproof and possibly bulletproof, realized that it was very warm, as I was sweating, and knew that if I asked to see whatever else he had I would not get back in the two hours. I asked how much it was. I didn't have that much cash with me. Tentatively, because he probably still thought in pounds, shillings and pence, even sovereigns, I asked if he could accept my credit card.

'Of course, sir. And if you'll take it off, I'll pack it – '

'No, no. I'll wear it. But pop the duffle coat in a bag for me, would you?'

And so I set forth to walk back. It creaked and it groaned as I moved. He'd said that would wear off, and had sold me a can of something with which I could spray it. 'It must breathe, sir. Breathe.'

By the time I got back to the tow-path, sweat was pouring from me. It was a relief to return to canal level, and bask in its rising chill.

I now had three quarters of an hour left. I felt I didn't need to hurry. With the new coat, mackintosh, whatever he would call it – certainly not an anorak – I prayed for rain. The sun shone in a clear sky. The creaking ceased. The material began to feel soft. I had to throw back the hood, just to cool my head, and forgot the woolly hat was still there. Thus, head down because I didn't want to see how far I still had to go, I plodded onwards. The sight of the row of boats was extremely welcome. I'd sweated off at least half a stone.

He was still there, that spaniel, and once more bounced from the partly open door. That was strange, now I came to think about it, that a steel hull, which was bound to be very cold in this water, should not have been closed up against any possible incursion of cold air. He barked at me two or three times, forepaws on the prow, but when I reached over to fondle his ears he ducked back, ran off inside, bounced out again for two or three more barks, then nipped back inside.

I waited. His head appeared. One yap.

I recognized this canine behaviour, having encountered it with our two boxers at home when they had something to show me, an otter or something like that. They're now getting rare in the Severn.

'Hello!' I shouted. 'Anybody at home?'

There was no reply.

The spaniel popped out again, with the same number of yaps. I stepped over on to the prow. There was barely foot room to stand straight.

'Anybody home?'

Silence. The dog went frantic. I opened the second of the pair of doors, and bent low. The head clearance was very little. A steep step or two down, then I could straighten. Just.

'Oh . . . Good Lord!'

This forward cabin had a bunk bed each side of the narrow walkway down the middle. Beyond was the kitchen, a compact area. One of the bunk beds had blankets – had held blankets, but they had been flung aside. The dog tramped over them, whining.

A woman lay on the bunk, barely covered, a young woman whose bruised eyes were wide, staring out above shrunken cheeks. She was wearing what looked like a crumpled and sweat-soaked T-shirt, and jeans. Her face was drawn thin, cheeks flaring hot and red, sweat on her brow. She moaned something, and moved one hand. I stepped over the dog. The hand was clammy. I bent low to her. My mind was running through possibilities. An overdose of whatever obscene drug she'd been using? Her lips moved, her eyes flicked wildly around, as though seeking for something.

I put the back of my hand to her forehead. Brown, tangled hair was soaked with sweat. Her flesh was burning. One eye was nearly closed, and there was a bruise on her other cheek. Her lips were moving, swollen lips, so I bent low, feeling the radiated heat on my own cheek. Her breathing was harsh and laboured.

'Den,' she whispered. 'Denny.'

I didn't know what that meant. Where had I heard that name? 'Den . . .' She couldn't complete it, and writhed her head in frustration on the roll of towel that was her pillow. Her lips drew back, horribly revealing two teeth missing from her upper gums.

'I'm going to get help,' I said quickly, to save her more effort. 'Help for you.'

She fought to reach my wrist. The grip was almost painfully hot – but she was shivering. I allowed her to draw me down, and she breathed in my ear: 'D . . . Den . . .'

'All right. I understand. But I must go now. Get help. A minute.'

I knew now how close I was to the house. She was drooling, fighting breathlessly to speak. I bent close again. With a desperate effort she managed to mumble: 'Col . . . in.' Her breath wheezed it.

'Yes,' I said. 'Right. Colin. I'll get Colin. I'll be as quick as I can.' And then I remembered where I'd heard the name, Dennis.

I bashed my head, trying to get out fast, and cursed the new coat for not being flexible enough, scrambled out on to the tow-path, and with my carrier bag once again in one hand I started to run. The spaniel barked at my heels for fifty yards, urging me on, then he ran back to the boat.

I galloped, coat flying now, as I had opened it, galloped, panting because I'd been smoking too much (and decided yet again to give it up) along to the forefront of Flight House, where Colin wasn't because I wanted him. People never are. I burst into the bar. Ted Slater was now interviewing Gerald, who looked round angrily.

'Colin!' I shouted, using all the breath I had left. Then I pounced on the phone and dialled nine-nine-nine. 'Ambulance,' I gasped.

'What *is* this?' Gerald demanded.

But I had no time for him, because they came on. 'Ambulance,' I said, 'to Flight House. Know it?'

'They will, sir. Have you any information?'

'I think we'll need the Paramedics,' I said. 'Young woman, living in a boat on the canal. I think she's got pneumonia. She's shivering, and her flesh is red hot.'

'Yes sir. Be with you shortly.'

'And I think she's been beaten up,' I added.

'Yes sir. Wait there, please, if you will.'

'Thank you.' I hung up, feeling a terrible, empty let-down. I'd been able to do so little for her. So little.

Then Colin burst into the room. 'What is it? Who's shouting for me?'

'Yes,' said Gerald, rising from his seat and eyeing me with disfavour. 'What's going on?'

I tried to speak to both of them at once. 'In the first parked boat along,' I said. 'The red and yellow one . . .'

'I know it,' said Colin, his voice dead. He gripped my arm. 'What?'

'There's a woman inside. I think she's very ill. Probably pneumonia.'

'Helen,' Colin breathed.

'You know her?' But of course he did!

Colin was white, lines drawn down his face, the stress of multiple incidents gradually undermining him. 'I told you.' He cleared his throat. 'She's the Helen I know,' he said, more explicitly.

'You're talking as though you knew she was there,' I said softly.

'Of course I damn-well knew,' he said angrily, impatiently.

'What *is* this?' Gerald interrupted, heavily authoritative. 'What does this mean, Colin?'

'Oh ... mind your own damned business,' Colin snapped angrily. The stress was getting to him – he was almost beyond control. He turned to me. 'The boat's mine. In February, I tour the canal, end to end, checking, checking.' He wasn't looking at me, his eyes hunting from left to right, back again. 'That's the boat I use.'

'And you lent it to Clare's sister?' I asked, having to restrain him now with a hand to his arm. 'Helen's Clare's sister?'

'Yes.' He bit it off sharply.

I didn't ask why. I could guess. Already I could hear the distant ambulance siren.

'You'd better get down there, Colin.' I released his arm.

Gerald moved forward a step. 'I want to know what all this is about, Colin. And this instant.' His chin was high. He had summoned up all his authority.

Colin was almost in tears from frustration and fury, and couldn't take much more. He spoke very quietly because inside there, somewhere, there was a whole bundle of emotions fighting for precedence, and he didn't know how to handle them. He simply shook his arm free, said, 'You'll have to wait,' and banged his way out through the swinging doors. I followed him, more slowly. In a second he was at a flat run.

Suddenly, Amelia was at my elbow. 'Richard?' She had heard it nearly all, I could tell that by her expression.

I filled in what she might have missed. 'I didn't spend much time with her,' I explained. 'All I know so far is that she's Clare's sister, and she's been living on that houseboat. It belongs to Colin, apparently. And love ... I've seen women like this before, and my guess is that she's been beaten up.'

She bit her lower lip, her eyes bright. 'We'll have to go along there and help.'

The siren was now close. I said, 'We'll be in the way.'

Then Inspector Slater was standing solidly in front of me. 'Did I hear you speaking about violence, Patton?'

'That was what I thought.'

He sighed. 'Then I suppose I'm going to be landed with it.'

'We don't know that,' I said. 'We don't know it's criminal violence.' I turned to Amelia. 'Can you put your hand on a length of string, love?'

'String?'

'Or the like. There's a spaniel along there, and he's going to get underfoot. The poor little bugger's probably hungry and thirsty, so I thought . . .'

'String?' she said. 'String, Gerald? Have you got any string?'

He stared at her blankly. 'I suppose. Behind the counter.'

He had been standing behind us, holding open the swing doors. Now he stood aside for her.

I was trying to work out what had to be done, what would happen first, and where I came into it. I heard her slam a drawer, then she came rushing out again. 'String!' she cried, waving a large ball of thick string.

I produced my penknife and cut off a couple or so yards of it. She understood what I had in mind. 'Wait for me,' she said. 'I'll dash and get my coat.'

'No time,' I told her. 'Here, try this.'

I pulled the duffle coat out of its bag, and tossed it to her.

'But it's Colin's!'

'Never mind. It'll go with your hair a treat.'

'Oh, stop your flannel,' she said. 'Let's get going.'

'I demand to know – ' began Gerald.

'You will do,' I told him. 'You'll know.'

Outside, the ambulance siren was dying to a moan. Appropriate, that was. They had driven round the building and stopped opposite the swing doors. I went forward to meet them, two men and a woman.

'Where is she?' asked one of the men, jumping down.

'Along the tow-path.' I pointed. 'Just round the bend – a red and yellow houseboat. A woman. High temperature. Shuddering, and having difficulty with her breathing. I saw bruises. You're going to have a hell of a job getting her out of there.'

'Never mind that. Better bring the portable oxygen, Fay. Right? Then let's go.'

They set off at a run, one with the stretcher, one with a black case, Fay with what must have been the oxygen equipment. I managed to get a double thickness of string, and tied the ends together. That ought to do it, I thought.

'Coming, love?'

But she'd already put on the duffle coat. 'I don't want to. Really, I don't.'

'Then wait here.'

'I can't. You *must* see that.'

I stared at her. There was nothing I could say.

We walked. Sedately, along the tow-path we walked, as though this might be a pleasant outing, Amelia clutched firmly to my arm. By the time we got there, all three were inside. 'Get that bloody dog out of here,' one of the men shouted.

So, after all, we served a purpose. The dog heard us, and burst out, barking still. I got a firm hold on him this time, was relieved to see he wore a collar, and managed to get my string looped through it. There was a brass plate riveted to the collar. His name was Bruce. 'Bruce,' I said, testing it out. The tail, which had been down, gave the faintest of movements.

Colin stood, still and white, on the tow-path. They got her out. It was a hell of a job. With the double doors open, it was wide enough for the stretcher, but the height of the sill wasn't generous, and there was little room for the foremost attendant to back out. His foot was perilously perched, right on the prow. He cursed. 'Easy, easy,' said a voice from inside. I relinquished the string lead to Amelia, and Bruce began barking again, frantically. I tried to help. With hands held high, I could just manage, from the towpath, to take one arm of the stretcher. He jumped down beside me, saw I had it, jumped back and helped to edge the rear end clear of the doorway. We lowered her.

Her face was inches from mine, but inverted. A hand clawed for my wrist.

'It's all right now,' I said. 'It's all right, Helen. We'll look after Bruce.'

'Denny,' she whispered. Her breathing was a little better. The woman attendant said, 'Let her rest.' I whispered, 'I'll see about Denny,' not knowing what the devil she meant. You promise anything, in such circumstances. Nevertheless, it was a promise, and she knew it. She moistened swollen lips and made a wry grimace. Perhaps it'd been a smile. It must have been, because I could see a gap in her teeth beyond it.

The taller man of the team was now on the tow-path. The rest was easy. They collected themselves together, the woman packing their equipment away. I jumped down.

'You the husband?' His voice was empty, controlled.

'No. I found her.'

He nodded. I couldn't see Colin anywhere.

They set off with her at a strange lope, not a run, not a walk. It disturbed the stretcher as little as possible. I walked briskly beside the woman – girl, not much more. 'Which hospital?' I asked. Amelia was very silent behind us.

'Haughton Grange. Who's Denny?'

'Her child, I think.'

We were nearly at the ambulance now. I ventured, 'Is it pneumonia?'

'Could be. We think there's a cracked rib. It could have punctured her lung. She's certainly in pain. She could have died.' She was a young woman of few words. What she used, she produced in a flat tone, almost painfully, as though she really wanted to shout out in protest, but her profession demanded calmness and quiet efficiency. 'A broken wrist,' she added emptily.

I turned away, looking back along the tow-path. Amelia said, 'What is it?'

'Colin. He ran ahead, and he hasn't come back. I'd better go and have a look.'

'I'll come . . .'

'If you don't mind, love . . . man to man.'

'You men! But don't be long.'

I walked back, rapidly and worriedly, unaware that I still had the string in one hand and the dog on the other end of it. I noticed him now because he hung back, looking for his mistress.

Colin was inside, standing there, just standing, but with his fingers fumbling with the poor blankets that Helen had flung aside. If he heard me enter, he didn't look up.

I said, 'I take it that I've just seen the young lady you were telling me about?'

No answer. He might not have heard me, for all the notice he took of my presence.

'Helen. You said her name was Helen, the woman you want to marry. But you didn't say she'd left her husband. I thought . . .'

He was not listening. 'I'll kill him,' he said quietly, with the decisive voice of a man who has finally made an important decision. 'Break his neck, or strangle him. Or drown him. Something. But I'll kill him, Richard, that's what I'm going to do.'

'I'm not sure that would be a good idea, you know,' I told him, assuming a casual voice. 'I mean, the police'd recognize it as murder, and with the motive you've got, they'd home in on you like wasps to a jampot. No, Colin. Think calmly, and later on. In the meantime ... they've taken her to Haughton Grange. Know it?'

'What? Yes, of course. It's our local hospital.'

'That's where she's gone.'

'Her name's Helen,' he said.

'I know.'

'The Helen I told you about.'

'I guessed that.'

'We're going to get married.'

'I rather gathered that was the idea. Before or after?'

By asking him a question, I had forced him to pay attention. 'What?'

'Do you intend to marry her before or after you kill him?'

'Are you insane, or something?'

'It matters. It'd be a pity to spend a lot of money on a divorce, and *then* kill him. Better the other way round. Cheaper, and very much quicker.'

'I think you *are* insane.'

'Kill him first,' I advised. 'And I'll help.'

'No. Myself. It's my job, killing Pierce.'

'All right, Colin. All right. Now ... let's get back to the house. I mean, that's where the phone is, and we'll need to keep in touch.'

'Then what're we waiting for?' he demanded, and managed a flying leap on to the tow-path.

'Give 'em time to get there,' I called after him.

But he took not a bit of notice, and all I could do was walk briskly after him, the dog panting at the end of the taut string, intent on trying to rejoin his mistress. Together, we marched on to the lodge frontage, Amelia now at my shoulder, as we'd met her half-way.

The ambulance was still there. They must have had to give Helen emergency treatment. I shuddered at the thought of how close I had come to discovering her too late. As I approached, the driver of the team jumped down from the back, shut the doors, and ran round to the driver's seat.

It was at this point that a tall, narrow and angular Rolls Royce, with a straight and uncompromising bonnet, rolled slowly round the corner of the lodge.

The driver, sitting sternly upright, viewed the ambulance with dour consideration. Gently, the Rolls backed up, sliding its bulk up the wider of the two bridges. It tilted steeply. He carefully eased it back to the exact spot over the hump at which the Rolls was level, drew on his handbrake, and got out to inspect the situation. There were three inches of clearance on each side. He was standing stiffly, about five and a half feet tall, and maybe carried around eight stone. He spoke to the ambulance driver, pointing to the toll booth. There was just room for the ambulance to back up, almost beside the toll booth. Then it was away. No siren yet. There was nobody to warn. Two minutes later, I heard it break in, distantly. And fade into silence.

When I turned round, the driver had drawn the Rolls into the exact position that he wanted, directly opposite the swing doors to the lounge.

Gerald walked out in stately welcome.

8

In situations such as this it is always advisable to stand back, hopefully not to be noticed, and wait to see what happens. The driver held open a rear door and two ladies emerged, neither of them above low-to-average height. Due to the generous clearance built in, and the running-board that ran all the length of the car from front mudguards to rear ones, they walked out of the Rolls rather than slid, as is necessary with modern cars. But the man following them was much taller, and found it necessary to back out, keeping a firm grip on both sides of the door-frame until his feet were well on the ground. Between them, these three could have notched up well-nigh on 250 years.

But they were far from senile, in spite of a certain stiffness of age, and I noticed that each took a quick look round to check that their property was in good order, and still a viable proposition. Then they smiled at each other, and nodded knowingly.

It seemed, at that stage, that greetings had to be performed with the correct degree of formality, though the two families must have met very many times, and knew each other intimately.

Gerald, of course, took it upon himself to be the chief welcomer. Colin must have dashed away to change out of his jeans and sweater, because he was suddenly there in what was for him more sombre wear, a shirt and tie, grey slacks and a hacking jacket, his face as grey as the slacks.

There was much cheek bumping and kisses planted on the air just below ears, and exclamations of delight that everybody seemed to be in good health.

'But where is little Mellie?' cried the old gentleman. 'Where are you hiding the child, Gerald?'

Mellie appeared, as if on cue. She had not exactly been hiding, it seemed, but rather had had to be retrieved from a quiet corner with Ray.

I was somewhat surprised to see Ray. When I had last seen him, about half an hour before, he had been heading out into the wilds of the countryside to rescue his super. He must have done some very rapid motoring, and some quick changing from uniform to suit. That he had not done a similar change the previous evening was apparent to Gerald as a personal insult. I saw that his cheeks were flushed with indignation.

All this was taking place in the open, which seemed to me to be strange, but it carried with it a quaint suggestion that bona fides should be established before entry was gained. Yet these people owned the place. They owned it all. Everything.

Then they flowed into the bar. Mellie, reluctantly, was persuaded to go with them, so that Ray remained outside with Colin. They came over to us quickly. Amelia hooked a hand under my arm.

'What's the situation?' Ray demanded anxiously. 'I didn't get to see much. The ambulance, and what-not.'

'It's Helen, Ray. Helen.' Colin's voice was strained, his lips set in a grim line.

I answered Ray's question. 'She's seriously ill, Ray.'

'Hell.'

Ray tugged at Colin's sleeve. 'I said, didn't I! Didn't I tell you, Colin? He oughta be put down. Like a mad dog.'

I glanced at him, surprised at his vehemence. 'You know about this, Ray?'

'Something.' He shrugged. 'What's he done now?'

'Who?' I asked. 'Who're you talking about?'

'That lousy husband of hers. Pierce.'

'How bad is she?' Colin cut in. 'How bad?'

'They were giving her oxygen,' I told him, that being sufficiently

107

expressive to cover it. 'She's seriously ill, Colin. It looked as though she'd been beaten up badly.'

'Again?' he asked hollowly. His eyes were bright and wild. 'Fresh injuries?'

'Yes.'

I was eyeing him cautiously. His eyes were flicking around and his arms were swinging about violently, exactly the behaviour of someone about to lose control.

'What did you mean?' I asked. 'Fresh injuries, you said. Was she hurt before – when she came here?'

'Yes . . . yes. That swine'd been at it again. Ray brought her, Ray and Clare – but for some reason or other they didn't bring Denny. That swine! He'd never have traced her to the boat – I could've sworn that.'

'I told you,' put in Ray. 'Denny wasn't there. So we brought Helen. Colin . . . we tried.'

'Couldn't ever have traced her,' Colin persisted.

'But it seems that he did,' I told him. 'And he had another go at her with his fists, by all the indications. Most of the damage was fresh, Colin.'

'It's Helen,' he said distractedly. He was unable to keep his eyes settled on one spot. 'The woman I'm going to marry.'

'Yes. You told me about that.'

But I hadn't got his full attention. He was darting glances around as though he ought to be somewhere else.

'For heaven's sake, Colin, stop worrying about your visitors. Tell me. Quickly , if you like – how long had you had her hidden away in your boat?'

'About a week. Ten days, perhaps.'

'So she came to you – '

He cut in eagerly. 'Ray it was who came. Isn't that so, Ray? I'm sure I told you that, Richard. Clare's her sister. Helen's sister. And Ray works with Clare. Ray knew all about it.'

'All there was to know,' said Ray.

'I'd asked Ray if he could get her away from him, and I'd have her here. Well – not in the house, of course.'

'Why of course?' I demanded, a little short with him.

'It wasn't a time for upset, with Mellie's engagement coming up. So I used the houseboat. Richard . . . she'd been beaten up . . .'

'When she got here?'

'Yes'

'With the dog?'

'Yes. Hell . . . why not?'

'But not with Denny? Denny's the little lad?'

'Yes,' he groaned. 'Look – I must – no, not with Dennis.'

He was very close to collapse and was completely disorientated. I wasn't certain he could organize his thoughts.

'What you must do is tell me. I'll say it for you, and you nod. Okay? She came, knocked about, not seriously, though?' Nod. 'Just with the dog?' Nod. 'You hid her away?' Nod. 'And now we find her very ill and severely beaten up?' A very weary nod.

'Didn't you go and see how she was doing, every day?'

'Of course I bloody-well did.'

'So, it follows that she must have been beaten up last night, or evening. In any event, after dark.'

'All right. Yes, yes to everything.'

'So . . . how did this Pierce creature suddenly know where to find her?'

'I don't know.' He shook his head violently. 'I don't *know*!'

'Then you get back into the fray, Colin,' I told him. 'Mustn't neglect your duties. We'll leave the boat locked up.'

If we could locate the keys, that was.

With a certain amount of relief, Colin turned and hurried back to the house. It seemed that he had no wish to have his relationship with Helen explored by his bosses, not at this time. And, as so many people do, he had completely ignored the presence of the family's driver, who had been standing quietly just beyond my right shoulder.

I turned. The driver – no, chauffeur, they would call him – smiled a bright smile, and he winked one twinkling eye.

'A complicated life the young people live, these days, sir.'

'Indeed they do,' I agreed.

I thought it better to wander away from his immediate presence if we wanted to speak our private thoughts, but he took the decision from us.

'It is my practice, sir,' he said, 'when we visit, to go round to the kitchen and brew myself a cup of tea. Then the master and mistresses will know where to find me. Should I be needed. I'll leave you now, if there's nothing I can do for you, and you can go about your own affairs. Of which, sir, I do not wish to be told.'

He was a tough, spry little man, who knew his place in life, enjoyed it, and had no wish to be involved in other people's concerns.

'You do that,' I said, and he ambled away.

I turned to Ray. He was standing stiffly, uncomfortably, his eyes empty of expression. 'I take it,' I said, 'that this business with Helen Pierce and the houseboat was all extra-duty stuff?'

He stared at me.

'Not undertaken in uniform,' I amplified.

'Of course not. Clare, my partner, was Helen's sister.'

'I know that.'

'So we helped her out. As friends, not as police officers.'

'Helped Helen?' I waited for his nod. 'For Clare's sake? If they were sisters.'

He shrugged. 'Partly. But I liked Helen. Like her,' he corrected quickly. 'Always have. I'd have helped Helen and Colin, anyway, on my own, but Clare said she wanted to help, as well. Demanded, actually. A bit bossy, Clare's always been.'

'But she couldn't boss you,' I suggested.

He gave a weak grin. 'She knew I would help Helen, with or without her at my elbow. So she kind of had to go along with it.'

'Yes. I see.'

'I'd better get along inside,' said Ray. 'Mellie'll want to show off her brand new fiancé.' He gave a grimace. 'I hope they're not frightened of coppers.'

'They didn't give that impression. It seemed to me that they'd treat policemen as their personal servants.'

'Hmmph!' he said.

He was about to move off, but I put in quickly, 'You did a quick job with that super of yours, Ray.'

'Yeah . . . well.' He suddenly grinned. 'You'll laugh. He'd been driving his own Rover, and he shunted it into the back of a big trailer wagon. Nearly took the top off the car, and his head with it. But it's outside our patch, and the local cops aren't happy. They were asking for statements. He must've been travelling too fast and too close. So they kept him, frothing with fury, and promised they'd deliver him at his own office, later. So I came straight here.' Then he winked at me, winked at Amelia, and said, 'I'd better get inside, and see if they approve.'

'I'm sure they will,' said Amelia encouragingly.' Then, after he

110

had disappeared she asked, 'What is it you intend to do, Richard?' She linked her arm in mine as we set off back along the tow-path.

'See if there's anything we can feed the dog with. Give him water. God knows how long he's been without food. And take a general look around. Tidy. And try to discover the address of this lout, Arnold Pierce.'

'Richard!' she said, using her warning voice.

'Don't worry. He'll surely want to know how his wife is faring. Now . . . won't he?' I managed to say this blandly, lowering one eyelid at her.

'I will not have you – '

'Getting involved? I know. But there's this Dennis they've mentioned. The kiddywinky, apparently. Quite frankly, I'm not happy that he should be with such a person, even though he's his father.'

'You surely can't be thinking – '

'Oh, but I am. I am.'

She shook my elbow in alarm. 'You're enjoying this, aren't you?' she demanded.

'No. No, I assure you.'

'You can't intervene in a domestic dispute, Richard. You've told me that.'

'That's police rules, Amelia, love. I'm not in the police now. Even if I was, I could intervene if requested. Now . . . don't you think the young lady – Helen Pierce, her name is – don't you think she'd *ask* me to intervene? If only to fetch the lad away from his father. It'd probably help no end with her recovery, if she knew the lad was away from the sort of man her blasted, rotten husband appears to be? As it stands now, she'll be worried to death.'

'But what . . . what can you do – what can *we* do with a little lad? Take him home with us? That'd be kidnapping.'

'No. We can't do that. But . . . take one step at a time. Depending on how the mother progresses.'

'Take *her* home with us, you mean?'

'Why not? If there's nothing else. She and the little lad, however old he may be.'

'And . . . Mary?'

'She'd love him. And Sheba and Jake would love this spaniel, here. Name of Bruce, by the way.'

'You live in a dream world, Richard. Fantasies.'

111

I had to ignore that. It was only too true. 'Here we are. Careful how you jump up,' I said.

'How long since I told you I love you?' she asked abruptly.

'Ages. Last night.'

'I meant, in words.'

'Ages.'

She smiled. I couldn't understand why.

We stood beside the boat. 'I haven't really taken a good look at it,' Amelia said.

'Looks smart, doesn't it? Colin told me it's his.'

'Is it really? A thing like this – they must be very expensive. I can't imagine how he'd be able to afford it, if the only payment he gets is the free tenancy of the lodge.'

'He gets tips, he told me. People he helps through with their boats, through his precious flight.' Yet as I said it I realized it would take a lot of tips to buy this vessel. A lot of years of tipping. Or perhaps, as he used it to travel on the canal on his employers' behalf, they had bought it for him.

The dog was pulling, his collar nearly choking him, so I let him go. He went like an arrow for that open door, clearing the prow with one bound from the tow-path. I paused to offer Amelia a hand, and heaved her aboard. Bruce was hunting up and down for his vanished mistress.

Now, with the chill of the water still in the metal hull, the boat seemed colder than the outside air. I looked round, and there was a small Calor gas fire. I traced the tubing back to the cylinder, and picked it up. As I didn't know how heavy it was when empty, its weight didn't tell me how full it might be. There was no sloshing sound of liquid from inside. How long had they been without heat? There was a spare cylinder in a cupboard, but there had been no one to connect it up.

I was looking round for a water supply. Logic told me it ought to be high, and there it was, to one side of the hull, and it had a tap. I tried it, Bruce's metal dish beneath it. Yes, there was water. But how long had it been since Helen had been capable of reaching it? When I put Bruce's metal dish beneath the tap, it rattled against it. My hands were unsteady, shaking with anger.

Water came, and filled the dish. I put it down and Bruce slopped at it noisily. He had access to the canal, but this was clear water. We ventured further inside. Here, in the kitchen area, there was a heater, one small ring to accommodate a kettle or a saucepan. The tube to this disappeared into the rear of a cupboard beneath. I tried the tap, and got a hissing noise. 'Ah,' I said, and turned it off while I hunted out my lighter. Then I lit the ring.

'No point in that is there, Richard?'

'Well . . . yes. See if there's any dog food, love. Ah . . . ah, yes. This is what I was hoping for.'

In the next compartment, perched on a table top, there was a large plastic carrier bag, packed with food supplies. Now, this explained . . .

I cut that thought off abruptly.

'What *is* it, Richard?' Amelia can almost read my mind. Certainly, my emotions.

'A theory gone up the spout, that's all. I was talking to Ted Slater about the intriguing way Clare's car had been left. It *was* her car, by the way. And there was the strange fact that it'd been left there in the lane, with the keys in. I explained it to myself by thinking it might be like that if the driver had been lifting out something heavy, and then shut the door with a hip. Well . . . wouldn't it?'

She was staring at me, and shook her head. 'I suppose so.' Contradicting the shake. 'Are you going to open that tin, or not?'

I reached out and hunted in a drawer, found a tin-opener, and also the bunch of keys for the boat. I popped the keys in my pocket, and opened the can. This released its smell, and Bruce went wild. But I had to take the chill off it, so I sloshed a drop of water into a saucepan and tipped in the contents of the can.

'Spoon?' I asked.

Amelia found one, and put it into my hand. Like a surgeon, I felt. I chopped at the solid mass, then I stirred it to stop it getting burnt. At the first sign of steam, I turned the lot into Bruce's metal dish, and barely got it to the floor before he pounced on it. Slop, slop, slop . . . and it had gone.

'The poor little devil's starving,' I said.

'Yes. He was. Now . . . what were you saying?' She was busy tidying up the blankets and towels and the rest from beneath our feet.

'Oh yes – why the car door wasn't locked. I thought it meant that Clare could've been lifting out a heavy weight, something bulky, so that when I saw that bag of groceries, I assumed that explained it. But it doesn't, does it?'

Bruce was whining for a repeat performance, but I didn't want to make him sick, and took no notice.

'Why doesn't the bag of groceries explain the unlocked door?' Amelia asked patiently.

'Because it would be a natural action to put the heavy weight on the ground, and then shut the car up and lock it. And this is a plastic bag, so it would come to no harm, being put down on wet ground. A cardboard box, now, she wouldn't have been able to put down. D'you get my point? The bottom would drop out, if it got wet.'

'Ah . . . I see. So you're getting nowhere.' Her eyes were bright as she pursed her lips at me. Teasing me again.

'No. Yes. I don't know where I'm getting. And I bet this bag's been here for days. Four or five. Even then, Helen Pierce must've been ill. Would her sister have left her like that? Just left a bag of groceries – and left?'

'You're asking me for guesses, Richard.'

'Yes. Sorry. But Colin's said he's been here every day. And he didn't think she was very ill. Not *really* ill. She'd been knocked around a bit before she even got here.'

'So?' She was frowning deeply. I was bringing it too close to her.

But all I could offer her was still no more than guesses.

'I'd say that Clare came, about five-thirty yesterday evening. She brought . . . something. I don't know. Perhaps that carrier bag of grocery. But certainly, Helen hadn't been beaten up so badly at that time. Couldn't have been, or Clare – a policewoman – would've got an ambulance. They were sisters. Surely she'd have done that much.'

'Sisters, Richard, often hate each other.'

'So I've heard, my love. But in that case, Clare wouldn't have helped her at all. Yet we know she did.'

'Do we, Richard?' Amelia was watching me with a gentle smile. 'We don't really *know* what she did for her sister.'

'I just can't understand her,' I admitted. 'Helping her sister out, and yet I was coming round to thinking of her as completely self-centred, and an unfeeling bitch into the bargain.'

'Richard!'

'The only word that seems to fit.' But damn it, Clare was beginning to sound like a vastly complex person, a strange and possibly violent mixture of strong emotions.

Amelia was silent for a few moments, then shuddered. 'Can we get away from here, Richard? And . . . look what I've found!'

She was holding up a small denim jacket, such as a child might wear. She had found it amongst the tossed blankets she'd been tidying. There was no need for words. Dennis had been here.

She was again silent for a few moments and shuddered. 'Can we get out of here, Richard?' she repeated.

'Yes, yes. Of course. But we'll take whatever dog food there is.'

There were four more tins. I now had reason to bless the multiple commodious pockets in the coat. Amelia watched me slipping them away. 'And why are you wearing that silly woollen hat, Richard?'

I snatched it off. 'I'd completely forgotten it. I must've looked a right fool in it.'

'Not', she assured me, 'if everyone thought you always went round like that.'

Trying to work out the logic in that statement, I thrust it into my pocket and carefully locked up, taking the metal dish with us.

'And why d'you need that?' she asked.

'Well . . . it might just be possible to persuade everybody that it's not a terrible thing to have an animal in the house, but you'd never persuade them to let him eat off their crockery.'

'You think of everything, Richard.' I could only wish she was correct.

So we walked into the bar lounge with the dog on his lead (my string), and me in my new coat, bulging strangely in unusual places.

They were all there. I managed to divest myself of the coat, and Amelia of Colin's duffle coat, before we were introduced.

The ladies were Victoria and Alexandra, the former a tiny old dear with a face much crinkled from too much laughter, it seemed, because she laughed at me frankly, having observed my previous discomfort. Alexandra was more severe, possibly the younger of the two ladies, but her eyes were kind and forgiving, her hand soft and intimate. The eldest, the tall, thin streak of a man, was Adolphus, grave, kindly and courteous, a man who would have difficulty thinking ill of anyone. He would not know how to deal with men like Arnold Pierce. From the names, I guessed the family had always revered the Royal Family.

'Oh, what a darling!' cried Mellie, swooping on Bruce, crouching to him, and allowing him to explore her face with his tongue.

115

'I do not approve of animals in the house,' observed Gerald distantly. 'And you shouldn't let him lick your face, Mellie.'

I glanced at him, and realized with a shock that he was simply afraid of dogs. So I turned to where Colin was sitting, to gauge his reaction. He wasn't worried about animals. He was clearly worried about himself, as he had had time to explain to his employers what had been going on here, and they had clearly not approved. A death in one of their locks was a terrible thing to have to contemplate. That it was possibly not a straightforward accident, but murder, must have shaken them to the core of their delicate respectability.

And I was just about to inflict on them another unpleasantness. I doubted whether Colin had told them the full details of Helen Pierce's illness. He would surely have played it down. But all the same, I asked him, 'May I use your phone, Colin?' And now they would hear for themselves.

'Of course.' But he frowned.

I went round the back of the counter. As there was a clean and empty glass there, and an opened bottle within reach, I poured myself a drink. It was, I realized, vodka. Not much taste, but a hell of a stimulant, which was what I needed. In the directory, I found the hospital's number, got them, and asked for Admissions.

When I got them on the line, there was some difficulty. They had admitted a woman without a name or address. She had been unable to tell them. Mid-twenties. I agreed she could be the one I was interested in. Was I the husband? No – I was just the one who'd found her. But I knew her name now. Helen Pierce. Address? Sorry, I didn't know. A lie, that was, because I did. I wanted to get there before the police made any enquiries. Injuries: abrasions and bruises and a cracked rib, a broken wrist – pneumonia, possibly. Yes, I agreed. That was her, and could I come along and see her? This afternoon? Hold the line a minute, sir, and I'll put you through to the Intensive Care unit. Which was done. Sister Morris – can I help you? She could, but we had to go through, once more, the business of my having no direct relationship with her patient. But could I come, anyway? Seeing that I was the one who'd found her. Later this afternoon, was the concession, and then she would decide whether she was fit to be seen. I thanked her, and hung up, looked around, and there were eyes centred on me from all directions.

Then the old gentleman, Adolphus, spoke on behalf of himself and his two sisters.

'You haven't mentioned this, Colin. I think we ought to have a chat about it . . .' He fished out from his waistcoat pocket a half-hunter, flicked open the cover, and frowned at it. 'After lunch.'

Ruby accepted this for what it was – a signal. She rose to her feet and said, 'I'm afraid it will be no more than cold meats and salad, but it will not take long to get ready. If you intend to stay the night . . . did you bring overnight things?'

Adolphus unfolded himself to his full height. 'Indeed we did, Ruby. One has to be prepared for eventualities, and it does seem to me that those eventualities have put in an appearance. Thank you, we will stay. And pray . . . do not forget that we have Jenkins with us.'

'Of *course* you have Jenkins,' said Ruby, laughing. 'How would you get around without him?' Then, realizing that this was not a vastly polite comment, she added, 'I meant in the car, of course.'

They filtered out into the hall, and Victoria placed a hand gently on Ruby's arm. 'Adolphus is always blaming himself for not having learned to drive a car, but I do feel he's a little old to take it up now.'

The voices faded off into the distance. When I turned round I saw that we were now alone, except for Colin. He caught my eye, glanced away, then deliberately captured me with a grimace of distress.

'A right mess you've landed me in, I must say,' he said, advancing on me.

'Me? I'm doing no more than trying to tidy up after you. No . . . don't go away, Colin.' I held up a hand to restrain him. He glared at it. 'Things that've got to be said.'

'Not now. Not now, damn it.'

I took his arm and led him to a table in the corner. It was Slater's favourite table, it seemed, though he was not there now, but one of the large glass ashtrays was full of his stubbed-out cigarettes. Amelia came to sit with us.

'Right,' I said. 'Facts, Colin. Dates and things. How long had Helen Pierce been here, living on your boat?'

He flicked a hand angrily. 'A week or so. I told you that.'

'And during that time you haven't been going along to visit her, to see how she was managing?'

117

He flinched at that, flinched at the realization that he could have done more. 'Several times. You know. Taking fresh gas cylinders – that sort of thing.'

'That sort of thing? Not food or the like?'

'She was all right for food and stuff. Clare was bringing that.'

'Clare was . . .'

'Pretty well every day.'

'And neither of you realized Helen had been beaten up, and was very ill? Seriously ill, Colin.'

'It got me worried.' He looked away, darting glances around as though spies might be lurking in the shadows.

'Only worried?'

'She *wasn't* seriously ill. Not at *that* time. It's all changed overnight. So I wasn't worried *then*. You know.'

'I do not know,' I said patiently, quietly. Very quietly, because of the effort required not to shout it in his face.

'My father . . .'

'Your father? What the hell's *he* got to do with it?'

He spoke heavily, his teeth nearly clenched. 'You don't think he'd have let it go on . . .'

'I would think not. *He* would have sent for a doctor – at least.'

'Of course,' Amelia agreed.

'And arranged for Helen to be sent home?' Colin spoke with heavily restrained anger. 'To that violent brute of a husband of hers. Arnold. Bloody Arnold.' He made a strange noise in his throat – a burst of disgust. 'Christ! Don't you understand my father yet? It wouldn't be right to do anything else. Right! What'd been right about it before? But you can imagine . . . hell, I hear him in my dreams. There's a word for it. Ponti-something.'

'Pontificating,' Amelia put in softly. Her eyes had not deviated from his face.

'Yeah, yeah,' he agreed. 'He'd have sprayed us with his law, the rights of the husband, the sanctity of marriage! All the bloody piffling laws we'd broken, assisting a woman to hide away from her husband. The sacred embrace of matrimony! Jesus, we'd have been bowled over with it, and the stupid bugger would've insisted we ought to take her back. Her and the dog. Of *course* we couldn't let him get one hint of Helen living here, on the boat. Oh yes . . . and don't look like that. It would be "here" to him. My boat – and only just round the bend along the tow-path.'

'How lucky for her, then, that I happened to step inside your

118

boat and find out what was in there,' I commented. I was having difficulty in making my voice sound right.

'Lucky!'

'Do you never think of anybody but yourself, Colin?'

'I lent her the boat. You know that. So I'd get all the backlash. Probably will.'

'But had you got any sympathy for Helen – any feelings at all?'

He gave a grunt of protest and slapped a palm on the table. 'I did what I bloody-well could. Don't you understand! I love her and I want her to marry me.'

I sighed. I had to suppose that he'd been somewhat restricted in his options.

'And finally,' I said, 'the husband – that Arnold – he realized that Clare probably knew where his wife was hiding. He'd only have to follow her, in his car.'

'*His* car?' He gave a short bark of derision. 'He'd have had to nick one.'

'A stolen car?' I considered it, and it didn't sound valid. 'No – not a stolen car. Not and have to follow Clare, on such a lousy evening as we had coming here. So much more simple just to wait for her – somewhere I don't know. Where he might expect her to be. Then force her to drive him to where his wife was hiding. Probably with a knife to her ribs. So she drove, to the nearest place where they could get on the tow-path, where I found her car. And *that* would explain why it wasn't locked, and why the keys were left in the ignition. She probably tried her only chance to get away from him in the storm, and didn't succeed. Then he'd have forced her to take him on, past the house here, to the boat. And then what? A few more punches and a few more bruises for Helen – '

'Richard, Richard!' cut in Amelia. 'You're talking nonsense. Are you saying that this Arnold Pierce forced Clare to bring him to where Helen was hidden? Nonsense! From what we've heard about her, Clare would've been quite a handful, knife or not. And anyway – what would that Pierce creature want to find Helen for – just to give her another beating – and heavens, Richard, he'd have simply taken her back home again, and done all his beating there.'

'But love,' I said. 'Dennis was there.'

'What?' Colin demanded. 'No . . . he wasn't there.'

'We found his little jacket, on the boat,' she assured him.

But Colin was shaking his head stubbornly. 'He wasn't there yesterday. I was along there yesterday morning. No Dennis.'

'But Clare *did* come, yesterday evening, Colin,' I said. 'We know that. Her car was at the crossroads – and she died in the pound. Perhaps she came for the engagement party, but didn't get that far. Perhaps she came to visit Helen, and everything was all right at that time, so Clare came away . . .'

Then I ran out of inspiration.

'And fell in the pound on the way back to her car?' asked Amelia meekly, smiling her little smile at me.

'Wouldn't it be so very straightforward if that were the case,' I said.

'Perhaps it is,' she replied.

9

Lunch was a misery, with Gerald demonstrating his ability to carve a side of beef into wafer-thin slices, and the conversation equally transparent. We ate in the dining room, of course, in honour of our distinguished visitors. Colin was grimly silent, and seemed not to be hungry. Ray and Mellie sat at opposite sides of the table. It seemed that their first lovers' dispute had raised its head and leered at them. Victoria, Alexandra and Adolphus did their best to lighten the atmosphere, they really tried, but nobody other than themselves seemed to be interested in the fortunes and misfortunes involved with their estate.

I gathered that a considerable number of acres were involved, and that their agent (it being inconceivable that they should manage the property themselves) had been proposing sundry considerations that did not please them. Rentals! The property seemed to include three farms and two villages. Some increase all round in the rentals would be necessary, the agent had explained, if his books were to show a satisfactory margin. But this was not acceptable to the family. The alternative was to consider the sale of meadowland for development. Nor was this acceptable. It was all very worrying.

Silently, Amelia and I worried for them.

Afterwards, I felt restless. No action, no progression, and Ted Slater was not around to be argued with.

'A walk?' I suggested. 'The dog could come.'

'But where?' Amelia asked.

'Along the tow-path.'

'It'll only upset him if he sees that boat again,' she protested.

'Then we'll go in the other direction.'

Bruce was asleep in the kitchen. They had rigged him out with a cardboard box, with an old blanket in it. He opened one eye. I said, 'Walkies?' and he was out of there in a flash.

Somebody had fabricated a better lead for him, out of a strip of leather. One end was formed into something to grip, by riveting it into a loop, and the other end had a clip for his collar. Colin's work, obviously. Good with his hands, was Colin.

We went out through the bar. Ted Slater and WDS Tomkinson were there again, talking to Ray, who was not a resident but had been a temporary one, and there when Clare died. They looked up.

'Going for a walk,' I told them. 'Getting anywhere, Inspector?'

He scowled at me, then returned his attention to Ray. 'Did you know that Clare had come here?' he asked. 'Or know she intended to?'

'I thought she might.'

'That wasn't what I asked. Did you *know*?'

'I've told you. She said she might.'

We walked out. Ray was in difficulties. Let him sort it out for himself.

Bruce, naturally, turned right, intent on getting back to the houseboat. He needed quite a little persuading, by which time I was getting flashes of light, coming from just beyond the end of the house. I investigated.

The old stables were not so dilapidated as Colin had implied. The one next to the lodge had been converted, probably by himself, into a workshop, complete with a long bench all the way down one side. He was wearing a leather apron, from neck to thighs, and his face was shielded by a large, dark-coloured welding mask. Sparks were flying, spluttering sparks.

'Don't look directly at it,' I said quickly to Amelia as we approached.

He was completely unaware of us, concentrating. As far as I

could sort it out, he was using a butane gas and oxygen torch, as I now recognized the shape of a Calor gas cylinder. We stood for a moment, watching. Then he straightened, flung up his mask on to his forehead, and switched off the taps. The flame died.

'What're you doing?' I asked, and he looked round, startled.

'By heaven, you gave me a shock.'

'What're you making?' I repeated.

He had bent curves at the ends of three strong lengths of rod, and had been welding the shanks together. The result was an anchor with three prongs. Then I understood. Two prongs to it, and it wouldn't have worked. Three, and it always offered two gripping points.

'I'm going to start dragging,' he said, a hint of pride in his voice. 'The locks,' he explained, when neither of us spoke. 'That missing handle, I'm going to have a go at dragging for it.'

'But didn't they bring – '

He cut in, annoyed. 'That's not the point. They brought one. Jenkins came round with it. There it is, look.' He pointed to one end of the bench.

There was a brand-new winding handle lying there, just waiting to be put to use. It was as he'd described it, a shank with a square hole in it, and a hand grip for turning.

'So why trouble about the old one?' I asked, reasonably, I thought.

He wiped sweat from his brow with the back of his hand. 'I've got to *try*, see. Such a fuss they make! A bloody handle! And them with their hundreds of acres. I've got to write out a full report. Can you believe it! Every tiniest damned detail has to be *right*. A murder in their lock and – '

I interrupted. 'Has that been confirmed? Is Inspector Slater taking that line?'

'Yes, he damn-well is. Now he says they've found traces of rust in her hair – at the back. Where she got hit. And there's nothing rusty where she went in. I keep all the metal moving parts greased.'

I laughed. Easy enough to laugh, looking back on it. I'd remembered the mess his grease had made of my anorak.

'So you thought the winding handle that's missing could have been the weapon?'

He grinned. He had the sort of face that wore a grin attractively.

'It's not the point. Don't you see! It's to stick under their noses. Give 'em back the new one. Indiscretion wiped clean.'

Amelia said, 'Is that what they called it – an indiscretion?'

'They did. You're getting to know them. Everything has to be right and proper. Lock-keepers don't lose their gate handles. Damn it all, it wasn't me who lost it.'

'Oh?' I asked. 'Then who?'

'The one who used it on Clare Martin. Belted her with it, then tossed it into the water. That's what I reckon, anyway.'

'But you do realize . . . they're mighty good at fingerprints, these days. For all I know they might be able to lift 'em off your winding handle, if you find it. A day under water or not. They might.'

'I suppose. Yeah . . . I suppose.'

'So, if you *do* find it, don't touch it. Let it lie where it comes up, and fetch the inspector. Okay?'

'Sure. All right. I'll do that.'

'But I don't fancy your chances. There's hardly anything to hook on to.' I picked up the new one, hefted it, and turned to face the lock. 'What's it worth not to toss this one in?'

He gave a yelp, and dived for it. 'It was a joke! A joke,' I told him, replacing it gently on the bench.

He didn't seem to appreciate it.

We walked away, firmly turning Bruce from the direction of the houseboat. I said, 'The funny thing is that Colin, with all his skills, could have made himself a new handle from scrap, though it doesn't seem to have occurred to him. But then, he needn't have reported its loss.'

Stranger still, he didn't seem to have mentioned it to Slater, the loss of the handle, or certainly Slater would be dragging for it already, with a whole team and proper equipment. Colin's mind was firmly locked on his responsibilities, and to hell with the police.

We crossed the locks by way of the narrow footbridge over the pound in which Clare had died, as the tow-path switched sides there. Then I realized what Colin had meant, when he'd mentioned easier access to the pound from there. A ramp ran down to the level of the bottom lock's coping edge. It would have been easy, from that lower level, for me to reach the low deck where I'd sprawled so frantically and uselessly, and from there with only the main gate's arm to edge round, and the rack and pinion.

Indeed, it would not have been particularly difficult to slide in the dead body of Clare – if it hadn't been for the chain from bridge to lock-arm. Which, I saw, the police had put back on its requested hook. So easy, and down there, out of sight from any of the lodge windows.

We walked on. Here, the canal was on our left, and overlooked by trees on the far side. I released Bruce from his lead. He was slightly disorientated, one tow-path being the same as another to him. He galloped ahead, searching for a houseboat that wasn't there, returned, seemed confused, and ran ahead again.

It was no more than a quarter of a mile to the bridge, over which the road ran. This was the crossroads where I'd looked for the signpost. There was access up to the roadway, a steep ramp cut into the high bank, with poor, collapsing steps, which were supported only by planking at the vertical edges. A rickety rail ran up, curving beneath the overhanging branches of a tree.

It didn't seem that it was a practical proposition to carry anything heavy down there from the road above. But I had already dismissed the proposition that Clare had been dead before arriving here. Gerald Fulton had seen her since, anyway. So he claimed.

We walked a little further along the tow-path, which narrowed considerably beneath the arch of the bridge. It seemed to be exactly the same view that side – a canal disappearing into the distance. The only difference was that the trees were now on our side, and only a thorn hedge at the top of the bank on the other.

And . . . 'Look, Richard!' cried Amelia, pointing.

Floating on the water, half submerged and half caught in bobbing peaks of paper-thin ice, was my hat.

'Heh, heh,' I said in delight.

'Ruined, now,' she said.

'Ruined . . . not it.' It had been a long way from pristine before, as I'd had it for years, a tweed trilby with all the stiffening worn out of it, lining tatty, but with the ability to be squashed down into a pocket and later emerge in all its former glory. Or rather – no worse than it had been. A night in the canal wouldn't have harmed it at all.

I looked around. Trees overhung us and dipped over the water, but I couldn't reach any of the branches. I tried jumping, but nearly fell in.

'Richard! It's not worth the risk.'

'Oh . . . but it is. It is.'

I went hunting further along the canal, but remembered the access steps beside the bridge. There, the trees encroached closer. I marched away, and returned with a branch I hadn't been ashamed to break free, as its absence merely improved the access.

'You can't reach it with that.'

Why is it that women always seem to concentrate on what you can't do, rather than what you can?

'I can try.'

It was a foot short.

'Hang on to my belt,' I said.

'No. It's ridiculous. You'll have us both in.'

And Bruce, having been watching these activities, supplied the answer. He had observed the objective, plunged in, and swum to it.

'Fetch!' I said, belatedly.

One quick chop with his teeth, and he had it. Then he was back, placed it at my feet with obvious pride, then shook himself thoroughly, soaking my trousers.

'He's wet through!' cried Amelia.

I patted his wet-through head. She didn't mention me.

'We'd better get him back into the kitchen,' I said. 'Before he gets a chill.'

'Richard – you're the limit. You really are.'

Then she took up his lead and began to run back along the tow-path.

'Watch your step!' I shouted, walking after her, but to no obvious response.

But my mind was still locked on the recovery of my hat, and quite naturally I recalled that the police had not found Clare's cap. Because of this, I walked along with my mind firmly on the possibility that hers, too, could have been blown away, so that . . .

'Hold on, love!' I shouted. 'Wait a second.'

She stopped, looking back. 'What is it?'

I pointed. Floating on the water, about a hundred yards back towards the lodge from the bridge, was a peaked cap. It had a checkered band around it.

'It's Clare's,' I called. 'Must be.'

She returned, breathing hard from her run. 'How very interesting.'

'It is, though. It means that she didn't walk along the tow-path,

125

with whatever she was carrying, she walked down the lane. That's the direction the wind was from. And she wouldn't be able to hold her cap on if she *was* carrying something. So she lost it. And therefore, she had no protection at all against a blow to the back of her head.'

'How very clever of you, Richard.' She gave me her little grin.

'And, my love, it also means that Gerald was lying when he said he saw her, because he mentioned the cap.'

'And won't you enjoy telling him that!'

'Perhaps you're right.' I pointed. 'Fetch,' I said.

Bruce looked up at me, showing me about six inches of tongue, and did nothing.

'Fetch the cap, Bruce,' I said.

Nothing.

'The one with the checkered hat-band,' explained Amelia, pointing. So I laughed at her, and changed it to a smile when Bruce plunged in.

'You see,' she explained to me. 'You have to be quite explicit.'

'I'll remember that.'

So I took the cap from Bruce, after a certain amount of tug and enticement, and off they went once more, Amelia and Bruce, but not before he'd shaken himself all over my legs again.

I walked, more soberly, after them. When I reached the kitchen, Amelia was rubbing him vigorously with a kitchen towel, which was rapidly taking on a darker hue, and Mellie was plugging in a hair dryer. Bruce thought all this was great fun.

Quietly, I waited. I glanced at my watch. Three-thirty. Too early. The ward sister had definitely said, 'Later.' I could come and see Helen later. Would four o'clock be considered sufficiently late? But she had hinted that I might be able to see Helen, providing ... Providing what, she had not specified. I had to guess that she'd meant: providing Helen was fit to receive visitors. So maybe she would be – at four.

I went up to change my trousers, and when I returned, Bruce had come up very much whiter than he had been, his markings a brighter brown. He rolled over on the floor happily, enjoying the warm draught of air. I left the hat hanging on one end of the radiator, the cap on the other end, and wandered outside to see what was going on.

Colin was standing on the wider of the two bridges, and had been dragging in the top lock. I could have told him how hopeless this was, fishing for his winding handle, when a whole team of police, with experience in such activities, might spend several days on such a task, especially as the only place a hook might catch would be the angle between the handle and the shaft. But . . . beginner's luck had triumphed again, and he began shouting at the sight of me.

'I've got it, Richard. I've got it.'

I approached. It was lying at his feet, and I couldn't see what all the fuss had been about. It was obviously very old indeed, the squared hole at one end very nearly worn circular, and the handle of brass tube showing cracks here and there.

'Don't touch it,' I told him.

'I haven't. You said not to.'

'So now you've got two of them. A spare.'

'I shall', he said with proud dignity, 'tell the three old penny-pinchers to take the other one back.'

I eyed him with amusement. He would delight in doing that, and probably, if I'd been the one to criticize them, would have given me a ticking-off.

'Why not keep both?' I said. 'It'd save you switching one around from here to there.'

'Yeah. Sure.'

'And on which of the rack and pinion things did you usually leave this one?' I was very casual about this, as I had a feeling what his answer would be.

'Oh – down by the lower pound. *Your* rack and pinion.' He laughed. 'It's 'cause I use that gate more often than the others.'

'Ah!' I said, nodding. 'Have you told Inspector Slater?' I guessed not. I didn't think it worth mentioning that his retrieved handle was probably one lost by a holiday boat, as it surely would not have been tossed into the top lock, if Clare had been killed – or at least knocked unconscious near the pound, some little distance away.

'Not yet,' he said. 'I only got it up a couple of minutes ago.'

So I told him to stand guard over it, while I located Slater. The most likely place was in the bar lounge, and there he was, at the same table as he'd used before, and with WDS Tomkinson sitting facing him.

Slater, clearly, had finished with his interviews. He was filling in a report, with the assistance of his sergeant's notes. This would have been done more correctly at his office desk, but if he stayed here he could expect less interruption and would be keeping in touch, and might, with a bit of luck, be offered a drink from time to time.

I said, 'I think we've got your murder weapon, Ted. Colin's found it. Come and see.'

He scrambled to his feet. 'Think you've got ... where ... where?'

Colin was waiting on the bridge, right opposite the swing doors. He was looking modestly pleased with himself.

'This?' asked Slater, staring down at it.

'Seems likely,' I told him. 'It was slotted on the rack and pinion down by the pound, yesterday. Thrown in the top lock after use. D'you think?'

Ted Slater grunted. He was nobody's fool. 'Then why toss it in here? Why not in the bottom lock? It was right there.' Like a flash, he was on to my own thoughts on it.

I shrugged. 'Can't say. Perhaps the attacker used it down by the pound, shoved poor Clare into the water, and walked up this way with it in his hand before getting rid of it. Kind of absent-minded.'

'Hmm!' He eyed me up and down. 'I know what went on at that houseboat, Patton. I thought to ask. Nosy of me. And somebody called Pierce was probably there, so equally probably might have had Clare with him, possibly under duress. They were sisters, you know, Clare and that woman on the boat. And they'd most likely come this way. How does that sound?'

'It sounds lovely, said like that. But it doesn't work, does it? If he was with Clare – if they were heading for the houseboat – how the hell would he know there was a weighty instrument, down there by the pound? The storm was probably still blowing, and only the amber light was on. It'd be a blank nothing, down there. And why kill her *then*? They wouldn't even have reached the boat. No, Ted, it won't do. Definitely not.'

'All the same ...' He smiled so pleasantly at me that I thought for the moment that I'd pleased him. 'All the same, I'll have to have a word with this Pierce character.'

'Yes, I think you will,' I agreed.

But I felt that I would have to see him myself, first.

'Oh ... and by the way, Ted,' I went on, 'I've found her cap. It was in the canal, further along.' I gestured in the direction we had taken. 'It's drying in the kitchen. But it does indicate she walked down the lane from her car, and she was probably carrying something bulky, if she didn't have a spare hand to hold her cap on. It was very windy, you know.'

He stared at me, cocked his head, and stared some more.

'You know, Patton,' he said, 'I quite enjoy these little theories of yours. But thank you. I was worrying about her cap.'

When I left him, he was staring down at the winding handle, which would probably more accurately be called a key. Then he turned and headed for the bar. He would have to phone somebody to come and collect it.

This would mean that Colin would be somewhat disappointed in his intentions. He would not have a rescued winding handle to show to his employers.

It was time I went back into the kitchen to see how they were getting along with Bruce. He was now all silky and soft – and no doubt longing to find somewhere filthy in which he could roll, and remove his disconcerting cleanliness.

I said casually to Amelia, 'How'd you fancy a little trip in the car, love?'

'If you wish, Richard. But where?'

I ran my hand up my neck. 'Well, I did promise myself I would try to see Helen this evening, but now something's cropped up that's made it necessary to go elsewhere in the evening, so . . . I thought it would do no harm to ask 'em at the hospital whether I can see Helen. They can only say no. But I'd feel better with my wife at my elbow, in case they think I'm Helen's husband.'

'Yes.' Amelia eyed me with her head tilted. 'You look like a wife-beater I must say. All right, we'll go and see what the situation is.'

'Can I come?' asked Mellie, who had been listening carefully from just behind Amelia's shoulder.

I glanced at her. My wife has an ability to nod with her eyes. 'Certainly,' I told Mellie. 'But . . . what about Ray?'

She pouted. 'He's had to go away. He said he's on duty.'

It was a strange time to report for duty, in the middle of the afternoon, but I didn't say so. It could be that he had his own private mourning to do. In that event, he would have had to invent an excuse. If that had not been satisfactory to Mellie, it would explain her obviously depressed state. Or had he been fool enough to admit to any sort of intimacy with Clare? Surely not!

But young men in love are notoriously unstable. He might have considered it as starting with a clean slate, though his slate would've needed quite a scrubbing.

I eyed Mellie cautiously. Was she capable of an attack with a winding handle? She most definitely was – and she would know where to put her hand on one, should the occasion arise. In this event, though, the occasion, if it had arisen, had done so after the event.

'Duty calls,' I told her cheerfully. 'If you're going to marry a policeman, I'm afraid that's one of the obstacles to be overcome. They do shifts. If they get on the CID, they work all hours, and the higher the rank, the more the hours. You have to allow for that and take it into account.'

'But I love him,' she said pitifully, as though that made any difference.

'Of course you do. Give me five minutes, love,' I went on to Amelia, 'and I'll be with you. Mellie, d'you know Haughton Grange Hospital?'

'Oh yes. Of course. I was born there.' As though she'd remembered it from that time.

'Fine. That'll save us getting lost.'

I took sufficient time to make myself respectable. Nothing gains the approval of hospital sisters so much as a clean and neat human, preferably in one of their beds.

They were waiting by the car. Mellie had Bruce with her.

'They won't allow dogs inside their hospital,' I told her.

'He wanted to come.'

'Hmm!' I said.

Amelia took her usual seat beside me, Mellie and the dog in the rear. I was a little concerned about Mellie and Bruce. They were becoming much too fond of each other, and if things worked out as I rather hoped, Bruce would eventually be restored to his proper mistress. It didn't seem fair to put the responsibility of choice on the dog.

Haughton Grange was a newish hospital, low and sprawled, but not too large. The car park was adequate at this time, and we had no difficulty finding somewhere to leave the Granada. Bruce we had to leave in it, though he wouldn't make a very fearsome guard dog. Before we reached the main entrance, he began his howling.

'Oh dear,' said Amelia.

Mellie looked worried. 'I'll go back to him.'

'I'm not sure you'd like it inside an Intensive Care unit, anyway,' I told her encouragingly.

So that was settled satisfactorily. I handed the keys to Mellie, and she returned to the car. Bruce stopped howling.

'There wasn't much point in bringing them,' said Amelia.

'Well no. But it gives Mellie something to think about, other than Ray. I don't think that engagement is going to last long, my love.'

Inside, there were direction signs everywhere, so that there was no need to ask our way. We simply followed the sign: Intensive Care – Females. On the way there I explained why I thought Mellie was on a bit of a loser with Ray. I told her about his exploits with Clare, rather more explicitly than I had before.

'Hmm!' she said. 'Doesn't sound good, does it?'

'It does not. I think this is it.'

The sister's office was immediately on the left, just inside the rubber swing doors. Sister Morris was probably in her thirties, looking rather young for her responsibilities. I explained who we were, and in what way we had an interest, and asked if we might see Helen. If not, we would go away.

'She's coming along fine,' she told us. 'There were multiple bruises, some of them old, the only worrying damage being a cracked rib. But it didn't puncture her lung, as we feared at first, and she's reacting to medication splendidly. Her breathing is much easier. There was a broken wrist that had to be set, and two of her front teeth had been broken. We had to extract the roots. She will not recognize you, of course, but you can explain to her. If it was you who found her, Mr . . .'

'Patton.'

'Yes, if it was you, she may recognize you. We mustn't expect too much, though. Please don't encourage her to talk. Ask her no questions, and don't encourage her to ask her own. I'll send someone with you . . . Oh, Nurse Simpson, would you take Mr and Mrs Patton to see Mrs Pierce. She's . . .'

'I know where she is, Sister.'

'I was about to say: she's not to be excited.'

'No, Sister. Of course not.'

And was there the hint of a wink from Nurse Simpson as we thanked the ward sister and turned away?

She was seven beds down on the right. A good sign, that was.

If your bed is too close to the swing doors, that might mean that you could be expected to require emergency treatment.

'Somebody to see you, Helen,' said the nurse. 'Now you be a good girl and don't over-excite yourself.'

We found two chairs and sat by her bed. Helen seemed much improved since I'd seen her. Gone the flush and the shivering, and there was more natural colour to her cheeks. She was on a drip, to her right arm, and with a drain tube in her right nostril.

'You may not remember me, Helen,' I said. 'I'm the one who found you in the houseboat. I want to tell you that we've taken charge of Bruce. He's in the car, and full of health. There's no need to worry about him.'

She whispered something. I bent close. 'Denny . . .' It was more a sigh.

I said, 'We know about Dennis. I'm going to see what can be done about him. Not to worry. Arnold can't reach you here.'

Another whisper. It sounded like, 'Please . . .'

I'm hopeless when people say please. And I knew what she meant.

'I'm going to have a word with your husband,' I said, spreading confidence all over the place. 'I'm going to persuade him. Then I'll bring Dennis to see you.'

All this, for the light of hope it brought to her eyes. The plastered wrist lay on the bedcovering, and helped me a lot. The still-swollen lips, the bruised eye, now black, the empty gap where two teeth were missing . . . these all helped. I was now more certain of my justification.

I felt Amelia's fingers digging into my arm. There were going to be words spoken.

'Sir,' said the nurse, 'I think that's enough.'

We got to our feet, and Amelia replaced the chairs as I bent over to whisper a final word or two.

'You'll see. I'll bring Denny.'

We left. I thanked Sister Morris. She smiled and said, quite mysteriously, 'You're not the first.' I told her we would be back again, later. Amelia was silent, all the way out to the car park. Then . . .

'Richard, I don't want you to go near that man.'

She usually forbids me. Somehow, this sounded more serious. I caught her arm, and drew her to a halt. We had to clear this out of the way before rejoining Mellie.

'What else could I promise, love?' I asked. 'That the police would see to it? Oh yes, they would. Fine. They'd go to visit that lout – and they'd be able to do absolutely nothing. A domestic dispute, it would be called. Inform the Social Services people? Oh yes, the police could do that. And *they* could do nothing. If the lad hasn't been too ill-treated, they'd have no complaint to make. If he has, then it'd be a Home he'd go to. Taken into care, they'd call it. And Helen wouldn't want any of that. If we leave it as it is – for Helen to recover enough to return home to him – it would simply start all over again, only with even less chance of her ever being free of him. So . . . what else can I do but fetch Dennis away? Tell me, and I'll consider it.'

'Damn it, Richard, you're being a fool.' She shook my arm angrily.

'I know.'

She halted me, her hand clasped on my arm. 'Then promise me . . . you won't go alone.'

'Promise. I'll not go alone.'

She seemed satisfied with this, perhaps thinking that I'd be taking Ray with me. But Ray wasn't available, and in any event was a policeman. I wanted no police authority in this. But I would not be alone.

I didn't tell her who I'd decided would be the best person to take along.

10

In the bar, after we'd had time to tidy ourselves, I explained the whole situation to the group.

Ted Slater and his WDS were outside at the locks, with two men, who had arrived in a small van. It was now dark outside. They had come to take away the winding handle, it seemed, and there'd been a right old upset about that, while we'd been away. There was nothing positive to indicate that the handle had been used as an offensive weapon, nothing but the rather thin circumstantial evidence that it had been on its rack down by the pound, and had been taken from there. But they were taking it away, and this had naturally brought Inspector Slater into head-on conflict with the old dears. What right had he to confiscate property that wasn't his? Could he specify his right to do so?

'It could be evidence in a murder enquiry, ma'am – ladies and gentleman.' Palely polite, was Ted.

He was on a very shaky foundation with this, as the handle must have been fingered, one time and another, by everyone at the house, and, during the past years, by scores of travellers who'd found it easier to locate than their own, so that it would be liberally covered with prints.

But poor Ted was in a delicate situation. Apart from interviews, he'd been able to do very little towards producing a murderer. There was nothing of a routine nature that he could pursue. Means and opportunity had been the same for everybody here. Motives were numerous, but were, apparently, being jealously guarded. Yet he had to be seen to be doing something.

All this was most upsetting, and it was fortunate that the three visitors had not been in the district at the time of Clare's death, otherwise they would have had to make statements, and submit to fingerprinting.

But now ... he was impounding the winding handle. The impression given was that this constituted the collapse of the family's remaining resources, and they would have to part with an extra hundred acres or so of meadowland in order to break even. They protested loud and long. That which was lost and is found, I suppose.

But eventually Slater had his way, and he and his men, who'd enjoyed it all immensely, departed with the handle, hermetically sealed in plastic, and a set of fingerprints from all but the later visitors. Including Amelia, mine already being on record.

After we'd all washed our hands, and Gerald had recovered most of his equanimity, we had a relaxing cup of tea in the bar, and we were asked about our trip to the hospital. But it was Amelia who told them all about it, as an independent witness, as she put it.

She told them that Helen Pierce was on her way to recovery, that was to say that she was winning the fight against the infection, and when her cracked rib healed, and her broken wrist healed, and when she had a small plate to replace the missing teeth in her upper gums, and when the various bruises and bumps had worn out their welcome, and provided, of course, that her legs were all right, as we hadn't seen her legs, then she would be fit to return to her husband.

'Return?' said Adolphus, glancing from one to the other of his sisters.

'They do, you know,' I told him. 'You'd be surprised. There are a great number of women who get divorces on the grounds of cruelty, and remarry the same man, and repeat the divorce and remarrying, and so on.'

'Surely not!' said Victoria, appalled.

'I can't believe it,' echoed Alexandra.

'Gerald,' I said, 'you'll know that, even though you don't handle divorce cases.'

'Oh, indeed,' said Gerald expansively. 'My fellow solicitors – we meet for lunch from time to time – they have encountered this.'

'How very strange.' Adolphus twisted his lips in distaste. He hadn't had a wife to batter.

'And it seems to me,' put in Ruby, 'that there's nothing to be done about it.' Her mind was firmly fixed on our own specific situation. 'But didn't I get the impression that you intended to have a few words with the husband? Wasn't that what you suggested, Richard?'

I couldn't remember being specific about it. 'That was my intention,' I nevertheless admitted. 'A few words.'

'Then I don't see the point of it.' Adolphus was uncomfortable. 'A few words.' Nothing like this had entered his sheltered life, or those of his sisters. I had no doubt that, of all their tenants, there must have been occasions of matrimonial upset, but their agent would have dealt with all that. It would not have brushed against them.

'But you see,' I tried, though not optimistic that they did, 'there's the little lad. The father has him. It might be a good idea to find out what the lad wants. You get what I mean?'

They all looked around at each other, wondering whether the rest of the group were as ignorant as themselves as to the stresses of life.

'We haven't heard about a little boy,' Victoria declared emphatically. 'Nobody's told us there's a little boy involved, have they, Alexandra?'

'Not in my hearing.'

'There you are then.' Victoria nodded to me.

'Well there is,' I told them. 'His name's Dennis, and he's now temporarily resident with his father, who can't keep his fists to himself. I simply thought I might visit, and ask the lad what *he* wants. It was just a thought.'

Amelia nudged me. I didn't turn to meet her eyes.

'How old is he?' I asked Colin. 'D'you know?'

'Between two and three, I think.'

'Ah! Then . . . after dinner, I thought I'd pay them a visit, and try to discover what the situation is.'

'Not alone, surely!' cried Victoria, clasping her palms together and putting the praying hands against her lips.

'Oh no. Not alone.'

'Ray,' said Mellie, looking round to see what her loved-one would have to offer. 'You?'

'I wish I could,' he said wistfully. 'But I'm a policeman. There're rules. And I'm afraid, if I was with Mr Patton . . . with Richard . . . I might get in his way.'

It was at this point that I realized that Ray was one of those persons who do not display their thoughts and their emotions openly. Perhaps Mellie was not yet aware of this. A solemn Ray was not necessarily a morose one. His humour was simply bone dry.

'I don't really think you would, Ray,' I told him. 'It might not be in accord with your position as a policeman, though. So I'm afraid it can't be you. Sorry.'

'That's all right.'

This was not greeted favourably by Mellie, who was at the romantic age when her man should rush into the fray and succour the ravishing, or ravished, maiden. In this event, herself as the ravishing one. She made a sound of contempt, and turned away.

Ray made a movement as though to go to her. He reached out and touched her shoulder, but she shrugged herself free, pouting.

'He knows me, Mellie,' he said. 'We've met – me as Clare's partner in the patrol car. He knows me. And I'm a policeman, and we're not supposed to get tangled up with domestic disputes. Isn't that correct, Mr Patton?'

I muttered an agreement, but Mellie would not relax, would not turn to face him. 'You just don't care, that's the trouble.'

'I care.'

'You wouldn't need to go in your uniform.'

'I told you . . . he knows me, uniform or not.'

'Hmmph!'

'So what would you have me do?' he asked, his voice taking on a shade of bitterness. 'Wear a moustache and a ginger wig?'

'You don't have to be sarcastic.' She said it close to a sob.

'Really, Mellie,' I put in, 'it's quite out of the question. Ray is definitely the wrong person to get involved with this.'

She turned, angry now with me, and probably glad of the chance to deflect it from Ray. 'You're all the same – you men.'

There was no answer to that. Amelia said, 'It's perhaps just as well.'

Mellie stared at her, trying to make sense of that statement, and reluctantly allowed Ray to rest a hand on her arm.

'All the same . . .' she mumbled.

'Some other time,' I suggested to Ray, as though he'd been deprived of a special treat.

He grimaced, and nodded.

'It's all a matter of convenience,' I said. 'Colin?' I asked. 'What about you?'

Colin looked startled. His eyes lifted to meet the neutral stares of his employers, who could not decide, it seemed, whether they approved of this use of their lock-keeper. He was theirs, body and soul, and they feared for the safety of his body. Besides, it would probably be difficult to find anyone else who could operate their flight, and maintain all the other locks as well.

He couldn't answer at once. They nodded solemnly. He had their support, whatever he decided.

'It's not really convenient,' he said. Then he looked around to see who might wish to dispute this. 'I've got to be here, you see. Any moment there might be a houseboat come along – hooting for assistance.'

The three sages nodded silently. He had their sympathy and understanding.

'But of course,' I said, snapping my fingers to indicate an annoyance with myself. 'They've been coming through all day, queuing up. We might expect another, any minute, preceded by an ice-breaker.'

He smiled bleakly. 'I knew you'd see my point.' I had seen his point exactly. He was intending to kill Pierce – but not today.

'Well now,' I said. 'That seems to leave you, Gerald. The ideal man, anyway. We'll go a little later. Better leave it till it's good and dark. I assume you know Crayminster?'

He was looking blank. 'My business premises are there,' he informed me distantly. He hadn't really understood what I'd said.

'You're just the man. I'll need guidance, on the location and on the law. We must remain strictly on the correct side of legality.'

He still wasn't sure that he'd heard me correctly, glanced at Ruby, who nodded, her lower lip caught in her teeth, and he compromised on my question, dismissing the preceding statement as an error on my part.

'I know Crayminster, of course. My business premises are there, as I told you.'

'Good,' I said with enthusiasm. 'So you're just the man. We must keep strictly on the right side of the law, as I've already said. Don't you think? Maybe you'll have to restrain my enthusiasm.'

I was talking in a pedantic and formal manner, such as I thought he would appreciate. But he clearly didn't.

'But ... but ...' He looked round frantically for assistance, encouragement. 'I couldn't allow myself to become involved with anything like this. My position ... my reputation ...'

'Will be enhanced,' I assured him.

'But I *can't* ...'

'I need a lawyer,' I told him. 'I had you in mind all the while, frankly, but I thought I had to give the others a chance. Somebody who can watch that no aspect of the law is infringed, who can advise me if I stray one iota from the straight and narrow of legal exactitude. Damn it all, Gerald, you're probably the only man I'd wish to have at my elbow – to advise. And perhaps, later on in a witness box, support what I'll have done with all the confidence your reputation must give you.'

'Witness box ...' He looked a shade green, I thought, but that had to be a reflection from the green surface of the table.

'Damn it all, Gerald, I wouldn't dare to go without you at my shoulder. This has to be right, strictly correct in all facets of matrimonial law ...'

I was well into my stride now, and could have gone on spouting this rubbish for ages. But I paused, because he'd have burst if I hadn't.

'I know nothing of matrimonial law,' he protested, raising his head, proud of the fact, flapping his arms to dismiss the idea.

'That's perhaps for the best,' I assured him, and had him stumped for a valid response. 'And . . . think of the glory . . .'

'That's enough, Richard,' said Amelia softly, into my ear. She knows what I'm like. And in the end it was Ruby who settled it, and quite calmly. 'You will go, Gerald,' she instructed, but smiling at him. 'It's your duty.'

He wiped a hand over his face. A different expression was revealed. 'If you wish, my dear.' And she smiled. She so wished.

But poor Gerald was sweating, and I was beginning to regret having pushed him into it. Behind and around us the others were muttering about what various affairs were demanding their immediate attention, and gradually the bar cleared. Gerald then came over and sat with Amelia and me at our table.

'You forced that on me, didn't you?' he asked. He did not resent it; he only deplored it.

'As I told you, I had you in mind all the while.'

'I can't understand that.' He was blustering a little. 'It's quite unfair of you, Richard. Quite.'

I smiled at him encouragingly. 'I might want legal advice, that's all. I thought I'd made that clear.'

'I told you – '

'I know. You don't practise in matrimonial law. But you'd have had to study the lot, and you'll know what constitutes legal consent and the welfare of the injured party.'

'You're referring to the young woman? Helen Pierce, I think you said.'

I looked to Amelia for guidance. She clearly didn't approve of my going, anyway, let alone taking Gerald with me. She shook her head. It was my idea, so I could sort it out with Gerald.

I took it on. 'The injured party, as you very well know, Gerald, need not be physically injured. Socially injured, welfare injured, reputation injured.'

'That'll be me.' Then he shook his head. 'And I don't know what you're trying to say.'

'The injured party in this case is not necessarily the mother. She's only suffered physical injuries, which'll heal. But what about the one in the middle, the lad, who's being psychologically injured every minute this goes on? And emotionally, and – I'm praying, not physically. Hasn't *anybody* got any thought for him! So all right. We're going along there, Gerald, simply to ask young Dennis what *he* wants. Quite clearly, it's not in his best interests for him to be left with both his parents. We're not trying to get them together, Helen and her husband . . .' I snapped my fingers. 'Arnold,' Amelia provided. 'Pierce,' she added.

'Yes. Thanks, love.' I went on, 'We're not trying to hold a marriage together. We're not marriage counsellors. We're trying to decide what's best for the lad. Perhaps it'll turn out that he's got no hope, caught between his parents.'

'Don't *say* that, Richard,' Amelia said sharply.

'All right, all right,' I agreed. I was stretched a little tight, myself. 'I'm just trying to get across to Gerald what we're going there to do. To find out how the lad is, and to ask him what *he* wants to do. And if there's anything illegal in that, I'm relying on you to tell me, Gerald. Very well, legal adviser. Do you get your fee now, or later?'

'Don't be stupid, please.'

'Yes. Sorry. I'm a bit on edge. Why don't we get going? Get it over with, that's my idea. Like having a tooth out.'

'All right.' Gerald looked round huntedly. 'I'll go and get ready.'

'Ready? What's the matter with you as you are, for heaven's sake? We just get in the car, and go.'

He sighed, and got to his feet. 'Ready for dinner, Richard,' he explained. 'It's about due on the table, and I still have to change.'

I'd been forgetting all about dinner. Now *that* was in the way, just when I'd built myself up for action.

'You don't need to change . . .'

'Not change? My dear man!'

'Then you'll have to change back afterwards.'

'Of course.'

I sighed. He had developed a way of life that consumed the empty hours, and would now feel uncomfortable if robbed of one iota of his routine, which was antiquated. No radio, no TV set, no CD player lived in this house. They were all too modern for Gerald, and thus had to be so for his family. It would be a waste of time to point out to him that although a CD player was a modern item, the Mozart it could reproduce was originated at about the same time as James Brindley was building his flights.

But I had to accept his idiosyncrasies.

This was the sort of delay that tears your nerves to pieces. I prowled. I washed and I changed, and I prowled a little more. And eventually the gong boomed us to the table. I never did locate that gong, or discover who bonged it.

140

I think I ate. It seemed that I did, because empty plates were exchanged for full ones, themselves to be emptied. The time was getting along. Wouldn't it be the lad's bedtime? Or would that wait until his father returned from the pub? Would *we* have to wait for that? In either event, or both, what might have been a smooth operation began to seem complicated.

And heavens ... we had to go through the port and cigars routine again, and then Gerald had to change into his utility suit, tailored for visiting great louts and other such occasions. I changed, too. Oldest suit I'd brought with me, and my heaviest shoes.

'It's not snowing,' said Amelia, viewing these.

'I know. But it might,' I told her.

They all came into the bar to see us on our way. Gerald was stiff and cool with me. Ray pouted his disappointment at having to remain behind.

Amelia reached up to kiss me. 'But Richard – you don't know the address.'

'Oh yes I do. It's 22 Brindley Street. It's on Bruce's collar.'

'Oh ... clever you.' It was that little sarcastic dig again.

'Ready, Gerald?' I asked.

'Yes, yes. I'm coming. Your car, if you don't mind.'

'No, I don't mind. But why?'

'I know Brindley Street. It's hardly a monument to the great man. I'd rather not leave my car parked there at night.'

'Nor me,' I agreed. 'But we're using Amelia's.'

She pouted at me, reached up and kissed me, and we went out into the night by way of the swing doors, then round to the side.

It was a reasonable night for driving, no fog or anything like that. 'Left at the crossroads,' he said, as we drove up the lane.

I did that. 'That's where I came across the unlocked parked car,' I told him.

'Was it, now? Take the left here, then the second on the right.'

Orientating myself from the lie of the canal, and recalling how the town spread from it, I realized we were coming into Crayminster from what one might call the rear. At that point, it was spaced houses in large grounds and the odd freeholding, but we were running down a long, winding road with a gentle slope.

'Still all right?' I asked, as he'd said nothing since the crossroads.

'Second right after here, then the first on the left.' His voice was uncertain. 'There's Brindley Street, look, with the lamp on the corner.'

It was a very poor street lamp, ancient, attached to a house's blank end wall. I turned into the street he meant. Lights along here were also meagre, and sparse. They hadn't got round to the orange ones.

'It'll be on this side,' he said. 'Yes. A bit further, I'd think. Yes, this will do.' He seemed reluctant to have the car stop, reluctant to get out now it had.

I put the handbrake on, and locked it up. Very few cars were parked along the street, not this far up the slope. Further down, light spilt on to the pavement. Noise penetrated dimly to our location. It would be a pub. It would be Pierce's local. I hoped he wasn't down there, as it would have been impractical to try to fetch him out of the bar.

I said, 'This it?'

Dimly, I could detect the number, 22, white, painted clumsily on a stone pillar, on which a wrought-iron gate should have hung, but didn't. The street was one long terrace of houses, perhaps smart when built, with a generous frontage of twenty feet or so, a slope of paving stones, then five or six steps up to a deep porch and a door set back inside it.

But now the low frontage wall was crumbling, the approach steps were cracked, and the original stained-glass insert to the front door was broken in several places, with paper roughly plastered over the gaps. We mounted to it and stood in the porch. Dimly, I could see light at the far end of the hall. The front window, to our left, gave the impression of being a bay-window, when in fact it was more likely a corner of the front room. The side pane of glass was cracked, with a length of wood nailed across it.

There was, I saw now that my eyes had become accustomed to the gloom, a bell-push. I tried it, but heard no response.

'This is most unpleasant, Richard,' said Gerald, from way back in his throat. I didn't reply. I'd seen worse places, and been inside them.

I found a door knocker, and discovered it was so stiff that it would barely move. With a little effort put into it, it did, producing a dead, bashing sound.

Way back, but opposite to me, I saw light appear as a door was opened. A voice shouted, 'Who the hell's that?'

In response, I banged the knocker again.

Footsteps approached in the form of clumping sounds. 'What y' want?'

'Open up, and I'll tell you,' I called back.

The door swung open a few inches, its hinge to my right. This was not a hall, as I could now see, but a room, with a little light filtering in from a street lamp on the far side of the street. The opening was a meagre foot. I could see one eye. His left arm was keeping out of sight behind the door. I didn't like the look of that, as it probably meant he was holding some sort of an offensive weapon, most likely a knife. I had not wanted violence, but it seemed that it was his natural approach to unwanted visitors.

'What the hell're you after? Sod off.'

'Are you Arnold Pierce?' I asked, quite quietly.

'Yeah. What's it to you?'

'I'd like to have a word with you. Can I come in?' Keeping it polite.

'Bugger off.'

The door began to close. If the latch clicked shut, I knew I'd never get him to open up again. On that eventuality, I had my weight poised, and as I now knew that the hinge was to my right, I kicked, flat-footed, at the left edge, as hard as I could make it given the cramped location I was in. The shoes were not heavy enough after all, but he had no firm grip on the door, only his left shoulder leaning against it, the right hand that I could see holding a can of beer. The door spun from his insecure grasp and crashed back against the side wall. Two panes of glass fell at his feet as I stepped quickly inside, crunching over them.

'Shut the door, Gerald,' I said flatly. I was having to attend to the movements and locations of two people at the same time. I heard it shut behind me, and Gerald's weak plea, 'Richard . . . really!' But he closed the door. I hadn't wished to use force, but clearly Pierce was a man who understood little else. A blade caught a glint of reflection, so I'd been correct about the knife.

Pierce had been thrown off balance, twisting round against the side wall. He was not moving, but waiting until his full responses recovered. His left hand, which had been behind the door, was now hidden behind his thigh, but I didn't give him time to think about using the knife, and went straight at him, hitting out with the heel of my hand to his shoulder, urging him, jolting him,

143

towards that lighted room at the rear, confusing him as to my intentions. I was recalling my first sight of Helen.

'What the bloody hell!'

He rubbed the palm of his right hand down the thigh of his denims. It was the hand that had held the beer can, and he'd crushed it in his automatic reaction to the slamming-back of the door. The beer had splashed back over his arm, and he stank of it.

I now realised that he was not so big as I'd expected. Images are subconsciously assembled from items of information, and I'd envisaged a large and powerful hulk. But he wasn't like that. Powerful, certainly, but two inches shorter than me, craggy, his shoulders wide and his neck short. He would roll as he walked, but he would roll straight into trouble and meet it head on. His expression now was of uncertainty. He shook his head from side to side in mystification, a shock of untidy, greasy hair moving with it. He had the large, scarred hands of a bricklayer.

There came a point where he decided he'd had enough of the jolting, and he stood his ground. The half-open door was a yard behind him.

'What y' want? What yerrafter?'

'In the other room,' I said. 'Then we can see what we're doing.'

'You coppers or somethin'?'

'Not the police. We've come for Dennis.'

'Who's Dennis?' But he'd slipped up, using the name. 'He ain't . . .'

'I want to go to momma!' It was a weak and tentative voice from the rear room. He'd heard his name mentioned.

It was all I'd needed to hear. The lad had made his own decision.

I pushed past Pierce and swung open the door. He grabbed for my shoulder as I passed him, but I twisted free, hoping that a display of confidence and authority might stay his knife hand.

Their rear room. Their living room. Beyond it would be a kitchen that I didn't wish to see. I looked round for the location of the voice.

The room was sparsely furnished. A table with a scrubbed surface stood in the centre, newspaper spread as a tablecloth on it, on that plates, used plates of more than one meal, and three cans remaining from a six-pack of beer. Knives were there, but no forks. Was it knives and fingers then? Beyond was the wall containing the fireplace. A meagre fire slumped in the grate. It was cold in that room, the chill of damp pervading it. On the mantelpiece were two vases, one at each end – no flowers, though. In its centre was poised a patterned plate on its edge. There was a single easy chair, its surface split in places, its padding leaking in sorrow. Two plain, rickety chairs stood at the table, facing each other.

It was a sparse room, a room empty of spirit. Boredom and despair seemed still to hang heavily in the stale air. A window, overlooking a back yard I guessed, was tattily draped with faded, ancient velveteen. The single light bulb hung miserably naked from the centre of the ceiling, mourning its lost shade, if it had ever had one. The air was heavy, and restless to get out of there, if only a window would open, but it wouldn't, being painted in solid. I doubted that it ever had. The neighbours might hear your voices, register the fear and the loathing, the cries for help that it was better not to hear.

The lad was standing in the corner to my left, his palms flat against the two adjoining walls. His friends, those walls. From those two directions a blow would not reach him. He might, as had been suggested, have been between two and three years old, but his face wore the age of ceaseless distress and fear, whilst his left cheek bore the inflamed puffiness of repeated slaps from a heavy palm. Enough of that and you go deaf.

'Are you Dennis?' I asked him.

'Want to go to momma.' Fear was in his eyes, that this might promote another slap.

It was clear enough. I glanced round for Gerald. He was just inside the doorway, and looked terrified.

'What d'ya want?' demanded Pierce. 'You're coppers . . .'

'We're not. I want to talk to you. You were along the canal, at the flight, yesterday evening. Late. Is that so?'

'I ain't talkin' to you.'

'Oh yes you are. You went there with Clare Martin, I'd say. Your wife's sister. She knew where the lad was. So I'd suggest you put a knife to her ribs, the one you're holding now, and forced her to drive you there.'

'No! It's a bloody lie. It's stoopid.' He gave a bark of derisive and empty laughter, which was more convincing than the words.

'You were there.'

Then he went for me. There was no warning. Usually you see it

145

in the eyes, but his were empty. He went for me with the knife in his left fist, pushing himself away from the wall with his other hand, helping himself along with his spare foot back against the wall.

I knew then that I'd taken on more than I'd anticipated. Pierce was a streetfighter, and he'd used that knife before, probably often. Suddenly, I was defending my life. He would know the law. He could plead self-defence, and in his own house, against intruders. I had to get inside his swing and disarm him, so I went at him head down, and got him in the chest. Then I twisted away, locking his knife arm in one hand round his wrist, the other at his elbow. He stumbled as he turned, dropping it. I kicked it along the floor towards Gerald.

'Get the knife!' I shouted.

But Gerald was rigid with fear. It wasn't what I'd promised him. To him, this was a hell wherein he had not previously ventured. He could no more have handled that knife than he would dive into one of the locks.

I had wasted one second in that glance at Gerald, and it nearly cost me an eye, as splayed fingers were jabbing towards my face. I caught them on their way to my eyes, interlocking my fingers in his, and threw Pierce back against the wall. His hands were the stronger. A multitude of bricks had been hefted by them. But I could bear down on him, being that small amount taller, and I watched his eyes go blank with pain, his mouth fall open, gasping. Then I broke free and stood back. He was busy trying to make a fist, which I watched all the way, ducked under, and threw my own fist deep into his beer gut, up under his rib cage.

'That's for her cracked rib,' I panted.

His eyes were going blank. The punch he threw at me was slow. When I stepped back a little, seeking more room in which to operate, his head came forward, so I hit him on the nose. Blood spurted. He licked his lips like a wounded animal, and made a snarling sound.

'That was for the teeth,' I told him, and put another fist where the nose had been. 'And that's for the broken wrist.'

He seemed to choke on his own blood.

Now, I had to keep on the offensive. If he landed a lucky blow and had me down, or even temporarily confused, he would pounce on the knife. I had to prevent that.

He managed a choked, burbling sound, and launched himself

at me. I stepped aside. It would need a lucky blow to put him down. I flung a punch at his face again, staggering myself, and got him clean on the chin. He shook his head, and stood still for a moment.

'And that,' I gasped, 'was for every damned bruise.'

Then I stood back, exhausted, as his eyes went blank. Slowly he tilted, rigidly, like a wooden toy, then he fell with a crash on to his face, his arms spread. I stared down at him, surprised that such a poor blow had finished him.

Panting, I turned my eyes to Gerald, who hadn't realized how close it had been, and couldn't, even now, bring himself to bend and pick up the knife. If he'd done that earlier, I might possibly have managed to end it more cleanly. I found I could barely speak, and knew I wasn't steady on my feet. I turned my head to the boy. He was still there in the corner, standing stiffly, his face drawn and sallow, huge brown eyes in a mask of wonder.

'Shall we . . .' My lips were dry, and I licked them. 'Shall we take you to your momma?' My voice sounded strange to me.

It was still there, inhabiting me, that distasteful monster of violence, which is in all of us to some extent. Sometimes it is let free – but is still there, waiting. I felt nothing but self-disgust.

Dennis ran out of his corner, stopped, looked at me, then at Gerald and ran to him, clasping him round the knees. Gerald stared across at me, horror in his eyes. He couldn't speak, but reached down, swept Dennis up into his arms, and turned away. I watched until he was out of the front door.

Then I followed, treading meticulously on Pierce's spread hands. It was like walking on gravel.

'And that,' I said for myself, 'is for the despair in her eyes.'

Then I followed Gerald, out to the car.

11

He was waiting beside the passenger's door. I reached past him and unlocked it, took Dennis out of his arms, and waited until he'd taken the seat.

'Fasten your seat belt,' I said.

This he did, his hands awkward and fumbling. I reached inside and handed Dennis to him. 'Hold him tight,' I instructed him. I was having to tell him every move, as he seemed unable to think for himself.

'I hope you're not going to do any speeding,' he said hoarsely.

I took that as a rather pitiful attempt at humour, but to Gerald that was what we would be doing; fleeing from this house. I went round and slipped in behind the wheel, fastened my own seat belt, and started the engine. We did a three-point turn, and set off back to Flight House.

I glanced sideways. In the poor light from passing street lamps, I could detect that huge, startled eyes were staring at me, Dennis's eyes.

'We'll take you to your momma,' I promised him. 'Not now – but soon.'

He relaxed limply against Gerald's chest. Ten seconds later he was asleep. The sleep of the exhausted, and of a hint of hope.

'Really, Richard,' whispered Gerald, 'that was quite uncalled-for. You told me – no violence.'

'Self-defence,' I explained.

'Is that what it was?'

'He drew a knife . . .'

'You know very well that it was lying on the floor.'

'Exactly.' I was holding the car at a steady thirty, aware that the tension was gradually easing its way from me – but leaving me uncertain and shaky. My reactions would now be very slow.

I said, 'The knife was there, Gerald. Still available. If he'd got me off my feet, or even unsteady, he'd have pounced on it. And what would the odds have been then?'

'All the same . . . that's specious, Richard, and you know it.'

'But we have the boy. That's the point. We have him.'

He was silent for a minute or two, then he said quietly, 'You should not have done this to me, Richard. You should not.'

'I thought it would be good experience for you. A solicitor practising in the criminal law area – you ought really to know about the people you defend in court.'

'Is that your attitude?' he asked with a hint of contempt. 'That I defend criminals! They are not so until found guilty, and you know it. Know it damned well.'

It had certainly shaken him, that he should have used that word. I said, 'I'm sorry it was a bit rough. But perhaps you will remember this little incident – '

'I'll never forget it! I feel . . . filthy. Yes . . . filthy.'

'I thought you might like to know about those mild, quiet and reasonably dressed people, who sit the other side of your desk. What they might be like in real life, I mean. *Their* real life. Such as you've run into this evening.'

'It is my duty – '

'Your duty to get them off on some vague technicality? Don't you *care* whether or not they're actually guilty? Do you ever ask them: did you do it?'

'If I know they have . . .' There was a little attack in his voice now. He was bitter. 'Then, I tell them they must plead guilty. As you very well know, Richard. This boy is all wet. I find it most uncomfortable.'

'I'm sorry. Not long now. But tell me . . . you said: if you know, you tell them they must plead guilty. But how do you know? Oh, Gerald, you're living in a different world. *That* was why I wanted you to come with me. To see for yourself. Now admit it – you didn't really believe that the lad's mother – Helen – had been brutally assaulted. Not really. You thought . . . oh, not directly, but way back in the depths of your mind . . . you thought I was exaggerating. That Amelia and I were. Because you'd never been within a mile of violence. Well, now you know what people can be like. You'll see, when you've got time to think about it quietly, you'll realize why I took you along. For you to *see*. I didn't guess he'd give you such a good demonstration, though.'

'He!' he cried. 'He? It was you who were so violent. You, Richard. I'll never be able to put it out of my mind.'

'And so . . . you make my point. You didn't know I had it in me. Admit it. So – in future – you'll know you have to look behind things. Around them. Anybody, Gerald, is capable of pretty well anything. It depends on the motivation driving them. Literally anything.'

He was silent. For two minutes, he remained silent. Then he said quietly, 'Will you stop the car, please.'

I glanced at him. 'He's wetter?'

'No. It's not that. But I can't go home like this. I . . . I feel sick. Weak and shaky. I don't know. They mustn't see me like this, at home. I feel I might even faint.'

'Hold on. That won't do. But you get my point now? You've stated it. People present their own selected image. And yours has been . . .'

'Tarnished,' he whispered.

I peered ahead. 'There was a pub we passed, on the way here, I'm sure. We'll stop and – '

'I couldn't go inside. Not like . . . like this.'

'I'll bring you out a drink. It'll help you pull yourself together. All right? Ah – there it is. I'll pull in.'

He said nothing as I drew on to their forecourt. The little pub seemed dim. There were only three other cars there.

'Whisky?' I asked.

'Brandy, if you don't mind.'

'Right. Won't be long.'

The bar was cosy and warm. The conversation was a mere hum, punctuated by the click of dominoes. A large and cheerful bartender watched me approach. I wasn't certain I was walking quite straight.

'Two brandies,' I said.

'Two singles, or one double, sir?'

He had assumed they were both for me. I tried to smile, but my face was stiff. 'There's somebody outside in the car. I'll take one out, if that's all right. Singles.'

He nodded, and presented two brandies. My loose change was in my right-hand trouser pocket, as I'd left my wallet behind. My fingers fumbled money on to the bar, fortunately sufficient. Then I saw that there was dried blood on my knuckles and realized he had noticed it.

'Anywhere I can . . .'

He nodded towards my right. Gents, the sign said. At that specific time I didn't really feel like a gentleman, but I headed there. They offered a wash-hand basin and liquid soap, but no towel or hot-air dryer. I used my handkerchief. Then I returned to the bar, trying a smile that felt a little stiff, and downed my own brandy. It hit me, way down, and I left it to get on with the repair work to my nerves.

'Be a minute,' I said, and took the other glass out to Gerald. He had the passenger's window well down.

'It's beginning to smell not too sweet in here, Richard.' His voice was, at least, a little more firm.

'Here. Get this down you. No hurry. No hurry at all.'

But they would be waiting anxiously, and they didn't deserve to have to wait. He handed the glass back to me, and I took it inside. 'Thank you.' The bartender nodded. 'Good-night to you, sir.'

I stood outside for a few moments, lit my pipe, and blew smoke into the night. It wouldn't be fair to inflict Gerald with tobacco smoke in the car. He was already complaining about a smell. Well . . . tobacco might cover it. No? Right . . . no in-car smoking, then.

I knocked it out and got in behind the wheel. He reached over and touched my arm. 'A minute please, Richard.'

I waited. He said at last, 'You're basing your remarks, of course, on what Ray told you concerning that episode in court. With Clare Martin.'

It was not a question. He knew I was naturally on the side of the police, hence my lesson on the basics.

'Perhaps you're right,' I conceded.

'But of course, that was quite a long while ago.' He offered that tentatively.

'So I understand. Months.'

'And things change. But Ray knew very well that my court encounters with Clare Martin were not confined to that one belittling episode.'

'Of course not.' I was wondering what he was getting round to now. 'She would've appeared many times as a police witness,' I agreed.

'And Ray deliberately didn't recall that I evened the score.'

'They'll be worried about us,' I said. That had been a strange phrase for him to use.

He ignored what I had said. People *did* wait on Gerald. 'More than evened. I got my own laugh in court. My own triumph – in spite of the fact that I lost the case.'

I knew that he had to recall some episode of which he could be proud, and in that way retrieve his self-respect.

'Tell me as we drive,' I said, starting the engine. 'It can't be all that urgent.'

'I'd like you to hear it.'

'I'm listening,' I assured him as I backed out. 'I'll go slowly.'

There was a slight hesitation. He was wondering how to put it. Then he said, quite softly, 'Of course, Ray was only trying to make me look a fool, to you and to Colin.'

'Why would he want to do that?' I asked easily, keeping it going.

151

'Because he knows that I don't approve of him as a husband for Mellie. And he knows why. But I'm allowing myself to wander off the point. There was another case, a month or so after that one, she again in the witness box. My client stood to lose his licence for driving under the influence of alcohol. Clare was telling the court that she'd asked him to use the breathalizer, and I felt I had to do something for my fee. This was a legal aid case, of course.'

'Of course,' I echoed. Why didn't he get on with it? My hands weren't steady. Reaction was setting in.

He went on, 'I queried whether that breathalizer was reliable, and pointed out that all these wonderful modern instruments . . . you'd call it that, Richard? An instrument?'

'Any word you wish.'

I was driving more and more slowly. Flight Lane was only half a mile ahead.

'Anyway,' he said, 'I queried its efficiency, and she answered that she could stand in that witness box, breathalizer or not, and still swear that my man was drunk.'

'Well . . . she *was* on oath.'

'Yes. But I had to ask her why she had reason (apart from the details we'd already heard of his erratic driving at that time) any reason at all to believe he was drunk. She said that yes, she had, and I asked: then what, exactly? And she gave me one of her smiles. Oh, she'd recognized me, of course. And she went on to tell the court that when she offered the breathalizer, and he pursed his lips, he said, "Give us a kiss, luv." And of course, laughter again, and I thought at my expense.'

'Is this going to take long, Gerald?' I was coming up to Flight Lane. 'They'll be waiting.'

'Does it matter?' he asked, sighing. 'A little anxiety – is that anything to set against what *I've* been through! You too, Richard, of course,' he conceded politely.

'So what happened in court, apart from the laughter at your expense?'

'Well . . . you see . . . I was sort of poised for conflict, you might put it, knowing her. And the response came to me, just out of the air. I said, and I can quote the exact words because they appeared in our local paper, verbatim, and I have *that* cutting in my office desk.'

The brandy had done him a world of good, apparently. His

voice was no longer unsteady, and he'd lost the tight, tense attitude he'd had before.

'And your exact words, Gerald?'

'I said: "I am sure that the court, who have been observing the witness closely, will agree with me that it was a very reasonable and sober request." And the magistrate laughed.'

'Well . . . good for you.'

'And Clare smiled at me, and inclined her head.'

'Well – that's fine. Shall we go on?'

'He's peacefully asleep.'

'I was thinking – '

'But Richard – that wasn't the end of it, you see – it was only the beginning.'

I couldn't feel that I wanted to hear any more, not just at that time. 'Can't you keep the rest for later, Gerald?'

'You're just not interested, that's the trouble. I offer you confidences, and you don't want to hear.'

'Oh, I do, I do. But later. You're forgetting, I'm the one who was in all the action, and I'm past the age when it comes easily. I'm tired, Gerald. I ache. Tell me later, there's a good fellow.'

He was silent.

I turned the car into Flight Lane, and increased the speed. Orange light ahead beckoned me, and as we came closer I saw that they had the white floods on again. That meant they expected us (if we returned fit and well and both in one piece) to drive round there. I did this. They had moved the Rolls further along, so that I could stop the car directly opposite to the bar entrance.

They had heard us, and in a moment had surrounded the car. Faces peered in at us, and grimaced, or smiled, whatever seemed appropriate. On the far side, Amelia was opening the passenger's door.

I could see that she would have difficulty lifting out the lad, as Gerald seemed bemused as to his actions in this crisis. But by that time I had my own door open, and as I stepped out I said, 'Slide him over to me, Gerald.'

With both of us leaning towards each other, we managed the transfer smoothly. I backed out with Dennis in my arms, and then slammed the door with my hip . . . and realized I had left the keys in the ignition lock.

Then I knew, and had a clear mental picture. Clare had reached across her driver's seat to reach out something bulky and weighty. Dennis, we knew, had been at the houseboat, as we had found his little jacket. He had not been there earlier in the day, because Colin had been there, and would surely have seen him. Clare, therefore, had been bringing him to Helen, her sister. But she hadn't wanted to be seen doing it, so she had not been able to drive down to Flight House. So she had carried Dennis, in her arms, Dennis . . . whom she had not been able to put to the ground while she locked the car door. And this must have been done at around 5.15.

It followed from this that Pierce must have fetched the lad back home. During the previous night.

But . . . if he had not known where Helen was hiding from him, how had he known where to come in order to fetch Dennis home?

He *had* come, because most of Helen's injuries had been recent. And he had not taken Helen home, for the simple reason that she'd been incapable of moving. He had come in the night.

As I stood there, unaware of what was going on around me, I realized that Gerald had managed to get to his feet, and was looking lost. I thought I understood why. He had expected to be the one who carried Dennis inside, the triumph his.

I stood and waited. He straightened, walked round, and I surrendered the lad. I could think of nothing else but that slammed door.

They flocked around him, the three old darlings and his family, and Gerald stood there, beaming. Hadn't he rescued the lad, as planned?

Amelia took my arm. She knew I wanted to keep well out of it. All I needed now was for the memory to fade.

'Has it been bad, Richard?'

I shrugged. 'I'm getting too old for it, love. Too old.'

But the swarm of faces around him had confused Dennis, and none of them was his mother's. The only words I'd heard him say had been, 'I want to go to momma.' Or something like that. Gerald lowered him to his feet, and now Dennis raised his voice and howled. He was confused, scared, and overwhelmed by faces.

Gently, I eased my way through. He recognised me as the big man who'd belted his father into unconsciousness, though perhaps he didn't use, to himself, that exact phrase. In any event, he smiled. That was thanks enough for me. I crouched down to his eye level. 'I want to go to momma,' he said, positively and lustily.

'And so you shall. Tomorrow. You know – tomorrow? When it gets light again. We'll take you to your momma tomorrow.'

His eyes were huge. I saw comprehension in them, a small hint of a smile on his lips. 'Tomorrow.' He had a little difficulty with the double 'r's.

Then Mellie, sensible girl, came in with Bruce on his lead. Why hadn't I thought of that? We parted for them, and Dennis shouted, 'Brucey!' That was it. The spell of shock evaporated, and memory was erased. Only the present existed for both of them, Dennis rolling on his back, Bruce pounding paws on his chest and frantically applying the tongue treatment. Now Dennis was screaming again, but it was with joy. Heavens, how this household needed screams of joy!

I drew back. Amelia was still clinging to my arm. 'A bath, Richard?'

'Yes. Oh yes.'

'And ... Gerald?' she asked. 'He's gone up already. How did he cope with it?'

'In the morning – maybe even later this evening – he'll be telling everybody what a splendid time he's had.'

We were mounting the stairs slowly, side by side, there being just enough room. 'And did he?' she asked.

'He learned a few things.'

'So, in the morning we can take Dennis to see his mother ... Then what? Have you given it one thought?'

I opened the door to our room, closed it behind us, and began peeling off my clothes. 'Run a bath for me, love, will you.'

She went into the bathroom, and called out above the rush of the taps. 'In the morning ... do you intend to take him to see his mother?'

'That was the idea. I thought we'd agreed on that.'

'Then what? Dennis can't stay here, and I'm sure Helen won't be discharged for a while.'

'We'll have to see. Take it as it comes.'

'And if it all comes about that she's still got nowhere to go when they discharge her, except back to her husband ...'

I stepped into the bath. She had it too hot. Stepped smartly out again. 'Bath salts?' I asked, shooting in a small amount of cold water.

'You'll have to manage without. There aren't any. And you're dodging the issue.'

I wallowed, and the pains seemed to retreat. I said, 'If she's got nowhere to go, I thought we might phone Mary and ask her to prepare that spare room . . .'

Quietly, she cut in, 'The house is mine, Richard. You mustn't forget that.'

I stopped soaping, and stared at her. She had never before thrown that fact at me. 'You surely wouldn't object – '

'Richard,' she said gently, leaning over and kissing me on the forehead, 'no wife likes a younger woman – and one who's probably very good looking indeed, when the bruises and the swellings go – no wife wants such a woman anywhere near her husband. Especially living in the same house.'

'For Chrissake! I'm twice her age.'

'Since when did that matter, Richard?'

Then, as women will when you're helpless to follow, she walked out into the bedroom. 'Amelia!' But she didn't return. Perhaps as well, because you can't do much, lying in a steaming bath, to persuade a woman that she's just plain crazy to think that anybody could possibly replace her . . .

Then she returned, just as I was levering myself up and about to chase after her, wringing wet or not.

'Yes, Richard?'

She made the mistake of approaching too closely, and you can do quite a lot in a steaming bath, I discovered, in the way of persuasion, even when the woman has her clothes on. I hoped nobody heard her screams and mistook them for appeals for assistance, because she didn't need any assistance at all.

A little later, towelled dry, and with dressing gowns over our pyjamas, we ventured out into the corridor to see what was or wasn't happening. Nothing seemed to be happening at all, except for the fact that one human being was standing at the end of the corridor, peering past a partly open door. We approached. It was Mellie. She gave a tiny cry when I touched her arm.

'What is it?' I whispered.

She stood aside, and gestured. In the bed they'd hurriedly made up was Dennis, fast asleep. Bruce was lying beside him, but on the coverlet, though he had managed to intrude his nose on to the pillow. What pressure had been applied to Gerald to allow this to have come about, I couldn't guess, but he'd been the one to rescue Dennis, hadn't he, and he could hardly grumble now. Not and be listened to.

From the fact that Bruce was again in his pristine and fluffy condition, as acquired by the use of a hair dryer, I deduced that they had been in the same bath together. All those years of experience in the police force had endowed me with these powers of deduction.

'Better leave them to it,' I said. Mellie smiled. 'Good-night. See you in the morning,' she promised.

Then we returned to our respective rooms, and Amelia said, 'We've decided nothing.'

'True. So we'll wait and see how things turn out.'

12

The following morning, it was Dennis who basically dictated the schedule. Everybody was anxious to attend to his welfare. He, with the adaptability of his age, seemed to have forgotten the previous evening's excitement, though he had not forgotten the one central issue, as far as he was concerned: there had been a promise that he would be able to go to see his mother. Go and *be* with her, he no doubt considered this to mean, as whenever I looked round, his two big brown eyes were fixed on me. I was the one who made things happen.

We ate in the dining room, and Ruby had produced a buffet-style affair, so that everybody helped themselves. This meant that you had the choice of where you sat. I was between Amelia and Colin. His choice, not mine.

'Settled it with your bosses, have you?' I asked him quietly.

'What?'

'The critical problem of the winding handle. Are they taking away the new one they brought, now you've rescued the old one?'

He dug into his bacon and eggs. 'They're leaving it. Somebody's told them that it might be a long while before the police let me have the old one again, so they're leaving the new one.'

'Hmm!' I said, and turned my attention to the tenth time that my jacket had been tugged. 'Soon,' I said. 'Your momma's got to have her own breakfast first. And then she's got to be all cleaned up and smelling nice, because where she is they don't believe in people smelling nasty.'

157

He frowned at that, and Amelia said softly, 'He's only a child, Richard. You mustn't tease him.'

'Mussen tease,' Dennis agreed, so I ruffled his hair and he ran off, laughing.

But Colin had been waiting patiently, in order to carry on where he'd left off. 'What d'you mean by that?' he asked stubbornly.

'By what?'

'You said: hmm. Something to do with the winding handle.'

'Ah yes.' I chewed, swallowed, and said, 'The police'll keep that one for ages. I know. Right up to and past any court case. And the old dears'll start worrying you about the new one.'

'What're you getting at?' he asked suspiciously.

'Something I've thought about. Thought, and thought, and thought, in fact, and hadn't got very far. It's that chain, you see.'

'What chain?'

'That length of chain down by the pound, where she went in. You know what I mean – it's supposed to hold the gate arm, or something like that.'

Colin was at once mentally involved with his technical expertise. 'It's like this, you see. When the pressure eases – '

'Never mind the technicalities,' I told him. 'It wasn't fastened when I was trying to get down there – trying to get to Clare.'

'It oughto've been.' He frowned heavily.

'Well it wasn't. Now think about it Colin. Think. The chain was probably unfastened just so that Clare's body – her unconscious body at that time, I'd guess – anyway, just so that she could be slid into the pound. Because that place would be a logical choice. It's about the only place that's really hidden from the upstairs windows of the house, way down there and at the other side of the footbridge. But it does mean that it was done by somebody who *knew* that, about the chain, and the way the pound was hidden from sight. Are you with me?'

He was no longer eating, and was glaring at me. 'What're you getting at? You're sayin' it was me!' Agitation was slurring his words.

'I'm not getting at anything specific.' I turned to him, smiling with my mouth full, and still chewing. 'Except that it's how I believe it was done.' I swallowed. 'And after all, you *did* say the winding handle was more often than not on the rack and pinion I had such a hell of a job getting past.'

'All right, all right.' He thrust back his chair.

I caught his arm. 'For God's sake, don't be so prickly. I'm only using your expert knowledge to confirm my thinking on it. But it *is* feasible, isn't it? Don't you think? Just because nobody saw anything of what happened – that adds a bit of authority to it.'

'Authority?' Colin blinked at me, not understanding. Authority, to him, was a group of three old people.

'Authenticity, then,' I said.

'All right, all right.' He attempted to smile. It didn't seem to him now that I was trying to trap him. 'So why tell *me* about it?'

'Just confirming about the chain,' I assured him, 'and telling you that the handle you found yesterday couldn't be the one used to attack Clare. Wrong lock, Colin. You ought to have tried the bottom lock first. Don't you think? It's right next door to that pound.'

He stood over me, then thumped his forehead with the heel of his hand. 'Fool that I am. I'll try that.'

'But it doesn't really matter . . .'

He was already gone, heading for the door. A little more dragging was now on the agenda.

It did, however, remove one from the number who wished to go to the hospital. Amelia and I had the precedence, I thought, because it was we who had already been to visit Helen, and I had been thinking in terms of three people for this visit. Amelia, Dennis and myself. But oh no – it was already assumed that everybody would be going. Well . . . everybody, now, bar Colin. And not Ray, as he hadn't turned up and was assumed to be back on duty. Was Mellie *never* going to get used to the fact that he would not always be there when she wanted him? In this instance, though, her attention was completely absorbed with Dennis.

But now . . . they all wanted to go. Gerald – hadn't he been the one to rescue Dennis from that terrible father? Ruby and Mellie said that the washing-up would have to wait until they got back. Nod, nod. So there! Amelia and I were going because we'd already visited, and Helen would know us. And the three old dears! Now . . . *that* I had not expected. Anything unpleasant in life usually had very little opportunity to brush against them. They were probably quite unaware of the existence of such streets as Brindley Street, at Crayminster. Yet they wanted to visit the young woman in hospital. Heavens! To them, hospital was a delicately pristine room, tended by one's own personal nurse. The sight of a whole double row of beds in one ward, all inhabited by women who couldn't really be considered hygienic, otherwise they wouldn't be in such surroundings, would probably send them running. Yet they wanted to go there, were looking forward to it as though it might be a coach trip to Blackpool – which itself would thoroughly upset them.

I sighed, and phoned to find out the morning visiting hours. Nine-thirty to ten-thirty. I didn't ask to be connected to the ward, not wishing to hear anything disconcerting.

'Oh . . . we'll have to rush . . . rush!' cried Alexandra.

It was only a quarter of an hour's drive away, and we wouldn't need the whole hour, anyway.

There would be eight of us, as Gerald still insisted on going. Hadn't he rescued the lad? He kept reminding everybody of that. And of course . . . Dennis. I'd forgotten him, the most important visitor, indeed the only one Helen would really wish to see. Nine of us, then.

It was to be hoped that Arnold Pierce didn't put in an appearance. This seemed unlikely. He wouldn't dare. Hospitals have their own means of ejection, and a meaningful gesture with a full hypodermic syringe usually did the trick.

Oh . . . and Bruce. I'd forgotten Brucey. Dennis hadn't, though. When we gathered outside, deciding on who would travel in which car, that was when the question of the dog arose. Dennis refused to go anywhere without his Brucey. 'Not even to see your momma?' Amelia asked. That really upset him. He was too young to have to handle such choices. So in the end we conceded the point, and loaded Dennis with Bruce into Amelia's car, along with Mellie and Ruby, Gerald sitting with Jenkins on the front seat of the Rolls, the other three in their usual places in the rear.

A complicated performance of backing-up and reversing then took place, with Colin enjoying himself no end, waving his three-pronged hook to convey instructions, and nearly backing himself into one of his own locks.

We reached the hospital at 9.45. Not bad at all. I had expected long delays whilst Gerald chose a hospital-visiting suit.

The car park was packed, and Jenkins and I both had difficulties in finding parking spaces, he being the most inconveniently placed in that he had three passengers who could not conceive the possibility of actually having to get out and walk. But Jenkins was magnificent. The apparition of the stately Rolls Royce, and Jenkins's dignity, attracted the assistance of an ambulance driver, who found them a space so close to Admissions that he must have expected three multiple-injuries cases to alight. The three old dears thanked him. I thought for one moment that Adolphus was about to tip him, but he was reaching for nothing more than his handkerchief. Already, there were smells around him that he found unfamiliar, and distinctly uninviting.

I thought to ask at the Admissions desk about Helen Pierce. There could, and I prayed not, have been a relapse. But it seemed to be quite the reverse of that.

'She's no longer in Intensive Care, sir. You'll find her in Brindley Ward.'

There he was again, that Brindley. He got everywhere. As did Brucey, apparently, because there *he* was, nudging against Dennis's legs. 'The dog?' I asked weakly.

'Oh . . . take him along. You'll have to ask Sister, though.'

'Ah!' I said. 'Yes. Thank you.'

Dennis marched along, very serious now, overawed by the bustling movement around him and by the fact that his mother had become an important person in this overwhelming and busy building, and somewhat subdued by the fact that he'd heard it said that somebody of huge authority had to be asked about Brucey. He held Amelia's hand, and kept glancing back. Yes, there was Bruce. Where else could he be? He was still on his lead.

In the event, there was no problem about dogs. Indeed, there was already a crowd of visitors, including dogs, and a clatter of cheerful conversation, cheerful because this wasn't so serious as Intensive Care, comparison elevating this ward to a mood of relaxation. Yes, there were dogs, not happy, and not pleased about these strange smells. One woman had brought a cat. So we joined the throng, Bruce at Dennis's heels.

Helen was right down the far end. We edged and manoeuvred our way through, Ruby and Mellie anxious, Gerald severe, and the three old darlings completely confused.

No more, now, the drip and the drain, and they had her sitting up, looking brighter, the bruises fading, the swollen lips thinner so that the missing teeth were unfortunately more obvious. But she could smile. Her ribs were still bound, and her wrist still lay in its cast on the surface of the bed.

'Told you, didn't I?' I asked Dennis. 'There she is, all snug and warm.'

And strangely, after his previous behaviour, Dennis advanced slowly, shyly, and with uncertainty, as though she might vanish like a soap bubble if he approached her with enthusiasm. And why the hell was I longing for a smoke, all of a sudden?

She wept, of course, Helen did, but silently and undemonstratively, with Dennis's head buried in her side, which must have been painful for Dennis and for her cracked rib, and Bruce, whenever he could get his nose in, managed also to intrude his tongue. Fingers or plaster cast; he didn't care.

Ruby and Mellie had managed to find chairs, which they now surrendered to the two old ladies. There had been much whispering and nodding amongst the three of them, but now Adolphus held back. Amelia and I retreated, giving way to Ruby and Mellie, who clearly regretted having surrendered their chairs.

Adolphus said, 'I feel distinctly uncomfortable in a ward for women, Richard. There should surely be more privacy for them. It is all . . . shockingly intimate.'

'There's not much privacy for anybody in a hospital, I assure you.'

'I cannot believe . . .' He dabbed his forehead with the handkerchief he was still carrying. 'I cannot accept that a man – a husband who has promised to cherish . . . cherish . . .' He paused, dabbed his lips. 'That *any* man could lay his hands on a woman, cause her suffering . . .' He allowed it to tail away. Not only couldn't he accept the facts, he couldn't even discover words to meet the situation. 'It is evil, of course,' he went on, having found one. 'Quite evil. Such persons should be punished.'

'He has been, Adolphus,' I said. 'And what the devil are they whispering about?'

Victoria and Alexandra were sitting one each side of the bed. Victoria held Helen's good hand, and was shaking it gently, as though in emphasis. Alexandra had to hold a forearm, had to reach past Dennis's head far enough, and resist Bruce's efforts to climb past her on to the bed. Dennis was saying, 'Oh yes, momma, yes.'

I edged closer. Amelia, without a chair, was crouched down at Alexandra's shoulder, shamelessly eavesdropping, and she was nodding, smiling a strangely vague smile. And Gerald was in dispute with Victoria.

'Indeed,' he was saying, 'I claim the right. I could add my own deposition . . .'

'But we have a most excellent man.'

And Helen's bright, dark eyes darted from one face to the other, whilst she tried not to smile too much in case it hurt. She attempted to bite her lip, but the two missing teeth hampered her.

'What *is* it?' I asked Amelia.

She glanced round, impatient, not wishing to miss a word. 'Hush, Richard.'

'I will not hush. What's going on?' Heavens, I had a prior interest in anything involving Helen and Dennis.

'They want Helen to go with them, Richard. To live with them. No . . . no. Don't look like that. Not as a servant – as a companion. And there's a mare for Helen to learn to ride, and a foal for Dennis to learn to ride, and . . . and . . . oh, a big man with a shotgun who guards the grounds.'

'A gamekeeper.'

'Yes, yes. He keeps the game that nobody's allowed to shoot, and Gerald wants to handle the divorce, and they want *their* man to do it . . . Oh, and lots of things.'

'Two solicitors? She could have two divorces,' I suggested.

'You do have these wonderful ideas, Richard.' And she patted my cheek.

'She could keep one in reserve,' I explained.

'Now don't be silly. What does *that* mean?'

I shrugged, my eyes on Helen. Such bright hope in her eyes! 'If they *were* divorced, he'd come for her, and – '

She shook my arm, her fingers digging painfully into my flesh. 'They wouldn't let him get near. And how would he know where to find her?'

'Her address would be on the divorce petition.'

She was frowning now. The assumption that I was simply playing around with my fantasies was being shattered. 'You really mean this?'

'I do. He would come for her – and she would leave with him.'

'No!'

'Oh yes. She's like that. Her husband's a complete lout – hopeless. But she would go back to him. They do . . . they do.'

She was annoyed with me. I could see it in her eyes. But – here – she had to control it. 'That's a philosophy of despair. You're a cynic, Richard.'

Trying to smile at her, I said, 'You're forgetting all those years I spent in the police force. Philosophy's a theory. An acceptance. I'm a realist – and I know how people are.'

'You make it sound . . . heavens, don't you ever offer anybody hope?'

'Oh yes. Yes. I'm on the watch for it all the while. Hope! It's like a bright light. I'll have a word with Gerald. He says he's not an expert on matrimonial law, but he can look it all up. Divorce. And maybe there're possibilities that her new address could go down as: unknown. Of no fixed address. I've seen that phrase used. Make no mistake, love, she'd be happy with what she's being offered, probably immensely happy – and for Dennis it'd be a fresh start, with hope over the horizon. But Arnold Pierce must never be given the chance to discover where she is.'

'And you . . .' she exclaimed. 'Criticizing Gerald for pontificating! You'd win a competition at it. First prize, a pedestal to stand on.'

Her bitter little laugh wasn't at all one of delight.

'Though of course,' I said, offering light where Amelia saw only darkness, 'she needn't apply for a divorce at all, then he'd never find her.'

She eyed me askance, wondering how seriously she could now take me. 'And if she met another man,' she asked, 'and wanted to get married again? What then?'

And I realized that I'd not told her about Colin. But . . . women, women! Always, they see happy marriage ahead.

'*That,*' I said, 'would be the time to divorce Pierce, and if her new man's got any guts in him – and perhaps a shotgun under his arm – then Pierce wouldn't be able to run away fast enough.'

'You and your happy endings!'

I made a mental note to advise Colin to buy a shotgun. Whatever these old dears wanted, I had a good idea where Helen would eventually be living.

I grinned at her. A bell tinkled, and Adolphus said, 'What's that, Richard?'

'It's the leaving bell. Everybody out. And when the ward's clear a whole gang of nurses swoop down on the beds, tidying, making sure nobody's comfortable, so that all these poor ladies here can smile and present a happy and hygienic ward to the big boss: The Matron.'

'Richard, you exaggerate.' Adolphus smiled, somewhat grimly.

'I've been told that I do.'

'So we have to leave?'

'Yes.'

He went to say goodbye to the young lady he hoped would soon become the mascot of the household, and I said to Amelia, 'Don't forget Bruce. I'll catch you up.'

'Richard? What now?'

I ran my hand through my hair. Time was running short. 'I must have a quiet word with Helen. I'll catch you up. A minute . . . please.'

She looked at me doubtfully, and said, 'They'll throw you out, Richard.'

'I know.'

She smiled very thinly, and hurried after the others. I fell to my knees beside Helen's bed, the more likely to be unobserved. 'Do you remember me, Helen?'

'Yes,' she whispered. 'And . . . thank you.' The missing teeth made her lisp a little.

'I'm not here for thanks, love,' I said. 'Questions. Will you try to answer a few quick questions?'

'Hmm!'

I took that for agreement. 'Tell me – how did you get to the houseboat?'

She leaned forward, in order to whisper. I noticed that she had a length of string around her neck, hanging inside the hospital nightgown. I wondered what was on it. And guessed.

'Clare,' she said. 'Clare took me in her car.'

She clearly didn't yet know that Clare was dead. It was not the time to tell her that.

'I know about Clare,' I told her. 'She took you in her car. Right. But . . . you didn't take Dennis. Did you?'

A spasm of pain twisted her lips for a moment, I didn't know whether physical or emotional. 'His . . . his father had him.'

'Had him? How? Where?'

'He'd . . .' Her voice was dying. She reached up with her good hand to touch her lips. 'He'd said I wasn't fit to leave Dennis with.'

'Not fit?'

'He'd been hitting me.'

How flatly she said that! No disgust, anger, complaint – a declaration of truth, like naked, chilled words spread out on a legal Statement of Facts.

'And he took him – where?'

'To the pub.'

165

'Public house? A child?'

'The yard behind it. They'd got an air pistol, and they were going to shoot rats.'

A quick bob of my head revealed that the ward was now empty. I went on quickly, 'So you had to leave Dennis behind?'

'Yes.'

'And Ray and Clare promised to bring him to you?'

This was my first mention to her of Ray, but she didn't react to his name. Helen associated Clare with Ray; they were a linked partnership. It began to appear that they'd worked together on matters unofficial as well as official.

'Yes,' she whispered. 'They promised.'

'And how long was it before they brought him? To you. At the boat.'

Her eyes clouded at that. Time had ceased to have any meaning to her. 'Ages and ages.' She sighed heavily. 'And ages.'

'But didn't Clare bring Dennis to you on the evening of the bad storm?'

'Umm . . .' She inclined her head, then she shook it. 'It was Ray who brought him.'

'And Arnold fetched him back – that same night?'

'Storm?' She was having to concentrate; her reactions were very slow. She blinked. 'Yes. Then. I remember. Arnold hit me.'

'I know, Helen, I know.'

I realized then that I was losing her. But it wasn't really surprising that she couldn't think straight.

'One more – '

'Sir!'

Oh hell, I thought. A huge and efficient-looking nurse was standing over me. I got to my feet. My knees were agonizing. I had wanted to ask Helen what was on the string round her neck.

'Sorry nurse.'

'You must leave . . .'

'Leaving,' I said contritely. 'Right now.' I turned to Helen and tried to smile. 'We'll come again.'

Then I limped out. Kneeling is not my forte.

'Richard!' cried Amelia, waiting out there in the corridor. 'What have you been *doing*?'

'There were questions I had to ask, love, and I didn't get much of a look-in with you lot arranging her life for her.' I looked round. 'Where are they all, anyway?'

166

'They'll be in the car park. They wouldn't want to be seen with a man who's been hiding in a women's ward.'

'And I don't blame them, either.'

She linked her arm in mine. 'I gave Ruby the keys so that they could wait in the car, and out of the cold.'

'I simply wanted – '

'I know. To ask questions. You've explained that, Richard. I hope it was worth the risk, and you got your answers.'

'I got answers that fitted with what I'd already guessed. I think of that as success.'

We walked out into the car park. Everybody seemed to want to get out of there first, to beat the crush, and thereby creating it. I slowed my steps. Let them get on with it.

From my right, Ray said, 'Can I have a word, Mr Patton?'

I turned, and he walked up to us. He was in uniform, was possibly on duty, and his new partner would be waiting impatiently in the patrol car.

'Yes,' I said. 'Of course. But you're on duty . . .'

'It'll only take a minute.'

'So?'

'I wanted to see Helen, but I couldn't see her bed for you lot swarming all round it.'

'See her?'

'I told you I'm fond of her. Fond, Mrs Patton. Amelia, isn't it? Yes. Fond. And interested in her – what she's had to put up with. How she's stuck it out. Mellie doesn't understand.'

Amelia's smile was more like a grimace. 'She wouldn't. She'd expect all your interest to be centred on her.'

I could have explained to Ray that although a man can admire a woman whilst loving another, he should not expect to be understood.

'She's improving rapidly,' I told him. 'But I'd keep away, if I were you. Leave it to Colin.'

'Yeah. I suppose.' He suddenly grinned. 'You got Denny all right, anyway.'

'Yes,' I agreed. 'I got him.' And I wondered how he knew that. I hadn't noticed him around when we'd brought the lad back to Flight House.

'Good.' It seemed to satisfy him, because he moved away quickly through the tangle of cars.

Amelia tugged at my arm. 'And what had you already

guessed?' she asked. 'You said you got answers that fitted what you'd already guessed.'

'Ah yes.'

'Well?'

'I just put two and two together. D'you remember, when Gerald and I got back to Flight House with Dennis – Gerald had him on his lap, in the car. I'd got the driver's door open, and I reached over, and Gerald slid the lad across. Then I slammed the car door with my hip – leaving the keys in the ignition. Don't you see?'

'No, Richard. They're all waiting for us.' She tugged at my arm.

'There's no hurry. Let the crush ease out. It must have been what Clare did, you see, on the night we found her car, left just like that. I thought perhaps she'd been lifting out groceries. But it wasn't that. It was something she couldn't put down on the ground. It had to be Dennis. Clare taking him to her sister, Helen. Clare lifting him out, but Helen says it was Ray who delivered Dennis to her. If that matters.'

'Richard! oh! – I've just realized. Helen couldn't know her sister's dead! Oh heavens!'

'Yes. She couldn't know.' But I guessed that Colin had been to see her, though it was unlikely he would tell her that. 'But love, you're not concentrating. If Ray took Dennis to Helen at the time of the storm, or just after it'd finished, and Dennis wasn't on that houseboat the next morning, when I happened to find Helen – and his father had him: then . . . how did he know where to go to fetch him?'

'You and your puzzles! Work it out for yourself, Richard.'

'Yes, love. I'll try to do that,' I said meekly, and she gave me a quick glance, her lips pursed.

We reached our car. The Rolls had disappeared, Jenkins now knowing the route. They hadn't waited for us.

'You *have* been a long while, Richard,' said Ruby.

'Yes. Sorry about that. But you know, I didn't get the chance of a word with Helen. You all monopolised her.'

'And it's quite upset poor Dennis.'

As indeed it had. The leaving had upset him, and his distress had communicated to Bruce, who was whining softly. I said, 'We can all visit again.'

'This evening?' cried Mellie, who'd missed her vocation, if she could be said ever to have had one. A nurse was clearly her

168

destiny. Or a copper's wife. My bet, just at that moment, would have been for a nurse.

I drove us back to Flight House. I'd had time to work out what was on the string around Helen's neck. Colin had been crafty about his activities, one of them being to drive to the hospital, out of hours, and in some way to persuade the sister to allow him to have a word with Helen. For one specific purpose, that would have been – to give her the ring, which I'd conveniently produced for him.

It had been essential to give Helen concrete evidence that everything was as it had been, and the engagement was still on. A long engagement, that would perhaps have been.

But I had to remember that Colin had plans for killing Pierce.

13

At Flight House there was complete chaos. Three police vehicles had driven round by the locks, leaving little or no room for parking either the Rolls or Amelia's car in any position that would maintain the sense of dignity expected by the three darlings. To them, the entrance at the bar lounge was the 'front'. Now they were offered the small door at the end of the house, which they would consider suitable more for servants than for persons of consequence.

Nevertheless, they had to use that door, and were pleasantly surprised to discover that access from there to the bar lounge was quite simple. Drinks all round were necessary to settle disturbed nerves, and I would have joined them if Gerald had not caught me by the arm.

'Richard . . . please . . . a moment.'

'Aren't you interested in finding out what's going on out there?' I certainly was.

'No, I am not interested in police activities. There were things we were discussing, you and I, Richard.'

'Things? Were we?'

He seemed annoyed that I should not appreciate the importance of this, and that I'd obviously completely forgotten it. 'I was telling you about my more recent encounter in court with Clare Martin.'

'So you were.' But I was unable to work up any interest in it. 'Surely it can wait.'

'I don't think it can.'

Now I eyed him with more interest. I had taken his general attitude as having arisen from our previous evening's expedition to Brindley Street, but it was not that. There was something he had to deal with, and now. Urgently. There was a possibility that the reappearance of the police had something to do with that urgency.

'All right,' I said. 'But where? Outside?'

'No. Oh . . . no! *They're* outside.'

'Gerald, out-of-doors is the best place to talk privately. Indoors, ears can be placed against doors. No, Gerald, I was just giving you an example. Outside ... although we'll be surrounded by policemen, nobody would hear a word. They'll be making their own noises.' I could hear them doing exactly that. 'Outdoors, Gerald, and before you take your coat off. It will seem completely natural that we should be there, if only to watch what's going on. Come along. It could concern you. All of us.'

I held open the swing doors for him, and we walked out to face the locks.

Talk? We were given little chance of that. At the first sign of us, Colin came striding over. He was gesticulating in anger, and yet with a light in his eyes that betrayed a certain amount of pride. After all, it had been his idea, and his success.

Inspector Slater had completely taken over the dragging operation. Colin, by merely standing there and watching, was able to observe how the job *should* be done.

The team Slater had brought along was dragging all three locks. Twelve officers, four to a lock, were using hooks specifically designed for the job.

'I was going to get all this going,' Slater claimed to me. 'But . . .' He glanced balefully at Colin, who was standing there, worriedly watching. 'But this idiot got in first. Heaven knows what harm he's done.'

He grunted fretfully.

His attitude was false, designed to cover the fact that he hadn't, himself, thought of dragging the locks for the murder weapon. That Colin, with his home-made hook, had succeeded in at least producing a possible weapon, and almost at once, had to be frustrating to Slater. But at least there was now demonstrable activity. Colin's success had been a million to one chance that had come off, and the winding handle he'd rescued was no doubt, at that time, producing frustration at the forensic lab. All the same . . . Slater was now doing a concentrated sweep. He was certainly succeeding, though not in producing a further possible weapon.

It was unlikely that the locks had been pumped dry in the past 200 years. Many items might, in that time, have fallen from boats in transit, and it was clear that other contributions had been made, but not one of them resembling a possible weapon. Indeed, a new mystery was being presented: how had it all got there?

Three piles of sundry junk were growing in girth and height, each opposite to its own lock, but fortunately Slater had exercised a certain amount of delicacy in this matter and had had it all dumped, not on the side occupied by the house, but on the stretch of grass beyond.

It was indeed interesting, if only in stimulating the speculation.

Pram wheels, two shopping trolleys . . . Shopping trolleys? How the devil had *they* got there? No canal user would load a trolley on to his boat; it would be a devil of a nuisance. And no ordinary shopper, too idle to return the trolley to the stores once it'd been emptied, would have walked it at least two miles to reach these locks. An electric fire was there. Two motorcycle wheels, bearing tyres. A child's tricycle, half a pram, and a good part of a wheelchair. Heavens, had somebody been in it? A length of hose, which emerged like a fearsome snake . . . 'That's mine!' shouted Colin. 'I wondered where it'd got to.' A chandelier – a complete chandelier with its crystal danglers apparently intact. A scythe, with half its handle rotted away, two cycle chains . . .

It all mounted up, and fresh offerings were appearing every minute. Not one item bore any resemblance to anything that could possibly have been the weapon.

Slater was in a dangerous mood. He had known that dragging would be futile, for the simple reason that a weapon for bashing people would most likely be straight, and would therefore craftily evade the prongs of the hooks. This, no doubt, was why he'd been suspicious about the winding handle. It had a straight shank, but with a two-handed grip at a right angle at one end. Possible to use, but unwieldly.

'The bloody chief super insisted on this,' he told me tersely. 'It's got now to the point where anything could have knocked her out. Oh yes, there was rust in her hair. Her hair! Could've come from anywhere. And only a single compressed fracture on her head. She could've done it falling in. And how's a bloody weapon going to help? Anybody could've used that bloody winding handle. Nah! I'm not going to make an arrest like that. It's got to be personal. Motives. And where people were. I tell you, Patton – '

'I know, I know,' I said soothingly. 'Means and opportunity, they're the same for everybody. So, it's motives. How're you doing in that line?'

We were talking as though Gerald, one of the possible murderers, was not standing stiffly at my elbow.

'Hopeless,' Slater said. 'Too many possibilities. She wasn't liked, you know. Too much of a spitfire, Clare was. Always on the offensive. She'll have made a lot of enemies.'

'And friends,' I suggested.

'Well yes,' he said. 'Yes?' He was eyeing me cautiously, though most of my attention was still on the dragging operation. 'You know something?'

'No. Oh no.' I gave him a quick glance. He was all eagerness. 'But I thought . . . there're people who admire a woman with a bit of fire in her. And determination. And that was Clare, from what I've gathered. You know about the sister, do you? Helen . . .'

'The one in the houseboat? Yes, I know. And that's another unpleasant mess. Mustn't let it distract us, though.'

'It was Clare who got her tucked in there,' I told him. 'Clare who would've protected her, nails and knees and whatever came to hand. Now . . . I admire her. I never saw her, but I've heard enough to make me admire her.'

That was not exactly true, but close enough. No it wasn't – it was a damned lie.

'You're saying . . .' He clutched at my elbow. 'You're suggesting . . .'

I laughed at him and shrugged myself free. 'If you're talking about Helen's husband – Pierce, his name is – if you think *he* might've done it . . . well no. I wouldn't think so. He didn't *need* to kill Clare, you see. I don't think this was a hatred murder. It wasn't a killing in a burst of anger. Pierce is good at anger, I believe. But it wasn't that. Do you think it could've been, Ted? Do you?'

'Well no.'

172

'Then what?' I asked, just to find out exactly what his thoughts were.

'I think it was a necessity. She *had* to die.'

'Ah!' I said. 'Yes,' I said.

And one of his teams broke up the discussion by shouting, 'Another of those damned winding handles, Inspector.'

'That's the fourth,' he told me gloomily. 'And from the look of them, they've all been there a hundred years.'

'Quite possible,' I said. 'Quite. Even two hundred.'

And they would have rusted almost to total disintegration, but all the same, Colin would welcome them with enthusiasm. The trawling exercise might be said to have justified itself.

'And they can't lift prints from the one they've got,' Slater said gloomily. 'Nor from the thumb impressions on her neck. I've got *that* to fall back on.'

'Oh yes? And how can you use it?'

'Size,' he said. 'Size of thumb. Shape. I'll get everybody to press their thumbs into wads of putty.'

'Yes,' I said. 'Very clever. But Ted – you know, I think you're on the wrong track for a murder weapon.'

'Oh? You think that? Well now, we've got to hear this.' He spoke somewhat tersely.

I grinned at him. His temper was wearing thin.

'It's just this,' I said. 'All the fuss about winding handles as a weapon, and all the other rusty rubbish you're dragging up . . . But – why?'

'I'll tell you why – '

'It's because of the rust in her hair,' I guessed. 'Go on – admit it.'

'Well . . . yes. Of course.'

'There's no of course about it,' I told him. 'There's a bit of rusty old chain, down by that pound she was found in. Now – isn't it possible she got rust in her hair from *that*? It seems very likely to me. If she'd been pushed in . . . oh hell, Ted, imagine it for yourself.'

'Well all right.' But he wasn't pleased to concede the point. 'All right, but we've got a rusty winding handle – '

'And *why* have you got it? Simply because it was taken from the pinion it was keyed to. The one down by the bottom pound. The body in there, the winding handle removed and thrown in a lock! It's a gift. But what say – just a suggestion, Ted – what say

173

she was knocked out with something entirely different? A chunk of wood, a broken tree branch ... heavens, there're masses of things like that around here. But what if she was? Wouldn't it be a neat little trick to throw away the winding handle, just to distract attention from the real weapon?'

'Tcha!' Slater was disgusted. 'So now – what d'you expect me to do? Hunt for weapons that weren't – and then that proves they could've been? Hell, you'd drive anybody crazy.'

I smiled happily at him. Then, because Gerald's fingers on my sleeve were becoming more imperative, I allowed him to draw me away. Once he thought we were far enough from Slater, he spoke in a tensed, hushed voice, almost stumbling over his own tongue.

'That was very clever of you, Richard.'

'Was it?' I stopped, turned and stared at him. I couldn't remember being clever. 'How? In what way?'

'The way you presented your case to him in such a convincing manner, yet you gave nothing away.'

'Heh, heh!' I said. 'Easy. You don't want to get the idea that there are different objectives, theirs and ours.'

'You'd have made a splendid lawyer,' he said blandly; he hadn't even been listening.

'Gerald,' I said carefully, 'you ought to realize that there are no sides in this: them and us. You're virtually presenting your family as enemies of law and order. Yes – I know. After my behaviour with Arnold Pierce, I'm in no position to talk about law and order. But I'm willing to stick my head out and take my chances. No ... please let me finish this. You're taking an unnecessarily defensive attitude to this thing. A death has occurred. Everybody ought to be offering what information they can give to help sort it out.'

'I didn't *mean* that,' he protested.

I eyed him suspiciously, but couldn't help smiling. 'Maybe not, Gerald. But it was in your attitude. Up to now, Slater's been very easy on the whole household. But that's because he thinks he's got a better way of getting at it than harassing your family. After all, the canal's almost a right of way. And the tow-path.'

'Legally ...'

'Yes, I know. People use it as they please, yet legally, it *all* belongs to those three old dears. Whatever's been done, it's been done on their property. But it's a practical fact that the public's got access, and the public includes a hell of a lot of people.'

174

'Are you trying to tell me something, Richard?'

Yes, and it was proving very difficult to get through to him. We were standing well back, now, still able to watch what was going on but out of hearing.

'As I said,' I went on, 'Slater's got another direction from which he can approach it. There's her flat, you see. And what it might reveal. There're friends she might have had, and not simply amongst her colleagues.'

Ray, at least, would qualify as more than a colleague, and he had been desperately worried about Clare's probable intervention in his engagement party. Certainly, I didn't dare use this as an example to Gerald. Worried, Ray had been, but not desperate, surely, not murderously desperate. Colin had considered himself as engaged to Helen, but had wanted to keep it a secret. Murder, though, was a little too permanent for the keeping of such a secret. It would take it into the realms of fantasy.

'You were saying?' Gerald asked politely, and I knew I'd been thinking it over for too long.

'Yes. Sorry. I was just saying that Clare could have had friends, or ex-friends – or even bitter enemies – all of whom Slater might care to chase up when they get through examining her flat, and sifting the contents.'

'*That* is what I wanted to talk to you about,' he said mournfully,' if you'll let me get a word in, Richard. I'm one of them, you see.'

'You . . . what?'

'You haven't let me tell you,' he protested. 'You've put me off whenever I've tried to tell you about it.' He said this in a voice of deep injury, as though I'd shunned him.

'Well . . . I'm sorry, Gerald. I didn't realise.'

'So now I'll tell you. And it's been weighing on me so heavily that I've near as dammit gone insane. I told you . . . I did tell you how I managed to get a laugh out of the court at her expense. Or to her benefit, look at it how you like.'

I didn't like looking at it from any direction. 'But your client was surely found guilty, anyway,' I reminded him.

'Yes, yes, I know,' he said impatiently. 'But that's not the point.'

'Then what is?'

He glanced around, to make sure we couldn't be heard. 'She and I were on opposing sides, and you can say we were, in every sense, adversaries. Yet . . . we understood each other, there across the courtroom. It was our own little secret. Shall we say ... we respected each other.'

I looked at him doubtfully. He was being at his pedantic best. 'From two minor episodes in court?'

'Yes – that. I felt it. I thought she felt it, too. And in the lunch interval, after our second encounter, we chose the same café. She was at a table alone.'

'You mean you chose the café you'd watched her enter?'

'If you wish to put it like that,' he conceded reluctantly.

'And you joined her at her table, to make sure she didn't feel too friendless?'

'Yes. And it grew from there.'

'What grew from there?' I asked, patiently, casually, and deeply troubled.

'Our relationship. We met in court again, after that, of course. Many times. We respected each other, as I said, but we fought our different sides – and the mutual respect grew to something, well, special. Do you know what it means to find somebody you understand completely, and somebody who can understand you? When mutual admiration enters into it, and complete trust – '

'Yes, I know,' I interrupted, but gently.

'I don't believe you can, Richard. Not as I encountered it.'

'Just as you say, Gerald.'

'And it grew.'

'To greater things,' I suggested brightly, though I was feeling distinctly depressed.

'At my age, Richard! With two grown-up children, and she about Colin's age ... it sounds quite absurd, I know.'

'Not at all,' I lied politely.

'You understand?'

'Completely,' I encouraged him. Because I did.

'Yes. Well ...' He had the grace to look embarrassed. I had realized he was leading me away from the police activity, the better to express his excitement at the experience, as though he had personally discovered, or invented, this situation. We were now on the tow-path, wandering slowly along the gentle curve of it.

'It's happened before,' I told him. 'By no means unique.'

'I've heard. But it could never have been how it was for us. Oh no. You'll say I'm too old for these strange ... passions. Is that the word I want?'

176

'If it describes how you felt, yes,' I assured him.

'Felt?' he asked. 'I don't know what I felt. It overwhelmed me – it completely took possession of me.'

'And she?'

'Can we say that she enjoyed being with me, being close to me, and . . .'

'And making love to you?'

He jerked a quick glance sideways. 'How did you know that?'

'Guessed. What else would all this passion lead to – but that?'

He was silent. We stood still, not facing each other, but staring at the still water. I waited. In the end, he spoke in a quite empty voice, having dragged his mind rather desperately from his treasured memory.

'You're trying to denigrate it, Richard. That's understandable, I suppose. Nobody who hasn't felt what I did – '

'I think I might qualify.'

But I might as well not have spoken. 'Could understand what she meant to me,' he finished it.

He began to walk slowly again. I paced with him. The towpath was too narrow to allow us to walk abreast, and I was just behind his left shoulder. I felt he was waiting for my response.

'I can understand your feelings completely, Gerald,' I said. 'And appreciate them. But you're too transparent. Too naïve, really . . .'

'What're you saying?' He came to an abrupt halt, and turned to face me. His cheeks were grey, his eyes haunted.

'It was originally presented to me by Ray,' I reminded him. 'That first paltry court episode . . . it was intended as no more than a dig, because he was aware of your dislike of him. But you realized later, after Clare's death, that it did give you some sort of a motive for having killed her. But such a paltry thing, that motive was, Gerald! Ridiculous. Nobody would have taken it seriously. And then you told me you had seen her from your window. That was also very naïve. You were only trying to suggest that if you'd been at your window, you could not be down there killing her, at the same time. And I know now that you couldn't have seen her, not from where you were. Didn't see her, in fact, because you mentioned seeing her cap with the checkered band, when in fact she had lost it, even before she reached the lodge. And you knew it would be considered to be feeble – as an alibi. But Gerald . . .'

'What're you saying?' he demanded, aggressively for him. 'I *did* see her,' he insisted. 'From my window. Hanging around by the bottom lock. And she *was* wearing her checkered cap. She was! I saw her. I could take an oath on it. I didn't go down to her – but I saw her.'

'All right,' I conceded, 'you saw her. But it doesn't help. It's neither an alibi, nor anything that adds to your ability to have gone down there to kill her. What I'm trying to tell you is in relationship to a possible motive – not an alibi. You produced a feeble motive, or rather you seized on it when Ray produced it – your first court encounter with Clare – in order to hide your other very strong motive. But now you've produced *that* motive – and very impressive it is.'

'I really must protest!'

'Though you've hidden it away in a camouflage of passion, as you call it.'

'How could I – '

'And now you're going to say that you couldn't have killed a woman that you loved so much.'

'Richard! How dare you!'

He had raised himself to his most distinguished height, his chin jutting and his cheeks flushed.

'I dare, because it's what you wanted me to say. Right. So I've said it. You could not have killed Clare – for whom you felt such a glorious passion. There. Does that suit you?'

'You don't – '

'Don't understand? Of course I don't. I'm a stupid, blundering ex-copper, so how could I possibly understand? Passion – you call it. Where I come from, it's called sex.'

'I . . . I . . .'

'And Gerald – you've offered this passion as a proof that you couldn't have killed her. Nonsense! There're more crimes based on sex than on anything else. Passion! It's passion that kills, Gerald, you poor idiot.'

'You don't understand.' He was gesticulating wildly. I had to watch that he didn't forget where his feet were in relation to the edge of the tow-path.

'Oh . . . I think I do understand,' I assured him. 'Only too well. You're having to cover for yourself, before people start asking around as to whose child she'd been bearing.'

He grabbed at my arm. 'What?' The colour had drained from his cheeks.

'She was two months pregnant, Gerald. Didn't she tell you? Or did you rely on the assumption that you're too old ... and that there'd be nothing to tell?'

'I ... I didn't.'

'But you're not too old, Gerald, and she *would* have told you. Eventually.'

Yes, she would, if she'd been sufficiently certain, out of the group she had similarly entertained, who was in fact the father. Indeed, it might have been a choice made on the question of who, amongst them, might be forced to contribute most towards her own and the child's welfare. Gerald, as a solicitor, would clearly have been near the front in that race. Yet, equally clearly, she had not informed him of her pregnancy.

Or so he intended me to believe!

'I ... I don't understand what you're trying to say.' He was waving his arms around frantically, and in danger of disturbing his physical as well as his emotional balance.

I sighed for him. 'Gerald, I'm trying to get across to you that she'd have had you by the throat. She could have choked you for your last gasp of maintenance. If you resisted, she could have ruined your treasured reputation, and ruined your home life. So she was in a position where she simply *had* to be removed.'

He was able to produce nothing now but a meaningless gabble. In court, he would not have been recognized.

'But maybe this won't reach Slater's ears,' I encouraged him. 'If it's any comfort, certainly not from me, because I know of at least one other man who could have fathered that child. At least. But ...'

I held up one hand in case he was intending to offer any comment.

'But ...' I said. 'If you'll turn round, you'll see the houseboat in which Clare's sister was staying. Hiding, if you like. This was a woman who was beaten up, and couldn't really look after herself – and you've seen that for yourself. And because she wanted her child with her, Clare took Dennis to her. A good and sisterly act, you would say? But Gerald – Clare left them. This was the evening of the storm, you realize. It'd just blown itself out. But Clare left them, without heat, it seems, a very nearly incapable woman, at that time, and a child too young to help. And Clare did – what? Nothing. She left them. And don't tell me she had no chance because she was killed before she could take any action, because that's not true. She had to pass your bar lounge, on the way back to where she'd left her car, and she did pass it, because she was clearly killed the far side of the footbridge. But did she look in? Did she ask for help, or to use the phone? No. In effect, she abandoned her sister and Dennis, calmly and coldly. She walked away from them, and by heaven, if I hadn't happened to walk past there the next morning ... damn it, Gerald, Helen would surely have died, because it was later that night that Pierce came along and gave her another beating.'

He was holding up his palm to stop me, but I ignored that.

'And what about Dennis? Think of *him*, damn you. As it happens, his father came along and collected him. But ... what if he hadn't taken him away? Ask yourself that. So don't come bleating to me to get you out of your paltry little difficulties, because I shan't be listening.'

I had been laying it on rather heavily, and on purpose. I hadn't seen much sign in him of grief for Clare. But if he did mourn her, maybe I'd helped to ease that a little.

I turned without another word, and walked away from him.

14

We were sitting together, Amelia and I, at her favourite corner table in the bar lounge, discussing the situation.

The house was strangely quiet, but outside were the splashes of tossed-in hooks, and the shouts of Ted Slater's team. I was no longer interested in their success or otherwise, because I was convinced that there was no weapon to be found in there.

I was still somewhat upset about Clare's behaviour.

'But she *did* take food to her,' Amelia pointed out. 'We saw that.'

'Yes, yes. And perhaps Helen wasn't in such bad shape at that time.' I was finding myself seizing on any minor point in Clare's favour, finding it so difficult to accept her character as being as bad as I'd drawn it for Gerald, though of course I had exaggerated it to him.

'And', said Amelia, understanding what I was reaching for, 'you've got to remember that Arnold Pierce came for the lad, that same evening.' She meant, after the pub shut.

'But how would he know where to come?' I demanded.

'I don't know that.' She was being very patient with me. 'What I'm trying to say is that Helen could have been very much more fit and capable before her husband came and took Dennis away.'

'Than she was after?'

I stared at my clenched fist, wishing I'd given it even more exercise than I had. It ached as I clenched it. Ached for more action?

'And of course,' I said, 'the whole business with the abandoned car was entirely different from what I originally thought.'

'What was that?'

'I rather imagined Clare, with Arnold Pierce beside her and with a knife to her ribs. I know now that he *does* carry a knife, but ... well, I thought he was forcing her to take him to wherever Helen was hidden, so that he could take Dennis home with him. I just had it backwards, that's all. Now I see that it was Clare and Ray who were *bringing* Dennis. And I mean, it all fits the timing, Ray being there, still in uniform. They'd both just come off duty, with Ray just in time for drinks before dinner, Clare delivering Dennis to his mother.'

'And Clare ...'

'Clare was killed on her way back to where she'd left her car.'

'Killed by whom?' Amelia gets right to the core of things.

'I don't know. And it's just about driving me crazy.' I thumped the table with my fist. 'I want to walk around breaking things.'

She tried to laugh, to make a joke of it, but it was a poor thing.

'Or throw things,' I compromised.

'If you want something to throw, why don't you go outside and start throwing that rubbish back into the locks,' she suggested.

'They'd take me into custody. Slap handcuffs on me. Unlawful disposal of litter.'

Now her laugh was a more wholesome thing.

I was beginning to feel more relaxed, and reached for my pipe. From behind me, Ruby said, 'What on earth have you been saying to Gerald, Richard?'

I got to my feet and turned to face her. She seemed flushed, her eyes too bright. 'Nothing much,' I tried to assure her. 'He asked for some advice and I gave it to him. I hadn't intended to upset him.' But oh yes, I had!

'Well, he *is* upset. I've sent him out with a list of shopping, to

181

set his mind on something else. To tell you the truth, I hadn't catered for the old people. There was no reason why I should, but all this . . . this chaos . . .' She flung her arms around a little. 'I find it all most unsettling.'

'Oh Ruby,' said Amelia, 'you should have said. We came for no more than an overnight stay. I'm sorry.'

Ruby grimaced. 'Now you're being quite ridiculous, Amelia. You know very well that you're always welcome . . .' And she cut herself off abruptly, twisting round with a start as the swing doors were flung open, and Colin stood there, dramatically holding them wide, one hand to each door.

'You'll never guess!' he cried heatedly. 'Not in a month of Sundays. Go on. Have a guess.' This he directed at me.

There was only one answer to that. 'You've just said it can't be done. So come on – out with it.'

He drew a deep breath. 'The buggers have given it up, and driven off to wherever they hide away – and left me to get rid of all their rubbish.'

'The police, you mean?' I asked.

At this point (the question not requiring an answer anyway) the three old dears came wandering in, and Adolphus, as their representative, spoke with chilling authority.

'Colin! Poor Alexandra has just looked out of her window. What *is* all that ugly rubbish lying around outside? It's a perfect eyesore. Get rid of it at once.'

Colin stared at me in desperation. He was no doubt now regretting that he'd ever thought of the idea of welding up his three-pronged hook. He had landed what had turned out to be no more than bait, and the predators had descended to scavenge the carcass.

'I . . . I . . .' Colin gabbled.

I got to my feet. 'It's all right. It's not Colin's fault. The police are investigating a serious and suspicious crime, Adolphus. A death. It gives them authority to search for evidence, and those unsightly piles outside consist of what they've found. And it was a useless waste of time, as it turned out.'

'Then', he declared severely, 'they should have taken their rubbish with them.'

I glanced at Amelia for support, but she had a hand clasped over her mouth, and her eyes were sparkling above it. So I had to manage myself.

182

'I'm sorry to tell you, Adolphus, that it isn't their rubbish – it's yours.'

'Well now ...' cried Victoria, making swinging gestures with one arm. 'That will just have to be clarified. Legally. Gerald! Where's Gerald?'

'He's gone shopping,' said Ruby.

'He has no right to go shopping,' declared Alexandra. 'Isn't that so, my dear?' she asked her sister.

'Now ... now,' put in Adolphus. 'I couldn't be certain about that. We do not employ him, Alexandra. It's Colin we employ. Colin. Colin, where are you?'

'Here,' said Colin, from behind my shoulder.

'Then Colin,' said Adolphus firmly, 'why aren't you outside, clearing away that unsightly pile of rubbish?'

'Three piles,' corrected Victoria, nodding.

Colin drew a deep breath. 'Ladies,' he said, 'and you, sir, I have something much more important to talk to you about than three piles of rubbish. I'd like us to go into the dining room, where there are comfortable seats and quiet, and where it's warm. If you don't mind.'

They stared at him. It was possibly the first time he had given them instructions, although they had been presented in the form of a request, and so very politely.

'But what is this about, my dear boy?' asked Adolphus.

'That's what I want to tell you. If you don't mind,' he repeated.

He went and stood by the door into the hall, opened it, and stood aside for them to precede him.

They looked at each other, eyebrows raised. Adolphus gave an almost imperceptible nod, and with massive dignity Victoria and Alexandra led the way. Once again, Colin managed to reach the door first and hold it open. Then, as he looked past them and saw that Amelia and I were hovering on the verge of following, he smiled, winked, and gave a little nod.

This I interpreted as an invitation to follow them in, and eavesdrop. Amelia was reluctant, but I urged her inside, and while the four of them were settling into the easy chairs that we – the four men – had used on the night of the engagement party, we slipped around the perimeter to a location where we faced Colin, and the three old dears had their backs to us.

'Now .. what *is* this, Colin?' asked Victoria. 'Do you have to be so mysterious?'

'It's the first chance I've had to get the three of you together, and where we can speak confidentially.'

They looked around at each other, then Victoria spoke again for them.

'Well – carry on, Colin. You can trust us, and you know that, my dear boy.'

Colin smiled. 'Of course I can. But for once we might not see eye to eye.'

They looked in astonishment at each other, then back to Colin, politely expectant.

'It's about Helen,' said Colin, leaning forward with his knees apart, elbows on them, his hands up beside his face to make gestures of emphasis.

'Dear child,' murmured Alexandra. 'So sweet.'

'Yes.' Colin grinned. 'Isn't she? And very sweet to me, I assure you. Now look – you must have realized that I was the one who let her use the houseboat as a hiding place from her husband. You do understand that?'

He had to wait until the three sets of eyes traversed around their group, and in some way signalled agreement. Then: 'We do,' said Adolphus, nodding.

'Right.' Colin beamed at them. 'Then you might have guessed that it wasn't just because her sister, Clare, was a friend of mine that I had Helen here. Well . . . not here. Father wouldn't have cared for that, but at the boat. No? You hadn't realized? Well, you ought to know – you have to know – that it's because Helen and I love each other, and we want to get married.'

The two ladies gasped, and Adolphus pointed out, 'But she's already married, Colin, my dear boy.'

'She wants to be rid of him, as you very well know. And . . .' He smiled around. 'And you dear people have done so much for her, just by offering her your home, and your love. She wants you to know . . . *we* want you to know how grateful we both are for the offer. But . . .'

'But, Colin?' asked Adolphus, lifting his head abruptly.

'But it wouldn't work, sir. Helen's a town girl. This house here, Flight House, is the sort of country she would be happy to live in. Fields and trees and the valley all round us – and the canal. She loves all this, as I do. And the town within reach. Ladies, sir, I want to marry her, and adopt Dennis – if that's legally necessary. I don't know about that.'

184

'But ... Colin!' Alexandra had her hand to her lips. A hint of distress had entered her voice. 'The child, Colin – Dennis?'

Colin positively grinned. 'Naughty thoughts, Miss Alexandra? No, Dennis is not my lad. I wish he was – but no. But I want him to be. Legally. And Helen to be my wife. And ... here. You do understand – it would break my heart if I had to leave here. But, if you will not agree to this, to having Helen and Dennis here until the divorce is through, and then my marrying Helen ... well, then I'll have to give you notice – '

'Colin,' burst in Adolphus sharply. 'What *is* this ridiculous talk of giving notice? We couldn't possibly manage – '

Victoria leaned forward and put a hand on his knee. 'Now Fussy, he doesn't mean that. You don't really mean that, Colin?'

'Only if you disagreed.'

They glanced at each other, but Colin got in first.

'I'm sure you were really looking forward to having Helen and Dennis with you – and I'm very sorry – but truly, she'd not be happy on your estate. Not after the initial delight, she wouldn't. So I'm asking you what you think.'

They did another of their mind-reading acts, nodded at each other, and Fussy spoke for them. It was the first time I'd heard their pet name for him, but it fitted him so well. Now he fluffed about with his hands, and did a lot of hems and haws, then he said, 'You must know, Colin, that we wouldn't want to lose you – we rely absolutely on you. So, do it as you wish, you and the dear young lady, and the boy, Dennis. If it'll make you happy, though I've never quite understood – '

'Fussy!' said Victoria gently. 'Of course they must be together.'

And Colin smiled. 'Thank you.'

'And here,' said Fussy.

'But ...' Alexandra touched her lips with one finger. 'Your own family, Colin – Ruby and Gerald and Mellie. I'm *sure* Gerald will not be pleased.'

'Then,' said Colin, raising his eyebrows, 'he'll have to put up with it – won't he!'

And they laughed. Then they got to their feet, Colin kissed two rather lined but flushed cheeks, and shook a crumpled and bony hand, and a contract had been sealed, in a way the family understood. Brindley had probably shaken hands with every one of his Navvies, though perhaps had not kissed their cheeks.

Quietly, Amelia and I slipped out, but hesitated at the door to hear the last part of it.

'And now, Colin,' said Adolphus, 'perhaps you can get outside and see about that mess the police have left.'

We were therefore back in the bar when Colin swept past us, on his way to the locks. He put up a victorious thumb. Full of bounce and energy, was Colin. Then came the wump, wump of the swing doors behind him, but he was not intending actually to do any clearing.

For that, he would need a very large rubbish-clearance wagon, and the assistance of a throng of muscular men. No ... not to do anything, just to stand out there with his beloved flight, with which he would not now need to part, and if he felt like it – as he probably did – dance a jig from one end to the other and shout out his happiness to the open sky.

Amelia and I followed him discreetly, and found him talking to Mellie and Ray, who had been surveying the rubbish piles, though not too seriously, I gathered.

It was no doubt a humorous situation, depending on your point of view. The rubbish had been doing no harm, slopping away in a about a foot of mud beneath, at the least, five feet of water. Now it was distinctly an eyesore. But it seemed farcical that Colin should get rid of it simply by heaving it back where it had come from. Fortunately, the three piles stood by their respective locks, and on the far side from the house. There was not much sign of healthy green visible beneath them at that moment, but at least, if the rubbish could not be disposed of at once, that was the best place for it. It was well clear of being tripped over or walked into, at night, as nobody had any reason for being over there.

'You could,' I suggested to Colin, 'simply leave it where it is. Call it a work of art. Put up a plaque and give it a name. Detritus. How about that? Art experts would flock here. Directors from every Art Gallery and Museum in the country would crave for it. You could hold an auction, and the highest bidder would have to take it away – and it would cost you nothing, Colin. In fact ... no, you wouldn't gain. The money would have to go to the family, as it's their rubbish. Though they might prefer to leave it ...'

'Richard!' Amelia prodded me in the ribs with a finger.

'Yes love?'

'Behave yourself.'

I winked at her. But Gerald was now with us, and would not

have appreciated my suggestion. He came walking round the house, carrying two large carrier bags, one in each hand.

'What on earth's going on here?' he demanded to know. 'Oh – there you are, Colin. What *is* all this?'

Colin sighed. 'The police have been dragging the locks for a possible weapon. Clare's death, dad.'

'I know they have. And did they find it?'

'No. Nothing.'

'There you are, then. Get on the phone and tell them to come and collect their rubbish.'

Colin clearly found the situation amusing. I saw his lips twitch. 'I'm afraid it's ours, dad.'

'What! Is it? Hmm! Perhaps so. I'll look it up. Yes. Perhaps we could get them under the Litter Act. Am I right, Richard? The Litter Act, 1983. It is an offence – '

Ruby said, from behind him, 'Now Gerald! It's not the time for you to be spouting your precious law.'

He dismissed the subject. 'That store you sent me to was packed, Ruby. I had to queue for ages, just to pay for these few items.'

'Gerald!' cut in Ruby briskly. 'Will you please go and take that shopping into the house ... oh, Mellie, do take your father into the kitchen, and show him where to put everything. You know he's quite helpless and useless.'

Mellie grimaced at me, and Ray, remaining behind because he'd not had instructions otherwise, gave me a wink.

'Stay a while,' I said to him.

'Oh ... sure. I'll be here, Mellie.'

She didn't look at him as she turned to follow her father. I wondered what could have happened between them.

'I wanted a word with you, Ray,' I told him.

'Sure, sure.' His favourite word.

'You're not supposed to be on duty, I hope.'

'No,' he said. 'Later.'

'They'll have to get you another partner.'

'I suppose they will.'

'Another woman?' I asked casually. 'Would you prefer to work with a woman, Ray?'

'What?' He seemed startled at the question. 'No. Not particularly,' he said, as I nodded encouragement.

'You'd never get another woman as good as Clare, anyway?' I made it a question.

He frowned, feeling I was leading him into a trap. 'She was a good copper,' he said warily.

'A good woman?'

Now everybody seemed to want to stand out in the rather weak sunlight. They gathered just outside the swing doors, the better to observe the art exhibit as an entirety, but standing back, perhaps because they were aware that I was exchanging quiet words with Ray.

He was shaking his head, and hadn't answered my question.

'I've had very different opinions on Clare, Ray,' I told him. 'From different people. I was rather wondering what yours would be.'

'We got along fine together.'

He made a movement to turn away, but I caught at his arm. With an abrupt flash of angry impatience he turned back. 'What the hell *is* this?'

He was trying to keep his eyes on Mellie, who had returned from helping her father put away the groceries. There was something reserved in her attitude, something that made Ray uneasy. She was hanging back, hesitant and worried. Dennis was clinging to her hand. He had recognized in me the strange man who had made his poppa lie down on his face, and who was looking as though about to make another man, whom he knew, do the same. His eyes were huge, he uncertain whether to be afraid or excited. Bruce sat at his feet.

Mellie asked, raising her voice a little, 'What's Richard asking, Ray?'

'God knows what he's after. He's always waving around his ideas. And what's the present idea, Richard?' he asked me, none too politely.

'It's just something I can't get clear in my mind. That night ... Do you mind if I remind you, Ray? No? All right, I'll go on, then. The night of the storm. Evening, rather – it was only just after five. Clare and you picked up Dennis and loaded him into her car, and brought him here. I don't want to ask him what he remembers – '

'Now ... Richard.' That was Amelia. She hates to hear me doing this kind of questioning. Pressuring, she calls it, but I thought I was being very casual.

'Ray's not protesting,' I pointed out. 'You don't mind, Ray? Of course you don't. Nothing to be ashamed of, was it, Ray. An errand of mercy, that's what it was. Weren't you and Clare doing exactly what her sister, Helen, had asked?'

'Well yes ... yes, it'd been Helen who'd asked. She'd said she wanted Dennis with her. Naturally, she was worried about him. It wasn't my idea. Damn it all, when we got him there to the boat, well, quite frankly Helen didn't seem up to scratch to me.'

'Up to scratch?'

'Well ... call it capable. Not really capable of looking after Denny, I thought.'

The impression was that we were alone. There was not a sound from the others. Even Dennis, somewhat repressed by the general atmosphere, was very quiet. He had heard his own name mentioned. It was all very puzzling. Bruce sat quietly beside him, his head cocked.

'Not really capable.' I repeated his words. 'With a broken wrist and two front teeth knocked out – and you thought she wasn't really up to scratch! Damn it all, Ray, she probably couldn't even stand. *Did* she stand?'

'Well – yes.' He looked round, as though for witnesses. 'She wasn't anything like what you're saying. There was nothing wrong with her teeth, or her wrist. Not at that time, there wasn't.'

'And so you thought she was capable? And you left him there, with his mother? You *did* leave him there?'

He stared at me as though I was insane. 'Well yes, of course. It was what Helen wanted.'

'So you'd made her happy?'

'What?'

'Happy. It was what she'd asked. You and Clare had made the delivery, so everybody was happy.'

'Yes.' He made a hissing sound out of it. 'And it was me who made the delivery. On my own for the last bit. Clare didn't want to see Helen. Said she made her sick, being such a weak ninny. Anyway, she'd seen her once that day. She took her groceries, in the morning.'

There was now absolute silence around us. Nobody really understood what I was getting at, or what Ray was saying. They couldn't realise that it was important. So there was silence. Not entire silence, though, as there was shouting in the distance, though I could not locate it, but for now I didn't want to relax my concentration on Ray.

'But Ray,' I said. 'All that trouble for you and Clare . . . oh yes, I was forgetting to ask about that. How did you manage to get hold of Dennis, you and Clare? I mean – in order to bring him to the houseboat.'

'Clare knew how to do it. We picked him up from Mrs Lloyd's, next door but one. She was the woman who looked after Dennis when the dad was away. Pierce. Away at work, and Helen out shopping, say. He's a bricklayer.'

'Ah, I see. And looked after him when Helen was incapable of doing it. Is that what you mean?'

Ray straightened his shoulders. 'Yes. Then. Those times. Too.'

'So all right.' And who the devil was that, doing all the shouting? 'So you brought Dennis to the houseboat. On the evening of the storm. During it, in fact, you brought Dennis here. Carrying him, I suppose? Taking turns, you and Clare? Down the lane – not the tow-path?'

I waited for his nod. He simply stared. I accepted this as agreement.

'But the next morning,' I said, 'he was gone. He wasn't there when I discovered Helen. Now, tell me, Ray . . . how could that have come about? How did Pierce find out about the houseboat? He didn't know before, or he'd have come for Helen. He came for Dennis that night, along the tow-path from Crayminster. That same night. What had been a secret, all of a sudden became something he knew in detail. So . . . how, Ray, how?'

Ray darted glances around him, as though seeking escape. I knew that he was searching for Mellie, to gauge from her expression what she was thinking about all this. But Mellie hung back, her face white, her eyes huge, her hand clutching Denny's possessively.

Woodenly, and barely moving his lips, Ray said, 'I wouldn't know – would I!'

'You didn't, either you or Clare, happen to mention to Mrs Lloyd where you were taking him?'

'Of course not. Ask yourself, Richard.'

'I'm asking you, Ray. You're the one who's got all the answers. And the answer I'm trying to get from you is how Arnold Pierce got to know where Helen and Dennis were hiding.'

'I don't know.' He shook his head violently.

I persisted with it. 'Only two people knew about the houseboat. You and Clare. No . . . three, if we count Colin, and *he* didn't know you'd brought along Dennis to his houseboat. And then Clare died, so that left only you, Ray.'

He shook his head stubbornly. 'I don't know how he found out.'

Now the shouting was very close. I had to take notice of it.

'Denny! Where's my Denny?'

They parted, the group that had drifted closer, and now edged back towards the house. As far as the three old dears were concerned, their actions were those of revulsion. Pierce, in the poor lighting of his own home, had not been very pleasant to behold. Now – in bright daylight – he was quite revolting. It was needless to guess that he hadn't had his clothes off the previous night. I had done so much damage to his vicious hands that he probably wouldn't have been able to undress, anyway. But when he tried to force himself into a run – and I hadn't harmed his legs – it was in fact a shamble. He hadn't washed and he hadn't shaved.

Whatever force that now drove him on (and I couldn't credit him with any affection for the lad) brought him stumbling along the tow-path to a point from which he could make his demands most forcefully, and facing the complete group of his enemies.

Because I had gradually moved closer to the house, so that nobody would miss a word of my conversation to Ray, it now left an obvious place for Pierce to use, to stop and stand with his legs apart, and stare balefully around an unsympathetic group of faces, his back to the centre lock.

There he stood, swaying.

15

'I want my Denny.' His voice was hoarse. I heard Mellie give a small and frantic cry, but she was well behind me.

I said, 'You can't have him, Pierce. You're not fit to have control of a child. You're not really fit to go on living.'

I advanced a pace towards him, and jabbed a finger in emphasis in the general direction of his chest. He backed a pace, a clumsy shuffle.

'You keep yer bloody hands to yerself,' he shouted. 'Got witnesses now, I have.'

I hesitated. I couldn't hit him, when I knew he was unable to use his hands. I prodded a finger towards his chest.

'Look at all them witnesses,' he cried. 'All the pretty ladies an' gennelmen. Witnesses. They'll say – you'm pushin' me. Violence, that's what it is. All I want's me lad.'

'How did you know about the houseboat?' I asked. Another little prod, not reaching him by a good foot, but it provoked another shuffle backwards. 'How did you know where to come to get Denny?'

'I bloody-well knew.'

'How?'

'Bugger off. Gimme the lad.'

Mellie produced another sharp eek. Pierce's eyes probed past me, towards the sound. 'There he is. Bring him here, me luvvie.'

Bruce growled, deep in his throat.

And Mellie – I caught the movement on the edge of my vision – captured and hypnotized by fear, took a step forward. So did I.

I didn't touch him, didn't need to, because his heels had reached the curved edges of the coping stones, and now they went an inch too far. With a scream, his arms flung wide, he fell backwards into the lock.

There was an almighty splash as he hit the water flat on his back, odd chunks of it rising high enough to splash on my trousers. The fall from edge to water was about eight feet. He plunged around wildly, but his feet would be able to contact nothing solid. Mud down there, surely. I had guessed at a foot of it. Certainly, it would not have felt like a firm surface, and he splashed with the frantic windmilling of arms that denotes a non-swimmer.

'Can't swim!' he cried out. 'Help me!'

'Help yourself,' I shouted back.

'Richard!' Amelia was now at my shoulder.

'He's safe enough, love,' I assured her. 'They always fit iron ladders, just in case anybody should fall in. Look. There's one right behind him. Fastened to the wall.'

In fact, it was six inches clear of the surface, in order to allow room for fingers.

'Oh yes . . . yes,' said Amelia.

'There's a ladder right by you,' I called out. 'At your shoulder. You can climb up.'

Splluttering and gasping, he struggled round for a sight of the ladder, and reached it, then raised his head and stared up at me, as I walked across to stand at the head of it. His face was distorted with terror, a mirror image of the many faces that had stared back at him in his time. Then I realized what his basic difficulty was. After the treatment I had given his hands, he was quite incapable of gripping the rungs.

For one moment I felt a chill, all down my back. I had no wish to watch somebody drown, not even this useless oaf.

'I'll have to go down to him,' I told Amelia. Though I couldn't see in what way I would be able to help him.

'No, Richard. I forbid that.'

I looked into her eyes. 'Forbid?'

'Yes, yes.' And this time she really meant it.

I smiled at her. 'He'll find a way.'

And as we had been exchanging these comments, he had. With his elbows crooked, he was hooking them over the iron rungs, and gradually climbing. Slowly and painfully. I watched.

Then I looked round, wondering where I might expect help. Not one of the group had moved. It was as though a spell had turned them to stone. The three oldies wore the identical expressions of offended distress that I'd noted before, but they did not turn away. Revulsion held them. Ruby was clasping Gerald's arm tightly, and leaned against him. Colin stood with his arms hanging loose, hands knotted into fists, which he had prepared just in case he found need to use them. Ray was a yard behind me, his face expressionless, and Mellie held back, Denny's hand in hers, and might have been cast in clay – in a rather white clay.

Pierce came up the ladder slowly. He must have been very nearly incapable of movement, first from the shock of the immersion, then from the wet clothes clinging to his flesh. I knew how it would be for him. But his elbow movements became more and more laboured, his face more and more distorted with effort and fear. My face, poised above him, must have offered him no comfort. Rope, I thought. But there was no time in which to search out rope. Yet ... slowly he mounted, until he reached the top rung. It was six inches below safety. He stopped, no doubt expecting me to lift him the last foot by grasping him around the wrists. The curved coping stones offered him no grip, even if his hands had been fully operative.

I stared down at him. I believe I smiled.

'Help me,' he whispered hoarsely.

Bruce, abandoning Dennis, came to the edge and snarled into his face.

'A question,' I said. 'Maybe two. Answer and I'll pull you up.'

'Richard!' Amelia appealed.

'It's known as extraction of evidence under duress,' I explained. 'Not admissable in court, but never mind.'

'Gerron an' say it, for Chrissake!' Pierce croaked.

'How did you know where to go in order to collect Dennis?' I asked.

'The boat . . .'

'Yes, I know that. But who told you?'

'Phone call . . .'

'You're not on the phone. Where?'

'Pub. The Blue Boar.'

'Phoned you at the Blue Boar?'

His teeth were chattering. He nodded.

'Who phoned you?'

'Ray.'

'Ray phoned?'

'Yes.'

'Say it good and loud. Who phoned?'

'Ray, for God's sake. Ray.'

'Right.' I crouched down, my knees protesting. I had offered him assistance, but now there was a distraction. It was a scream, a stifled and choked scream. In this situation I found it difficult to look round. Pierce croaked, 'For Chrissake!' I managed just to turn my head.

Ray was standing directly behind me, staring back towards the house. It was Mellie who had screamed, Mellie who had now released Dennis's hand, needing both hands to tear the ring from her finger, but only one in order to hurl it at Ray's head. Like a fool, he ducked. Women are notoriously bad at throwing. This time, as it happened, and unfortunately, she would have hit him directly in the face. But he ducked, and the ring sailed past his head, to make a small and insignificant plop into the lock.

'For pity's sake!' whispered Pierce.

I kneeled now, muscles and bones crying out, my balance not secure, not certain I could manage it. Got my hands clasped around his forearms, and now both of us were groaning. 'Don't struggle,' I gasped. He would have had us both in.

'Richard!' Amelia screamed, and I felt her hands grasping my coat, pulling, pulling. I reached lower and hooked hands beneath his armpits. 'Now!' I shouted at him. 'Climb, damn you.' Then Colin was clutching at my one shoulder, Gerald at the other. 'Climb!' I cried. 'Your legs, man, use your legs. That's it. Another step.' I shuffled backwards. Amelia nearly had the coat off me. 'Climb,' I groaned, and Bruce barked frantically into Pierce's agonized face.

And he came up, one painful heave at a time, until I rolled over, Amelia scrambling free, and Colin and Gerald got an arm each and hoisted him out, dumping him, face down and gasping, beside me.

Gerald, who had been so afraid of this creature, was now grinning in triumph at having saved him, and Colin, stolid, was unmoved but smiling. 'Good show, pop,' he said, and his father slapped him on the shoulder.

Then, grappling with each other, we helped ourselves to our feet, and we stood, looking down at the sodden wreck at our feet.

I felt fine. Strangely, the feeling was very like the hectic triumph with which I'd beaten him the evening before.

Beyond Ray's stiff shoulders, I could see that Mellie was now standing at the half-open swing doors, Denny's hand still firmly grasped in hers, and Bruce now peering round the closed half. She was staring her last agonized farewell to Ray. Then she was inside, and the door did its wump-wump.

Beside me, Pierce was stirring. I said to Gerald, 'Anywhere you can dry him off, before he catches pneumonia?' I didn't want man and wife in the same hospital at the same time, however much their wards might be separated.

'There's the old Gents, through the back.'

'There, then. Dry him off – and if you've got any old clothes . . .'

'There's a pair of corduroys in my wardrobe, dad,' said Colin. 'And that old hacking jacket – and some old shirts in the drawer. You'll find something.'

'And we can send him home, all clean and tidy,' I said.

So . . . with Gerald tentatively clutching an elbow, and Adolphus gently fingering a lapel, they took him, unsteady, inside. Victoria and Alexandra were giggling behind their hands at this audacious venture on the part of their brother. Pierce was assisted through the bar.

I realized that I had been left alone with Ray, apart from Amelia, who was keenly aware of the tension between Ray and myself and prepared to intervene.

'Well Ray?' I asked, turning to him. 'You realize – do you – that you've now put yourself into the position of being the only one in close contact with Clare, at the time she died. You came here, with Clare and Dennis. You went with them to the boat, and delivered Dennis to Helen. All as planned. Then you walked back to here, to the locks. Then what?'

He simply stared at me, with a despair that was mainly based on Mellie's action of angry rejection. But I realized now what burden he had been carrying, every moment of that evening. That evening! It seemed so long ago.

'Ray,' I said, 'it seems very clear that you walked back with her after delivering Dennis to Helen. Back to the lower pound . . .'

I realized that I was repeating myself, but he didn't seem to be taking in what I had said.

He interrupted abruptly. Now that he knew there was no way out for him, he was going to make sure of his own situation being presented accurately. He was going to tell me the exact truth.

I looked beyond him. One of the swing doors was open a foot or so. Somebody was watching, listening, from behind it. It had to be Mellie. I didn't tell Ray, who had now begun pouring it out – but I wished she wasn't there.

'You never understood Clare, did you?' said Ray with a lofty contempt. 'Not really. You never ever met her – alive. And that's just the word. Alive, Richard, full of life and energy and the joy of living. And she had guts. Nobody, absolutely nobody, would ever get the best of her, physically or verbally. She was a fighter, Richard. Pierce, that lout they're now tidying up, he'd have stood no chance with her, if it'd come to it. If he'd raised one hand to her, she'd have had him in agony on his back in a second. And Helen . . . she was so different. Never fought back. Clare hated her, you know.'

'Hated?' said Amelia. 'Her sister?'

Ray shrugged. 'Had contempt for her, if you like. She was always on at Helen. "Get the bastard with a knife," she told her. "Go for his guts." As though Helen could've been even remotely capable of doing such a thing! No imagination, Clare hadn't got. Not a bit.'

'But Ray . . .' Amelia touched his arm, a signal for me to let her take it on. I smiled at her.

'But Ray,' she said. 'Clare *did* help her. She took Dennis to her. You can't deny that. It wasn't your doing, was it? Clare's idea, surely.'

'Sort of.' He looked from one face to the other. 'But most of the work – that was me.'

'Explain, Ray,' I said. 'I'm not getting a clear picture.'

'Aw . . . the hell with it. Clare came early in the day. *That* day. Brought groceries, you know. And Helen said she wanted Dennis. Well . . . from what Helen said when I got him there, she'd asked her before, but Clare had done nothing about it. This time, I suppose, she thought we'd do something about it. I would, that is. Get Dennis for her. That wasn't going to be all that difficult, because we knew Dennis would be with Mrs Lloyd. Poor old dear, she got lumbered with him all the time, but she said he was company. I wouldn't have thought an old lady'd want a kid around, but she didn't seem to mind. Anyway, all we had to do, Clare and me, was go to Mrs Lloyd and pick him up. Pierce wouldn't be home for ages.'

'Home? He's a bricklayer. Surely they wouldn't be working in *that* sort of weather – what we had that day.'

I glanced at Amelia. She simply shook her head gently. I took that to mean: don't question it – let Ray say it. So I did.

'They seem to be able to find something to do, whatever the weather. In any event, we just told Mrs Lloyd we were taking Dennis to his mother, and she said it was about time, too. And we took Dennis along. Of course, he knew Clare. Auntie Clare, she was to him. So – no difficulty.'

He stopped. His eyes were wandering. Where was Mellie? He wanted to get to Mellie.

'You said, no difficulty,' I reminded him.

'Well . . . yeah. There shouldn't have been. But all of a sudden it was sort of *my* idea. I thought I knew Clare, but now, abruptly, she seemed to be backing off. On the drive here, oh – she was grumbling all the while. It was *me* who'd fixed up the boat for Helen, fixed it up with Colin. We'd worked it out together. Me who picked her up and brought her.'

'Now Ray,' put in Amelia, 'you make it sound all straight-forward, so why didn't you bring Dennis with you, at the time? With Helen.'

'Aw hell!' he said, provoked by the memory. 'He wasn't there. Wasn't.'

'Then where was he?' I asked. 'Round at Mrs Lloyd's?'

'No, no. That would've been a doddle. Pierce had got him. This was an afternoon, you see. A Saturday afternoon. Just me. Clare'd parked her car around the corner, and said she didn't want to get involved, so she stayed in the car. She was going all funny on me, and didn't want to do it, after all. I was beginning to worry about Clare. A month before, I'd have matched her against anybody, but now ... well, she seemed scared of getting the wrong side of Pierce. Scared! That was what really worried me. I couldn't do it, without Clare, for back-up, you know. But there I was, all worked up to take Helen and Dennis away, and Dennis not there. But I just *had* to get Helen away. And Dennis wasn't there, and Clare was acting funny, just sitting in the car. Oh hell, it was just a bloody mess. Helen in tears. Grabbing some of her clothes to take, and stuffin' 'em in a plastic bag, and all the while weeping 'cause of Dennis. And me all worked up to do it. It was then or never – and in the end she came with me.'

'And where *was* Dennis?' I asked. 'If he wasn't at home.'

'His father had taken him down to the Blue Boar.'

'A little lad? To a pub?'

'Well ... Pierce'd got hold of an air pistol, and he took Dennis along. Him and his mates were going to have a go at shooting rats in the yard at the back. He thought Dennis would enjoy that.'

'I see,' I said. 'Yes, I see.'

It was now very silent around us, with not a sign of anybody keeping an eye on us or an ear behind a partly open door. The swing doors were firmly closed.

'Go on,' I said. My voice sounded flat to me.

'I got Helen in the car,' he said, 'Clare didn't say a word. I got in the back with Helen. Most of the way she was crying, grabbing my arm and leaning against me. And Clare ... she said she had no patience with her. Said Helen should've taken a kitchen knife to him. The same old thing. All that and secretly, I discovered, Clare was just as scared of him. But that was a bit later. A bit later, when I found that out.'

'Yes, Ray,' I said patiently. 'But *was* she?'

He laughed emptily. 'Was she just!'

'But she *did* bring Helen groceries, from time to time,' Amelia reminded him.

'Oh sure.' He gave a brief laugh of contempt. 'Once we knew Pierce hadn't got a chance of finding Helen.'

'But in the end he *did* find her,' I pointed out. Pierce had received a phone call.

'You're too right,' said Ray, grimacing. 'He found out. He was told. But – you see – he'd guessed that Clare had been in on it, helping Helen get away. And he found out where Clare lived. A flat, she'd got. And he started hanging around. If she went out, he wouldn't be far away. And letting her see him. But of course, not expecting her to lead him to Helen. Oh no. Just terrifying her, simply by staring at her.'

'Intimidation,' I said softly. 'And she told you this?'

'She did. And sometimes I saw him, too. If we were out for a drink. In a pub, say, he'd be there . . . in a far corner. Staring.'

Amelia said, 'But he never managed to follow either of you, the times you visited Helen?'

'No. How could he? We both had cars, and he didn't. He'd have needed to nick a car, but he hadn't got the talent for that. For all I know, he might not have been able to drive.'

It was all very substantial, and there was no reason why Ray shouldn't be telling the exact truth. Mellie's rejection of him had hit him hard. There was nothing else worth his while to worry about.

'So,' I said, 'let's come to the evening when Clare died. You'd taken Dennis to his mother that morning. You said that.'

I paused, hoping he would take it from there. He did.

'Well . . . yes. Helen'd said she couldn't go on with it. Ten days, it'd been. She said she'd got to get back because she didn't know what was happening to Dennis. That time, I was on my own, visiting her, in the boat. I promised to get Dennis. All right. Fine. That suited Helen a treat. But when I told Clare . . . well, she started to go all strange about it. Reluctant. But she did go and see Helen. That morning, before we fetched Dennis. On her own – I suppose so that she could try to persuade Helen it couldn't be done. Something like that. But that was what Helen wanted and there was no getting away from it. And I suppose it was then she took the ring from Helen, or borrowed it. You know: "Lend me your ring and I'll do it." That sort of thing. Perhaps. But she had it on her finger at the time of the party.'

'And did she tell you what she'd said to Helen?' I asked.

'Well . . . sort of. It was a kind of sulky temper she'd got on her, had Clare. Said she'd told Helen she ought to go home to Dennis, and not have Dennis at the boat. But Helen had been scared to go back. And then we got to talking about when we'd pick up Dennis. She cussed me out for offering. Said we were getting into it deeper and deeper. And if we took Dennis away, Pierce would know who'd done it – and he'd wait to get her ...' He shook his head in disbelief. 'I just didn't understand her. It was all ... well, kind of different. Unusual. Clare was certainly acting awfully strange. There was the engagement party, that evening. She was ... well, not demanding, but sort of possessive. Didn't I think anything of *her*, she'd been saying. As though I'd ever thought once of getting married to Clare, or even mentioned the possibility. I couldn't understand her. She'd been so positive – and even bossy – only a month or so before. Aggressive, you know. Acting like a man.'

He gave a shy smile, implying he didn't really mean that.

'But now, all of a sudden,' he added, 'she seemed scared of everything. Particularly Pierce.'

'I believe', said Amelia, 'that I can explain that. She was two months pregnant, Ray. Women change. They need to look after themselves more carefully, because they've now got more than their own life and welfare to protect. Didn't she tell you she was expecting a baby?'

He took a deep breath, and let it out with a sigh. 'She did. And she said the baby was mine.' He smiled sadly. 'She said I'd got no right to promise to marry anybody else, when I'd made *her* pregnant – and we both of us knew damned well she'd had other men. God knows how many. *That* didn't worry me. I didn't feel anything for her in that way. But ...'

And now he grimaced sourly. He shook his head, apparently unable to go on.

'But,' I said, 'I do know that she was wearing the ring when she went into the pound. Did you know she was wearing it?'

He lifted his head in disgust, whether with Clare or of himself I couldn't tell. 'I told you. I knew she'd got it. She waved it under my nose. Swore she was going to break up the engagement party. Walk in there and claim a prior contract – the fact that she was pregnant. You know all this, Richard.'

'I know it. But you wouldn't have killed her for *that*. Not to stop her breaking up the party. But you *did* kill her.'

He didn't answer that. After a few seconds of silence, he seemed to go off on another tack.

'I couldn't understand what had happened to her. We picked up Dennis easily enough, but then Clare seemed to go to pieces. Driving here . . . I was doing the driving . . . it was her car, though. She had Dennis on her lap. Driving here, she was moaning and groaning about it all the way. Dennis was asleep. When we left the car, the storm was blowing like mad. I put my slicker on, and I carried him all the way. Under it, to keep him dry. My cap blew off.'

'It's in the kltchen, drying. So what's that one in your hand?'

He laughed disgustedly. 'It's Clare's. I've got to have one to carry.'

I didn't take him up on that. 'Get on with what you were saying, Ray.'

'Yeah. Well. There's not much more. We walked down to the locks together. Clare wouldn't go any further.'

'The dog!' said Amelia abruptly. 'You haven't mentioned Bruce.'

He gave a short laugh. 'They wouldn't go anywhere without each other. Yes, I'd got Bruce. His lead was on my wrist. And I left Clare waiting at the pound, where she couldn't be seen.'

'She *was* seen, Ray. By Gerald.'

'Yes. It doesn't matter. I made the delivery, stayed a minute or two, then went back to Clare. She said she'd made up her mind, and she wasn't going on with it.'

'What did she mean by that – not going on with it?'

'I didn't understand at first.' He rubbed a palm over his face, as though to provoke deeper thought on it. 'It was just that Pierce had really got under her skin. He'd know that Clare and I had been the ones who'd collected Dennis. Well . . . Mrs Lloyd would say – wouldn't she! And then, said Clare, he'd be after *her*. And this was the Clare who'd told Helen to stick a knife in him! At *that* time, Clare would've been able to do it herself. But now . . . hell, she was going to pieces. I tried to talk her round. No, she said. I just didn't know what to do. Time was running on – the party, or rather, the dinner first. About due. And she started to say she was going to have done with it.'

'Have done with it?' Amelia asked. 'In what way?'

He sighed, lifting his shoulders with it. 'She said, quite simply, that she was going to phone Pierce at the Blue Boar – and tell him where Dennis and Helen were. Then she'd be able to get some sleep, she said. I don't know what she meant.' He shook his head miserably. 'I mean – it wouldn't just have ruined everything, it meant he'd be getting his filthy hands on Helen again.'

'So?' I said.

'I tried. Really, Mr Patton, I tried to get her to see sense. But no. She was going back to her car and use her car phone to tell Pierce. Leave a message if he wasn't there. You know. I pleaded with her. Pleaded. But no. She turned away and I grabbed her arm – and suddenly she was her old self. Well ... sort of. Snarling and vicious. "Touch me ..." she said, threatening, and in a second she'd got her peg out.'

'Her what?'

'The ladies carry a smaller baton than ours. Call 'em pegs.'

'Oh?' They hadn't in my days. 'And she threatened you with it?'

'More than that. Got me on the arm. Left arm. It's still bruised. And – naturally – by instinct I suppose, I had my own baton out – and she'd turned away as I struck out.'

He sounded very weary. His shrug barely moved his shoulders. 'I'd killed her, Richard. These caps are no protection at all. She just went down, and I'd killed her.'

I shook my head. 'No. She was only unconscious.'

'It's not so!' He sounded frantic. 'I tried. Tried for her pulse. Wrist and neck. I couldn't feel a thing. Dead – and ... oh, I don't know. I had to get to that dinner and the party. My head was going round – all the working out, and Helen, and Dennis. So ... so that she wouldn't be found, I pushed her into the pound. And that's that.' He ended on a note of despair. Then he looked haggardly from one face to the other, but we were both silent. Amelia had my hand firmly grasped in hers.

'But Ray,' I said, 'you'd killed her to prevent her from phoning Pierce, then you went and phoned him yourself. Why?'

'Well ...' He looked round, then found the words. 'I thought about it, you see, and decided it might not be such a bad idea, phoning Pierce, but with a different end in mind. A better idea than Clare's.'

'And what was that?' I asked quietly.

'It would bring him there, you see, along the tow-path, and at some time after eleven, when the pub shut.'

202

'And?'

'Well . . . I'd be waiting for him, wouldn't I! A quick tap on the head, and then drown him. If it meant holding him under. Don't you see, it was the only thing to do – kill him. Because I didn't know about Colin's plans for Helen and Denny, and all I could see was Helen and the lad back in that lousy dump of a house, and the violence going on and on, and I couldn't have done anything legal about it, because it was domestic. You know damn well that the police can't interfere in domestics. Till it gets criminal, till somebody dies – Helen or Denny, or both. All I could do was kill him. Then it'd all be over. I'd be doing somebody some good, anyway.' His voice fell away to a whisper. 'And – by God – how I hated him! And it seemed to me I was on my own with it – the responsibility all mine – and I wanted an end to it. Oh Lord . . . a positive end.'

'So you phoned him, with that in mind. Good. But you didn't carry it through, did you? Why didn't you go ahead with it? Did you simply decide that Helen wasn't worth the trouble?'

'No, no! It wasn't that.' He gave Amelia a sudden, almost delightful smile of embarrassment, flicked a glance at me.

'We'd just got engaged, you see,' he went on after a slight pause. 'Mellie and me. And . . . well . . . I was staying the night. You know this, Richard, and Mellie knew which room I was in . . . and she came to me. To kiss me good-night, she said. Quietly, in the night. I knew Pierce wouldn't leave the pub until after eleven, so I thought I didn't have to worry about time. But Mellie came. And she was warm . . . you know. And – well, she didn't go back to her own room until about six. I mean . . . I couldn't unwrap her from round me, couldn't say, "Excuse me, love, but I've got to go out and kill somebody." Now . . . could I? I was stuck. It was dawn before she decided she ought to get back to her own room.'

His voice had sunk lower and lower. It was a secret. I could wish it had been said louder, so that Mellie might have heard. But she wasn't at the swing doors now. To her, Ray had been the one to phone Pierce, and launch a vicious attack on Helen. Yet she'd been a little to blame, herself.

'Well Ray,' I said, after a few moments to think it through, 'it seems to me that you've got two explanations to make, here. Or rather, one confession and one explanation. The confession to Inspector Slater, to explain how Clare died, and the explanation to

Mellie, to explain the phone call and why you didn't go through with it.'

I waited for his reaction, but he stared at me blankly. Disaster faced him from both directions – and he was lost.

'What say,' I suggested to him, 'that you and I go to find Inspector Slater. Right now. And Amelia can go to see Mellie, and explain about the phone call, and why you didn't carry it through. What d'you say to that?'

But it was Amelia I was asking, not Ray. He had no choice. She raised her eyebrows at me and tried to smile. But gently she nodded her head. It was going to be difficult to persuade Mellie that she need not blame herself too severely for what had happened to Helen. But I knew Amelia could do it.

And soon, it now seemed, Helen would be living at Flight House herself, and would be able to offer her own forgiveness.

204
Newport Borough Libraries

MOBILE LIBRARY)1/96

HOUSEBOUND   2/98

0143062